The Summertime Soldiers

Also by Susan Kelly
The Gemini Man

The Summertime Soldiers

Susan Kelly

Walker and Company
New York

First published in the United States of America
in 1986 by the Walker Publishing Company, Inc.

Published simultaneously in Canada by John Wiley & Sons
Canada, Limited, Rexdale, Ontario.

Library of Congress Cataloging-in-Publication Data

Kelly, Susan.
  The summertime soldiers.

  I. Title.
PS3561.E39715S8   1986   813'.54   85-26365
ISBN 0-8027-5646-8

Book design by Irwin Wolf

Printed in the United States of America

10 9 8 7 6 5 4 3 2 1

Prologue

September 19, 1970

Blast Rocks Police Headquarters; Radical Group Claims Responsibility

CAMBRIDGE, MA (AP)

An explosion caused extensive damage to the first floor of police headquarters last night, moments after a telephone caller warned that a bomb had been placed there.

The caller identified himself as a member of the Peoples Revolutionary Cadre (PRC). The PRC, a Boston-based radical organization, has also claimed credit for last month's bombing of the Global Airlines termi-nal at Logan International Airport, in which four people were injured, one of them seriously.

Police said the blast at headquarters blew out one wall and shattered most of the windows on the first floor. There were no reports of injuries.

Captain Thomas Grassi said the explosion was caused "probably by dynamite." The device had been placed in a lavatory closed for repairs.

October 7, 1970

Police Officers Gunned Down

CAMBRIDGE, MA (AP)

Two police officers were shot and killed early today as they sat in a parked cruiser on Massachusetts Avenue.

The victims were identified as Patrolman Gordon Clancy, 27, and Patrolman Anthony Gianelli, 39.

Investigators said that the incident, which occurred at the intersection of Massachusetts and Somerville Ave-nues at Porter Square, took place at approximately 2:20 A.M.

A witness to the shooting, whose identity is being withheld by police, told authorities that he saw a late-model sedan pull up beside the cruiser. Moments later the occupant of the passenger seat opened fire on the two officers. The sedan then sped north on Massachusetts Avenue.

Patrolman Gianelli was pronounced

1

dead at the scene. Patrolman Clancy died shortly after being admitted to Cambridge City Hospital. Both officers sustained multiple gunshot wounds to the head and chest.

Police have no motive for the double slaying.

Patrolman Clancy leaves a wife, Kathleen, and two children. Patrolman Gianelli leaves a wife, Angela, and three children. Mrs. Gianelli is expecting a fourth child in January.

October 8, 1970

Caller Ties Radical Group to Slaying of Two Police Officers

BOSTON, MA (AP)

A talk show host for a local radio station today received a telephone call from an individual claiming responsibility for yesterday morning's murder of two Cambridge, MA, police officers.

The caller identified herself as a member of the Peoples Revolutionary Cadre (PRC), a Boston-based radical organization linked to last month's bombing of a Cambridge, MA, police station and to the August 9 explosion at the Global Airlines terminal at Logan International Airport.

Talk show host Peter Kandelis, of station WCSK, said the caller informed him that the attack on the two police officers was "only the beginning," and that further "warrants for the execution of fascist insects and agents of the oppressors" would be served shortly.

Kandelis said that the caller's voice was apparently that of a young woman. A tape of the conversation has been turned over to police for study by voice experts.

Detective George Shostek, a member of the team investigating the deaths of Patrolmen Gordon Clancy and Anthony Gianelli, said that police were pursuing several promising leads.

A reward of $5000 for information leading to the arrest and conviction of the killers has been posted by the Cambridge City Council.

2

Bank Robbery Leaves Police Officer, Teller Dead

By STUART CONNELL

Globe Staff

A Somerville police officer and a bank employee were shot to death when three men and two women held up the Davis Square branch of the Middlesex County National Bank this morning and fled with $58,000 in cash.

Dead are Patrolman Stanley Dubrow, 35, of Powderhouse Boulevard, and Miss Donna Cherufisi, 23, of Kidder Avenue. Patrolman Dubrow was shot twice in the chest as he attempted to pursue the suspects on foot down Highland Avenue. Miss Cherufisi was shot once in the head when she apparently attempted to alert a customer at the drive-up window of the holdup.

Patrolman Dubrow's partner, Patrolman James McMullen, was not injured.

A bank spokesman said three men and two women, armed with carbines and handguns, entered the bank at 10:45 A.M. One of the women shouted, "This is the Peoples Revolutionary Cadre. The armed struggle begins now." She then fired a shot at the ceiling before taking up a post by the bank entrance. A second woman stood guard over the bank employees and customers, while the three male accomplices took money from the tellers' cages.

Seven customers and ten employees were present in the bank at the time of the holdup.

According to witnesses, the three men and two women escaped in two cars bearing New Hampshire registration plates. One car was found abandoned in the parking lot at the Porter Square shopping plaza in Cambridge several hours later.

Susan Williams, of Day Street, was crossing Highland Avenue when she heard gunfire. Several moments later she saw three men and two women emerge from the bank and run toward a waiting car driven by a third woman. Miss Williams said Patrolman Dubrow gave chase and was shot by one of the male accomplices.

The woman said to have identified the gang as the People's Revolutionary Cadre is described as 20 to 25 years old, about 5'7", with a slender build, wearing a tan coat and black boots.

The second woman was 20 to 25 years old, about 5'3", with reddish-brown curly hair and dark glasses. She wore a green jacket over gray slacks.

Patrolman Dubrow's alleged assailant was reported to be about 35 years old and six feet tall with a medium build and receding brown hair. He wore a blue sweatshirt and work pants.

The second man was about 20, with a slender build and long blond hair. The third man was described as 20 to 25, about 5'8", with a slight build and dark hair and a birthmark on his chin.

The driver of one of the getaway cars was described as a woman about 20, with light-brown hair.

Patrolman Dubrow, a twelve-year veteran of the police department with two citations for bravery, leaves a wife, Jean, and six children. Miss Cherufisi, a 1969 graduate of Bridgewater State College, leaves her parents, Helen and Daniel, and two brothers.

The Peoples Revolutionary Cadre is the Boston-based radical organization that has claimed credit for last month's slaying of two Cambridge police officers, Patrolmen Anthony Gianelli and Gordon Clancy, for the September bombing of Cambridge police headquarters, and for the August bombing of the Global Airlines terminal at Logan Airport.

November 7, 1970

Members of Radical Group Sought in Somerville Slayings

By STUART CONNELL

Globe Staff

The two female suspects in yesterday's robbery of the Davis Square, Somerville, branch of the Middlesex County National Bank, in which a police officer and a teller were shot to death, were identified today as Sarah Clarke Olmsbacher, 23, a graduate student in political science at Boston University, and Linda Ruth Spahn, 21, a sociology major at the University of New Hampshire. Two of the male suspects, Jeffrey Alan Goldman, 22, and Prescott Harris Forbes, 20, are students at Harvard University. Murder warrants have been issued for all four.

The third male suspect, Charles Roy Mitchell, 34, of Everett, was arrested late last night and arraigned this morning on a charge of murder.

Mitchell, who was paroled from the state prison at Walpole three months ago after serving two-thirds of a fifteen-year sentence for armed robbery, was taken into custody as he left a bar in Revere.

The driver of one of the getaway cars used in yesterday's robbery, described as a young woman with light-brown hair, has not been identified.

In a raid at 329 Marlborough Street this morning, police found a box of hand grenades, several sticks of dynamite, an M-16 rifle, four army-issue Colt .45 pistols, three boxes of .45 caliber ammunition, and explosive detonators. The apartment had been leased in the name of Miss Olmsbacher.

Miss Olmsbacher, Miss Spahn, Goldman, Forbes, and the unidentified female suspect, all believed to be members of a radical group calling itself the Peoples Revolutionary Cadre (PRC), are also wanted in connection with last month's slaying of two Cambridge police officers, the September 19 bombing of the Cambridge police station, and the August 9 bombing of the Global Airlines terminal at Logan Airport.

Miss Olmsbacher's father, James, is an executive with Global Airlines.

An intensive manhunt throughout Massachusetts, Connecticut, Rhode Island, New York, New Jersey, and Pennsylvania has so far failed to uncover any trace of the five suspects. Yesterday's robbery netted the thieves $58,000 in cash and resulted in the deaths of Patrolman Stanley Dubrow, 35, and Miss Donna Cherufisi, 23, a bank employee.

Mitchell has told police that the purpose of the robbery was to expropriate funds to finance the "revolutionary activities" of his group.

A spokesman for the Federal Bureau of Investigation says that the members of the gang should be considered armed and "extremely dangerous." Anyone having information concerning the whereabouts of any of the suspects is requested to get in touch immediately with the nearest FBI office.

January 20, 1975

Inmate Stabbed During Prison Melee

WALPOLE, MA (AP)

Convicted murderer and bank robber and self-styled revolutionary Charles Roy Mitchell was fatally stabbed yesterday during a brawl that erupted in the dining area at the state prison here.

Prison authorities said the incident was the result of an argument between Mitchell and another inmate regarding seating arrangements in the dining area. Witnesses said that the alleged assailant, Robert Whitney, 27, approached Mitchell and demanded that Mitchell give up his seat. Mitchell refused, whereupon a struggle broke out between the two men. Whitney then allegedly drew a knife and stabbed Mitchell four times in the chest and abdomen before being subdued by guards. Mitchell died several hours later while undergoing surgery at a local hospital.

Mitchell was serving a life sentence stemming from his 1971 conviction for the armed robbery of a Somerville, MA, bank, in which a police officer and a bank employee were killed. Four of Mitchell's accomplices, who, like Mitchell, claimed membership in a radical organization calling itself the Peoples Revolutionary Cadre (PRC), have never been found. A fifth female suspect, Linda Ruth Spahn, was killed in an automobile accident on the New Jersey Turnpike last December.

5

Contents of a message sent to the editors of the *New York Times,* the *Boston Globe,* the *Washington Post,* the *Los Angeles Times,* the *San Francisco Examiner,* and the *Chicago Tribune:*

Greetings,

We are the Peoples Revolutionary Cadre (PRC), a band of communist men and women dedicated to the smashing of imperialism, racism, and sexism. Though hounded underground by the fascist oppressors in 1970, we have nonetheless sustained the struggle against the bloodsuckers of the ruling class. The pig media have labeled us thieves and murderers. But the people know the truth.

We mourn the deaths of our sister Sonia, whom the pigs knew as Linda Spahn, and our brother Jorge, whom the pigs called Charles Mitchell. Sonia and Jorge were beautiful in their revolutionary zeal and in their love for the people. They understood that only out of blood will come peace and freedom for all peoples.

DEATH TO ALL WHO OPPOSE THE ARMED STRUGGLE, FOR THEY ARE THE ENEMIES OF HUMANITY

Peoples Revolutionary Cadre

1

For the first time since college, I had a summer job. I was teaching report writing at the Cambridge Police Academy.

I had twenty-two students, same as I would have in any freshman composition class. We were going over pretty much the same material as we would have in any beginning writing course, too—sentence structure, diction, and organization. Scintillating stuff like that. We talked about paragraph development and denotative and connotative language. The students wrote brief essays. I corrected them.

In fact, the only real difference between this class and the ones I'd taught elsewhere was that my students at Harvard and Tufts didn't carry guns. At least, I assumed they hadn't.

Today we were discussing why it was important for the details in a police report to be set down in chronological order, a subject on which I could get quite passionate. The recruits were attentive. Maybe they thought the subject was interesting. Or maybe they just liked watching me make a spectacle of myself. I'd broken four pieces of chalk and tripped over the lectern twice in the first twenty minutes of class alone.

We finished up our two-hour gig at 12:30. The sergeant who was the assistant director of the academy came in to dismiss the recruits for lunch break. I waited for the initial stampede to moderate and then gathered up my papers and went back to the academy office. No one

7

was there. I tossed my lecture notes on top of a filing cabinet and plumped down in the chair behind the assistant director's desk. I'd have kicked off my shoes and put my feet up on the blotter, but the space was already taken up by ten boxes of .38 caliber ammunition and an empty black leather hip holster. Somebody's teaching aids, no doubt.

If I haven't made it clear already, I'm not a cop. My name is Elizabeth Connors. I used to be a full-time assistant professor of English. Now I'm a free-lance writer and a part-time teacher. It's less money, but it's more fun. And I don't have to attend faculty meetings or receptions at the dean's house.

I looked at my watch. 12:45. Jack and I were supposed to be going for lunch about now. I ran a comb through my hair, put on some lipstick, and tucked the tail of my blouse back into my skirt. Then I walked downstairs to the Criminal Investigation Division on the third floor.

A black detective in faded Levi's and a yellow T-shirt printed with the advice FEEL SAFE: SLEEP WITH A COP was dialing the phone on the secretary's desk. He looked up as I pushed through the swinging doors and said, "Hey sugar, when you gonna dump the lieutenant and be my lady?"

"Soon's I get permission from your wife, Lewis," I replied.

He laughed and returned to his phone call. He and I went through variations on that little routine every time we ran into each other. Which was nearly every day since I'd started teaching in the academy.

As a lieutenant and as second-in-command of the detective bureau, Jack had his own office, a sparely furnished eight-by-eight cubicle that had once been an interrogation room. Through the plate glass window I could see him at his desk, head bent over a stack of yellow papers. Arrest reports.

I stuck my head through the door opening and said, "Hiya."

He looked up and smiled. "Hi, Liz. Come on in."

I took the chair across from his desk. "You look busy."

He shrugged and made a face. "Just the usual crap. How'd your class go?"

"Oh, fine. They're a good group. Most of them seem to know the difference between a noun and a verb, anyway."

He raised his eyebrows approvingly. "More than I can say for the guys who wrote some of these things." He pointed at the pile of reports.

I laughed. "That bad, huh?"

"Jesus," he said. He leaned forward and picked up the top sheet. "Listen to this. 'Motor vehicle pulled into a private lot. Operator got out of motor vehicle and was staggering around and could not produce or pronounce. Registration was glassy-eyed with a strong odor of liquor on his breath.' The registration was glassy-eyed? *Jesus.* Now will you tell me what the hell that's supposed to mean?"

I widened my eyes and held out my hands, palms up. "Sorry," I said. "I don't do translations from Urdu or whatever."

He grunted and shook his head in disgust. Then he tossed the paper back on the desk.

"You ready to eat?" I asked.

He looked at his watch. "Sure. But I'm expecting a phone call. Mind waiting a few more minutes?"

"Not at all," I said.

"Okay." He picked up another report and scowled at it. I settled back in my chair and crossed my legs, watching him as he read.

Jack was John C. Lingemann, and I had known him for a little over two years. We'd met when I wandered into the police station one afternoon looking for information on how missing persons investigations were conducted for an article I wanted to write. He hadn't exactly warmed to me during our first interview, partly out of a natural reserve and partly because cops tend to be guarded around strangers. *Especially* strangers who claim to be magazine writers or reporters. My second get-together with him was, however, a lot more relaxed. So much so that we ended up going out afterward for drinks and dinner. We had been together without interruption since then.

He was forty-three, eight years older than I. He had been a cop for seventeen years and a widower for five. His wife, Diana, had been hit by a drunken driver while crossing Garden Street on her way to a photography class at the Cambridge Center for Adult Education. They'd never had any kids.

Jack was tall, very lean and well-muscled, with light-brown eyes and light-brown hair that was starting to gray around the edges. I thought he was one of the handsomest men I had ever seen. The attraction lay less in any regularity of feature than in the character that informed his face. The world is full of good-looking window dummies, and they all leave me cold.

The phone rang. Jack picked it up and said, "Lieutenant Lingemann." He held the receiver cradled in the hollow of his shoulder and continued leafing through the reports as he spoke.

I slung the strap of my bag over my shoulder and stood up, preparing to leave. I was *very* hungry.

"Okay," Jack was saying. He glanced at me briefly. "Yeah. No, don't do that. Yeah, that's good." He was silent for a few seconds. "All right. I'll be along." He hung up the phone and let out a long, heavy sigh.

"What's up?" I said, although I had a feeling I knew what was coming.

He leaned back in his chair, gazing at me a little ruefully. "You mind very much if I cancel out on lunch?"

I shrugged. "I had the feeling you were going to say that." I nodded at the telephone. "Was that the call you were waiting for?"

He shook his head. "Uh-uh. This one was something else."

"What?"

The left corner of his mouth turned down. "There's a body in a vacant lot off Kendall Square. Behind the transportation department building."

I could feel my face screw up involuntarily. "God."

"Yeah." He had gotten up and was rolling down his shirt sleeves.

"Who discovered it?"

"Some guy walking his dog." Jack took his suitcoat from the back of his chair and shrugged into it.

"Was that who was on the phone?"

"Uh-uh." He gestured at me to precede him out of the office. "One of the patrol officers over there."

"Oh."

A detective sergeant named Flaherty was standing outside the captain's office, his back to us.

"Hold on a sec," Jack said, touching my right elbow lightly. "Sam?" Flaherty turned to us. Jack went over to him and began speaking, keeping his voice low.

Flaherty was a tall, skinny, stooped man in his late forties, with graying red hair and one of those uniquely Irish faces that seem cast in perpetual melancholy. It got even gloomier as he listened to Jack.

Jack came back to me and said, "We gotta go now."

I nodded.

"Sorry about lunch."

I made a dismissive gesture. "You can still come to dinner tonight, can't you?"

"Well, I hope so. If I don't get tied up with this—with the business in Kendall Square."

"Why don't we shoot for eight-thirty?" I said.

He smiled. "Sure. I'll call you if there's a screw-up."

"Okay."

He gave me a sort of half-pat, half-squeeze on the shoulder. Flaherty ambled over to us, hitching up his pants. "Hi, doll," he said to me, and then to Jack, "Whose car?"

"Mine," Jack said.

I waited till the two of them were through the swinging doors and then yelled, "Behave yourselves."

Jack's voice floated back to me. "Got no option."

2

Apparently there wasn't any screw-up, because the doorbell rang promptly at 8:30 that evening. I answered it, accompanied by Lucy, my runt Weimaraner–chocolate lab cross. She's very protective of home and hearth, which is a comfort in a city where house breaking seems to be the highest-return venture after bioengineering.

Jack was leaning against the porch railing, a bottle-shaped package in his left hand. Wine? Probably.

"Hello, sailor," I said. "Is that a concealed weapon in your pocket or are you just glad to see me?"

"Well, police officers are supposed to carry a weapon at all times."

"Yeah, I heard. Will you show it to me later?"

"Depends on how good the dinner is." He handed me the wine and reached down to pat Lucy. She was grinning and capering around and thrashing her tail in an ecstasy of canine welcoming. Unlike Jack and me, Lucy and Jack took to each other at first sight.

The dog bounded up the stairs to my apartment and we trailed her, hand in hand. When we were in my living room, I said, "Would you like a drink?"

"God, yes," Jack breathed.

I stared at him. "Dumb question. Maybe I should just offer you the whole bottle and let you slurp from that."

He smiled, but not very broadly. "No, a glass is okay." He dropped down on the couch and put his head back and closed his eyes. I peered at him curiously for a few seconds and then went to the kitchen to get some ice.

I returned with the ice and two big squat glasses on a tray. I put them down on the coffee table and got the bourbon and the vodka from the booze cabinet. Then I dumped three ice cubes in one of the glasses, added a hefty slug of bourbon, and handed it to Jack. "Here's your plasma, honey." I made a slightly less lethal vodka on the rocks for myself.

I settled down next to him on the couch, took a sip of my drink, and said, "Bad day at Black Rock, huh?"

"Not the best," he agreed.

"What was it? The body in Kendall Square?"

He nodded and drank about a quarter of his drink.

"Why don't you tell me about it?" I suggested.

"All right. But it's very weird." He took another swallow of bourbon and set his glass on the table. "The guy's name was Andrew Morgan. He was a senior staff engineer at Gordon Labs."

"Gordon Labs? What's that?"

"They're one of those federally funded think tanks. They have a plant over on the Fresh Pond Parkway. They do a lot of work for NASA and the defense department. Star Wars stuff, you know? I think they had something to do with developing a part for the MX missile."

"Uh-huh. So what about Morgan?"

"He's—he was a young guy. Thirty-six."

I felt that special twinge you always do when someone close to you in age dies a needless death. "And?"

"Well, he was shot twice. In the back of the head. Then dumped in the weeds in that vacant lot. But that wasn't where they actually killed him."

"*They?*" I repeated. "It sounds like a mob execution."

Jack looked at me. "Well, in some ways, yes, it does. But not the kind of mob execution you're probably thinking of."

"Oh?"

He picked up his glass. "Ever hear of a group that called itself Peoples Revolutionary Cadre?"

"No," I said. I paused, my drink halfway to my mouth. "Wait a

13

minute. Wa-ai-itt just a minute. There's something familiar . . . oh, Lord, of course. Weren't they some sort of terrorist group in the late sixties and early seventies? Like the Weathermen?"

"Yeah, that's them."

"Sure, I remember now." I furrowed my eyebrows in thought. "They robbèd some bank in Somerville."

"That and a few other things."

I nodded. "It's all coming back to me. They set off some bombs and assassinated a couple of cops, didn't they? To strike a blow at fascist America or some such worthy cause?"

"You got it."

I was puzzled. "But they went underground years and years ago, like all those groups. Nobody's heard from them in ages. They probably don't exist anymore."

He smiled without humor. "You wanna bet?"

"Huh?"

Jack leaned forward and dug his wallet out of his hip pocket. From the wallet he took a piece of paper and handed it to me. "Read this. It—the original, anyway—was tucked into Morgan's shirt pocket."

I took the paper and unfolded it. It was a photocopy of a typewritten note. It read:

Pigs:

The time has once again arrived for the oppressed peoples of Amerika and the Third World to rise and strike a blow against Amerikan imperialism and fascism. We greet our courageous brothers and sisters of the Weather Underground, the Black Liberation Army, the Popular Front for the Liberation of Palestine, the Red Army, and the Red Brigade, and salute the memory of all those warriors who have given their lives in the struggle against neocolonialism and oppression.

Reactionary forces have seized control of Amerika. Military spending has reached a new height. The government of the U.S. is waging secret and open war in Central America and the Middle East. Workers, young people, and women must unite to fight U.S. domination of the world.

For too long we have remained passive. Events of the past have all too amply demonstrated that rallies, protests, strikes, even bombings and sabotage of military installations, government buildings, and nuclear facilities are useless against the genocidal policies of the Amerikan government. Direct action is necessary.

The Peoples Revolutionary Cadre has therefore determined that for every million dollars spent on defense, the life of one pig will be exacted. Andrew Morgan, a lackey in the service of imperialist war preparations, is only the first. Others will follow, until the streets of fascist Amerika run red with the blood of the oppressors.

Peoples Revolutionary Cadre

Below the signature was a rough pencil drawing of a hand clenching the hilt of a saber against a background of what appeared to be flames.

"Good *God,*" I said. I folded the note and returned it to Jack. He stuffed it in his pocket.

"No chance it's just some sort of sick gag, is there?" I asked.

"I doubt it," Jack said.

"How can you be so sure?" I was playing devil's advocate.

"I can't. But I have to operate on the assumption that that note means exactly what it says. There's nothing to tell me it doesn't. And what else do I have to go on? I can't afford not to take this thing seriously."

I got up and paced over to the window. "I know. But it's so . . . bizarre. Almost archaic, even. I mean, I haven't heard anybody use phrases like 'fascist Amerika'—spelled with a 'k,' yet—and 'blood of the oppressors' since when? 1971? I thought all that stuff ended when Vietnam did."

"Some of it did. Some of it didn't. It just hasn't gotten the kind of publicity in the past few years that it used to."

I stopped my pacing and frowned at him. "What do you mean?"

"The Black Liberation Army is still shooting at cops in New York. And there's some group in California that's been trying to blow up public utilities all up and down the coast."

I leaned against the window sill. "Okay. But even so . . . "

"Even so what?"

"Why should this particular crew of PRC crazies suddenly crawl out of the woodwork now? It's been maybe fifteen years, Jack. That's a long time for them to sit around waiting for the revolution to arrive."

"Not really. A committed, organized terrorist group has a lot of staying power."

"Well, sure. If it's Al Fatah or the IRA it does. But this isn't the IRA or Al Fatah we're talking about."

He gave me a curious look. "What difference does that make?"

"How big and organized can this PRC be? How much damage can it do?"

"On the basis of what happened today, I'd guess a fair amount," he replied dryly. "Anyway, that's not the point. A terrorist group operating in a city doesn't have to be big to do a lot of damage. In fact, the smaller they are, the better they can move around."

I nodded. "Okay. But that still doesn't answer my original question."

He smiled and shook his head slightly. "Jesus, you're contentious tonight. What was the question?"

"Why are these loonies doing this now?"

"You read the note. The defense budget *is* up. It's higher now than it ever has been."

"And that's supposed to be a good reason for killing someone like Andrew Morgan?"

Jack shrugged. "It probably makes sense to the PRC. Is Palestinian liberation a good reason to blow up an airplane with four hundred tourists on it?"

We were silent for a moment, finishing our drinks. I picked up the bourbon bottle and waved it at Jack, and he nodded. I put a few more ice cubes in his glass and covered them with bourbon.

"Was Morgan married?" I asked presently.

Jack let out his breath with a long whooshing sound and said, "Yeah. With two kids."

I winced. "I'm sure the whole family will be enormously comforted to know that Daddy died in the struggle against fascist imperialism and militarism."

"Uh-huh. You know, the hell of it is, Morgan wasn't even working on defense."

"He wasn't?"

"No." Jack shook his head. "His last big project was the space shuttle. And—get this—he was very active in the antiwar movement at Swarthmore in the late sixties. That's what his wife said, anyway. She ought to know."

"Oh, God," I said. "Looks like the PRC isn't too selective in picking its targets."

"It never was."

"No," I agreed. "In that bank robbery in Somerville, wasn't one of the people who got killed a teller?"

"Yeah. A girl named Donna Cherufisi. She was going nights to Boston State to get a master's in education."

"Terrific," I said. "Another mighty blow struck against the capitalist warmongers." I looked at Jack. "And they're striking out again, apparently. Alarm you?"

"What do you think?"

"Alarms me, too," I said. "What do you know about the PRC?"

"Practically nothing."

"Oh, come. You must have *something*."

"Not really. Two of them are dead. There are warrants outstanding for the other four, but hell, we don't even know the name of one of them. There could be more. The last time they surfaced was in 1975, and that was only to send a message to the papers. They use code names like Leilah and Esteban and Sonia and Jorge." He shrugged. "And there's no guarantee that this bunch today is the same as the original one. It could be a whole new group that just decided to call itself the PRC."

I sighed and rubbed my forehead. "But if it isn't . . . ?"

"I'm still not that much ahead."

"You know they're somewhere in the area. And you have pictures and descriptions of three of them."

"All of which are over fifteen years old."

"Still."

He took a swallow of bourbon. "Yeah, well, you can change your appearance a lot in fifteen or so years. There's plastic surgery, and you can gain weight, or lose your hair, or . . . just aging will do it."

I didn't say anything. Lucy, sensing that we were troubled in that way that dogs do, slithered out from her favorite resting place under

17

the wing chair and walked over to the couch. She gazed at us for a few minutes, her tail waving gently, and then rested her muzzle on Jack's right knee. I suppose she figured he needed her sympathy more than I did. He scratched her behind the ears, absently.

I got up. "I guess I should see about dinner."

"Huh?" Jack blinked, as if he'd been in a trance and the sound of my voice had called him out of it.

I laughed. "Dinner, cookie. Before it burns to a crisp. You must be more hungry than I am. You never did get any lunch today, did you?"

"Yeah. I mean, no, no, I didn't."

He was only half answering the question. I sat back down on the couch and put my hand under his chin. I turned his face toward me. "This really bugs you, doesn't it? I haven't seen you look so preoccupied in ages."

He shrugged and lifted his chin from my hand.

"Yeah," I said. "It bugs the hell out of you."

3

The report of Andrew Morgan's death got top billing on the eleven o'clock news that night and occupied half the front pages of the Boston papers the following day. Both papers reprinted the text of the letter found on Morgan's body. The *Globe* featured a sidebar on the history of the Peoples Revolutionary Cadre, comparing its goals and method to those of other urban guerrilla groups past and present. The *Herald* ran an editorial taking a strong stance against the rising tide of terrorism abroad and now, it seemed, at home.

I was sitting at my kitchen table finishing one of the articles in the *Globe* when the phone rang. The caller was a man named Brandon Peters, a feature editor of a magazine called *Cambridge Monthly*. Sometimes I write for him. I wish it were more often. *Cambridge Monthly* isn't the *Saturday Review,* but any magazine that publishes the work of Liz Connors can't be all bad. That's what I tell myself, anyway.

"I'm really glad to hear from you," I said. "I was sort of wondering how I was going to pay my electric bill."

"What do you know about sixties radicalism?" Peters asked. He's not big on idle chit-chat.

"About as much as anybody else who graduated from college when I did," I said. "Why?"

"I'd like you to write something on it."

"Oh? Anything special?"

"Well, I was thinking in terms of a sort of where-are-all-the-activists-now piece."

"Where have all the flowers gone," I murmured.

"What?"

"Nothing. Go on."

"Yeah, well, you know, something along the lines of whatever happened to so-and-so who was so big in the Boston peace movement and had his face on the tube every night and then just dropped out of sight."

"Hmmmm," I said. "This wouldn't by any chance be in response to the murder in Kendall Square yesterday, would it?"

There was silence on the other end of the line.

"Okay," I said, smiling to myself. "Sure, I'd like to. It sounds as if it'll be really interesting."

"Good," Peters said. "Haven't you got a friend who used to be some kind of big radical?"

"You mean Abby Henderson?"

"Yeah, her. Why don't you talk to her and get some background."

"Thanks for the suggestion," I said, rolling my eyes at the ceiling. "It never would have occurred to me on my own."

"And while you're at it, why don't you see what you can get from your connection in the police department. The cops must have kept pretty close tabs on all those jokers."

"Now that's a *really* novel approach," I said.

Peters laughed. It was one of his virtues that he didn't get offended easily. He could be a pain in the ass sometimes, but at least you could kid him.

"What sort of focus do you want this thing to have?" I asked.

"How about this PRC group?"

"I don't know if you'd call them activists," I replied. "I knew a lot of activists in college, and not one of them ever blew up a building or shot a cop or a defense worker. I think the PRC think of themselves more as revolutionaries or urban guerrillas."

"Well, whatever. It's all part of the same thing. See what you can get in the next few days and we'll talk about it again." He hung up without saying good-bye.

I called Jack. He wasn't in his office. It took the person who answered the phone a little while to track him down. When he got on the line, his voice sounded less depressed than it had the night before. Not exuberant. But more alive.

"Guess what?" I said.

"I don't have the time," he said.

"Okay. I'll be brief. Peters called me about ten minutes ago. He wants me to do something on sixties radicals. With special reference to the PRC."

"Son of a bitch," Jack said. "Where'd he get that inspiration?"

"That's what I asked him. He thinks you can help me with my research. He calls you my connection in the police department."

"Yeah? I may throw up."

"Well, you are, aren't you?"

"In a manner of speaking," he said. "Look, I really can't talk now. Whatever I can tell you, I will. But it'll have to be some other time."

"How about tonight?"

"Sure."

"Okay. See you later." We said good-bye and hung up. I went back to the kitchen, got a pair of scissors from the utensil drawer, and started cutting the articles on Morgan's death from the two papers. When I'd finished, I put the clippings in a manila folder along with a pad of white narrow-ruled paper and some five-by-eight index cards. Ready to roll.

I spent the afternoon in the microfilm room of the Tufts University library, reading newspaper accounts of the movements of the Peoples Revolutionary Cadre from August to November of 1970. In four months, they'd accomplished a lot—a bombing at the airport, a bombing at the police station, a bank robbery, and four murders. A good record for terrorist activity even by Black September's standards, I reckoned. After the November bank robbery, nothing, until a communiqué about sustaining the struggle against the bloodsuckers of the ruling class got sent to the major papers at the end of January 1975. Following that, silence.

Both of the papers had names and photographs of five of the six alleged PRCs. I studied the pictures carefully, searching the five faces for some trace of what made normal people into terrorists. Charles Roy Mitchell, the oldest of the group and an ex-convict, looked like what he was—sullen, stupid, and vicious. He had a receding chin and hair to match and heavy-lidded, expressionless eyes. Adorable. Linda Ruth Spahn had a corona of frizzy hair, wire-rimmed glasses, and a round, scared face. Some revolutionary—she looked like a Future Teacher of America who'd found a cobra in her desk. Prescott Harris Forbes had an arrogant expression and shoulder-length fair hair restrained by an Indian band. Jeffrey Alan Goldman had an unkempt Caucasian Afro, an Oscar Wilde mustache, and a large dark mole on his chin.

Sarah Clarke Olmsbacher looked like an Episcopalian homecoming queen, except that she wouldn't have condescended to be one. The girl was gorgeous. She looked like Meryl Streep on a very good day. Long blond hair, almond-shaped luminous eyes, and the kind of cheekbones and jaw that people call chiseled. She was smiling and wearing a dark turtleneck sweater with a single sixteen-inch strand of pearls. I would have bet my bank account that the pearls were Oriental and not cultured. The photograph looked like a Bachrach. When had it been taken? Well before Sarah had joined the urban guerrilla movement, I was sure.

What the *hell* had made her into what she'd become?

I rewound the last of the microfilm tapes, covered the reader with its plastic shroud, and signed out of the reading room. After that I went down to the stacks and rummaged around until I found some books on terrorism and on the student movement. I checked the material out, left the library, and walked down Professors' Row to catch the bus back to Harvard Square. I took my time about it—the warmth of the early June air and the beauty of the campus combined to give me a stab of nostalgia for the time when I thought I might grow up to be a Famous English Professor. Sometimes I missed that old life and older dream. But only sometimes. If I were still in it, I'd be spending most of my time bitching about all the stupid papers I had to correct and the even dumber meetings I had to go to.

When I got back to the apartment Jack was there, lying on the couch reading a back issue of *Esquire*. There was an empty bottle of Molson Ale on the coffee table. He tossed the magazine aside and started to get up.

"I didn't expect you so soon," I said. "But I'm glad you're here. Like a drink? Though I see you've already helped yourself."

"Sit down. I'll get them."

"Oh, you're so good to me," I said in a silly baby voice. I flopped down on the couch, put my head back, and massaged my temples. My eyes were probably permanently crossed from all the microfilm reading I'd been doing.

Jack came back into the room with a glass and another bottle of beer.

"I'm really tired," I said. "Let's send out for a pizza, huh?"

He nodded and made me a vodka martini on the rocks. Then he sat down next to me and put his arm around my shoulders.

"You seem cheerier today," I remarked, leaning against him.

He shrugged with his free shoulder and drank some beer. "Tried to call you earlier. Where were you all afternoon?"

I pointed at the manila folder and the books. "Hot on the trail of the Peoples Revolutionary Cadre. In the Tufts library."

"Sounds like fun."

"It was. Remember I spent four years in graduate school learning how to do research. This was easy in comparison to the kind of thing I used to have to do. What can you tell me about Sarah Olmsbacher?"

He smiled. "Well, she's one hell of a good-looking woman."

"I know," I agreed. "I made a copy of her picture. Who does she make you think of?"

"Meryl Streep?"

"Yeah, me too. Okay, we know she's beautiful. Or she was. What else is there to know about her?"

Jack rubbed his chin thoughtfully. "She came from a very rich family."

"I figured. How rich?"

"Well, the father was a vice-president at Global Airlines. Still is, as far as I know. The mother was an heiress to some pharmaceuticals outfit. Sarah herself had all the advantages, as they say. Born in Westchester in June 1947, went to the Brearley School and after that Vassar. Spent her junior year at the Sorbonne. Came back, and in her senior year got involved in the peace movement. By all reports, became radicalized very quickly. Moved out of the dormitory and in with some guy who had a reputation as a big-time dope dealer. Graduated from Vassar in 1969 and applied to and was accepted into a doctoral program in political science at B.U. Helped organize some strikes and demonstrations there, but never got busted for anything.

Nobody at B.U. even knew she was in the PRC. In fact, nobody knew the PRC even existed until they tried to blow up the airport. There were some rumors floating around Boston and Cambridge about some new terrorist group that was real heavy, but nothing anybody could pin down."

I had picked up my lined pad and begun to write. "Go on, this is just what I need."

"That's pretty much all I know about her, except that she was probably having an affair with one of the PRC men."

"Oh? Who?"

Jack smiled slightly. "Charles Mitchell."

I dropped my pencil. "Are you kidding me? That creep? That yuck?"

"Well, that's what Mitchell told the Somerville cops when they picked him up after the bank robbery."

I shook my head. "He was probably hallucinating."

Jack shrugged again. "Maybe. Maybe not. If you look at it from Sarah's standpoint, what better way to stick it to the establishment than by screwing somebody like Mitchell. Why the hell else would a girl like that get involved with a dirtball like him, unless it was to get back at somebody or something."

I raised my eyebrows. "It was probably more complicated than that. But I see your point. I don't suppose it was any coincidence that her father worked for Global Airlines and it was the Global terminal at Logan the PRC tried to blow up."

"No, probably not."

I picked up the pencil. "So what was her position with the group?"

"From what Mitchell said, she was sort of chief theoretician and strategist. Her apartment in Boston was where they kept their armory. They called her Alexa."

"Alexa?"

"Uh-huh. I told you they all had code names. Goldman was Raoul, Forbes was Esteban, Mitchell was Jorge, Spahn was Sonia, and the last one was Leilah. Leilah's the one we never identified. Mitchell didn't know her real name or where she came from. She was a latecomer to the group, apparently. Only in on the bank robbery. All anybody could get out of Mitchell was that she had light-brown hair and blue eyes and talked a lot about Mao."

"Swell description," I said. "Sounds like a quarter of the 1970 graduating class of Brandeis."

He laughed and squeezed my shoulders.

"About this Leilah," I continued. "She drove one of the getaway cars after the bank robbery, didn't she?"

"So Mitchell claimed. And the description of her, such as it is, tallies with what the witnesses said." Jack finished his beer and set the bottle on the coffee table.

Something elusive was darting around the outer limits of my consciousness. I reached for it and grabbed. "One of the articles I read this afternoon said that after those two cops were assassinated, a young woman called a radio station and told the deejay or whatever that the PRC was responsible. You know who that was?"

Jack glanced at me. "Oh, Christ, yes."

"Well, who?"

"Mitchell said it was Sarah."

"Sarah who made the call?"

"Nope. Sarah who blew away the two cops."

4

A week later, a guy on his way to work at the Internal Revenue Service in Andover was about to make the turn off Route 93 onto Route 133 when he spotted what looked like a bundle of clothing on the verge of the wooded area alongside the highway. Part of it was snagged in the branches of a low-growing bramble, like something that had fallen off the back of a pickup truck and rolled away unnoticed by the truck's driver.

Afterward, the man told a *Herald* reporter that if he'd been running late or even on time, he'd never have bothered to stop. But with ten minutes to spare, he could indulge his curiosity. And so he pulled over into the breakdown lane, put his Datsun in park with the emergency lights blinking, got out, and walked toward the roll of clothing. He wasn't apprehensive, nor even slightly wary. It was an early summer morning in an expensive suburb. The buzz of the cicadas was louder than the traffic noise.

Ten feet away from the roll of clothing, the man stopped. And stared. He took one big gulping breath and then turned and ran back to his car. Shaking, he drove to the Mobil station on Route 133 and yelled at the attendant to call the police. Then he went to the men's room and threw up twice. He was five hours late getting to work that day.

The bundle of clothing was a body. In the back of its head were a pair of holes drooling a lot of gray and red semi-liquid matter. The left eye was missing, by all appearances blown outward from the skull. The body belonged to a forty-six-year-old ex-Marine captain named Stephen Burmester. Burmester had been a vice-president for research and development at the Centron Missile Systems plant in Andover. In the pocket of his shirt there was a brief typewritten note. It read:

Pigs,
        This is number two. Remember what we said. We mean business.

Peoples Revolutionary Cadre

No fancy Marxist–Leninist rhetoric this time, but the note made its point more than adequately. Beneath the signature was the logo of a hand brandishing a saber against a background of flames.

The killing of Andrew Morgan had gotten a lot of publicity. But with the murder of Burmester, the press really pulled out the stops. And who could blame them? The six o'clock news shows devoted half their air time to an examination of the phenomenon of terrorism in our time. Channel Five borrowed a forensic psychiatrist from the staff of Beth Israel Hospital and trotted him out for a ten-minute discussion of the motives of what he called "destructive deviants." Channel Seven did a retrospective on the antiwar movement and ran some file footage of the Harvard Square riot in 1970. Channel Four sent a reporter to interview a political science professor at B.U., one who'd had Sarah Olmsbacher as a student in one of his seminars. You could tell he was straining to remember something dramatic about her. Or anything at all.

After the local and national news, the governor pre-empted *Entertainment Tonight* and made a rock-jawed speech about standing foursquare against a sweeping tide of anarchy and lawlessness. I liked his hardy nautical metaphors. The governor said he was establishing a special investigative unit to look into the activities of suspected terrorist groups operating in the Bay State. He sweated a lot as he spoke. It could have been just the klieg lights.

I watched the whole surreal pageant alone. Jack was up in Andover at the state police barracks, comparing notes with their detectives, I figured. They'd established very quickly that the bullets that had killed Morgan and Burmester had been fired from the same gun. Certainly the styles of execution were identical—two shots to the back of the head at close range. And it was a good guess that both men had been ambushed as they left work.

The messages found on the bodies had been typed on the same kind of paper (an erasable variety that every five-and-ten sells) and on the same machine. The hand that had drawn the logo was the same in each case. There were no fingerprints on the paper that matched any on record.

It was a great case. The cops knew who the bad guys were, they knew why they'd done what they'd done, and how.

But with all that knowledge, nobody could think of a way to catch them.

5

I did my part. When I wasn't teaching my academy class (I assigned the recruits a research paper on terrorism), I continued getting background for my article. I ripped through the four books on urban guerrillas and revolutionaries that I got from the Tufts library and checked out another five on the same subjects. I discovered that there was a scholarly journal devoted exclusively to the study of terrorism. I talked to a professor in the Harvard government department whose specialty was "low-level violence"—meaning the kind of spectacle to which the PRC had just treated us. I wound my way through about two million miles of microfilmed newsprint. I read transcripts of hearings before the Senate Subcommittee on Internal Security.

And I talked to Abby Henderson about student radicalism in the Boston area in the late sixties and early seventies. She was an expert on the subject.

It had the potential for being a funny situation. I mean, you're not usually in circumstances that require you to call up a close friend and ask her to sit for an interview and then shove a tape recorder in her face. Abby was good-humored about it, though. Well, we'd known each other for eight years, and there were few surprises we could spring on each other.

Abby was, in many ways, a remarkable person. A political radical and feminist long after it was fashionable to be either one, she'd graduated from Radcliffe in 1971 and gone on to take a Ph.D. in Asian Studies from Harvard. We'd met while she was teaching history and I English in the humanities division that existed as a sort of afterthought in a small business college in one of Boston's western suburbs. It was the first teaching job for either one of us, and Abby's last. We'd both hated the place. The difference between us was that while I'd stayed in teaching, at least for a bit, Abby'd gone as far from it as she could. She'd enrolled in medical school. After a year among the slides and test tubes, however, she'd decided that medicine wasn't for her, dropped out, and signed up for some sort of computer training program. She now had a job at American Aerodynamics so top secret that even Cal Sanders, the man she'd lived with since 1975, didn't know quite what it was she did. I sure didn't.

I'd often wondered at the apparent ease with which Abby'd made the transition from political activist to corporate figure in what she used to call "the military industrial complex." Not that I thought there was any element of hypocrisy or opportunism in the shift. Abby's socialist convictions seemed intact. But somewhere along the line, she'd acquired flexibility, or at least a willingness to accommodate herself to the things she couldn't immediately change. She'd learned the necessity of compromise, the way I suppose we all do just in order to live. The dinosaurs couldn't, and look what happened to them.

The softening process Abby'd undergone had led to other transformations, although these were ones of style rather than substance. Her appearance had altered considerably in the time I'd known her. The long loose hair was now short and blow-dried, and the elderly jeans and T-shirts that had once constituted her entire wardrobe had given way to suits and dresses, at least for work. She even wore make-up now, something she once would have scorned as demeaning. When I asked her why she'd given in on this point, she'd shrugged and said she liked the way her face looked with color on it.

We met for lunch in Passim, the underground (literally) coffeehouse in the alley that runs between Church Street and Brattle Street in Harvard Square. Passim is a sort of refugee from the early sixties, when Cambridge was the folk music capital of the East and Joan Baez was packing them in at the Club 47. Like everything else that had survived the end of the sixties, Passim had adapted. I figured it was as good a place as any for the kind of conversation Abby and I were going to have.

She was waiting for me when I got there, a bowl of chili and a glass of cider on the table in front of her.

"Sorry I'm a little late," I said. "I made the mistake of taking the bus instead of walking."

She shook her head. "It's okay. I only got here a few minutes ago myself."

A waitress wandered over and gave me an inquiring smile. I ordered a salad and an iced tea. Somewhat to my surprise, she returned with both almost immediately. Service here was normally a lot more laid back.

"Well," Abby said. "Where do you want to start?"

The abruptness of the question startled me a little bit. I reached into my canvas shoulder bag and took out my portable tape recorder. I set it on the table next to the salt and pepper shakers and the sugar bowl.

"You're kidding?" Abby said, eyeing the tape recorder with an expression of exaggerated incredulity.

I laughed. "Not really. I want to make sure I get everything down accurately."

She raised her eyebrows and then shrugged. "Okay." She smiled. "As long as it's not going into any FBI files."

"I'd go to jail first," I assured her.

"That's good." She sipped her cider and set the glass on the table with a decisive-sounding click. "Look, I'm not really sure what it is you want. Why don't you ask me some questions?"

"All right." There was a little silence, during which we stared at each other blankly. I felt remarkably silly. Then, self-consciously, I cleared my throat and punched the "on" button of the recorder. "First thing, I guess, is how did you get involved in the antiwar movement?"

She settled back in her chair and laughed. "In 1967, it would have been hard not to. I really hadn't thought much about Vietnam before then." She paused and ate a spoonful of chili. "Anyway, the first few weeks I was at Radcliffe, I met a bunch of people who were pretty active politically, and I went with them to a couple of teach-ins and discussion groups, and that got me started on the whole thing."

"Did you think of yourself as an activist then?"

"No, not really, not till I joined the SDS."

"When was that?"

"Uh, let's see." She leaned her chin on her right fist and closed her eyes. "Sometime in the winter, I think it was. January, February? Something like that. Anyhow, it was early in 1968."

"And what happened after that?" I ate some of my salad.

"Well, you know, the war was escalating, with the Tet offensive and all, and then Martin Luther King got shot in April, and that just seemed to turn things around completely, for me and for a lot of other people."

"How?"

She gave me a curious look. "You were around then. Don't you remember?"

"I'm more interested in what *you* remember."

"Yeah, well, the whole movement up to then had been pretty—oh, passive, I guess. There was a lot of rallying and leafleting and organizing, but nobody was seriously talking revolution at that point. After King was shot, though, and Bobby Kennedy, all that changed. Everybody was saying that the assassinations just totally destroyed the concept of nonviolence, and that you couldn't work within the system to change anything, and that maybe all we could do was blow it up and start from scratch."

"But nothing happened here like what happened at Columbia University," I interjected. "Not on that scale, anyway. I mean, sure, yeah, there was that takeover of University Hall, and the cops came and dragged everybody out, and the square got trashed, but . . . "

"No," she agreed. "But you could sense the potential for something really heavy was there. In fact, now that I look back, it seems funny that things didn't explode."

"Did you go to Chicago for the Democratic convention that summer?"

"God, no," she replied. "Though I knew a lot of people who got into that whole street-fighting scene, and they went. Got their skulls bent, too."

"Off the pigs," I said. "All power to the people. And didn't the press just love it all? All you had to do was stand in the middle of Boston Common and yell 'strike' and three seconds later both papers and all the TV networks and the entire Boston police department in riot gear would be there. Carnival time."

"Well, we were going to bring the war home, you know."

"What about you personally?"

"Huh?" She resumed digging into her chili.

"Where did you fit in with all of this?"

She looked slightly puzzled, and then shrugged. "You know, I can't really say. Things sort of started to fall apart the next year. The Harvard–Radcliffe SDS chapter was a frigging disaster area. There was a lot of infighting, and nobody could get together on any kind of strategy. Plus the Progressive Labor Party was very big in all the Boston and Cambridge SDS chapters, and they were opposed to most of the stuff that the other part of SDS supported, like women's lib and the National Liberation Front and the Black Panthers. They even hated rock music, for God's sake. But they ended up pretty much in control of the organization."

"And?"

"Well, the SDS meetings just turned into brawls, more or less, with Progressive Labor saying that the rest of the SDS had to be smashed— that was the word they used, smashed—because SDS were tools of the imperialists and just as antiproletarian as the Harvard administration. Then the other side would start screaming that PL was racist and sexist and anti-Hanoi and a lot of other crap like that." She shook her head in reminiscent disgust. "PL was Maoist, which is what I was— still am, basically—but I couldn't take any more of that factional shit. So I just dropped out. At that point, I'd gotten involved with one of the Cambridge feminist groups, and that was taking up a lot of my time . . . " Her voice faded and she shrugged.

"No wonder the revolution never arrived," I said.

She smiled. "No. But for a while, it really seemed close, didn't it?"

Actually, it never had to me, but I couldn't say so, even to her. I remembered how that same lack of faith had always made me feel apart, back in college when everyone I knew had an ideological answer for everything. Destroy one social order and replace it with another, a guaranteed nonsexist nonracist nonmilitaristic noncapitalist worker's paradise where everybody did dope and smelled flowers and made love not war in the streets. My problem was I thought *all* systems were by definition shit. And that there was something vaguely ludicrous about people with a blind commitment to them.

On the other hand, most of the college students I met nowadays didn't have a blind commitment to anything but a portfolio of blue chips and a house in the Hamptons. Maybe even misguided idealism was preferable to that.

"Those were the good old days," I said, finally, neutrally, and in a strange but totally sincere way, I meant it. "Tell me something. Do you recall ever hearing anything about the Peoples Revolutionary Cadre?"

"Those crazies? Oh, sure."

I stared at her for a moment.

She gave me a slightly surprised look. "What's the matter?"

"Well, you seem so matter-of-fact about it, that's all. I mean, nobody seems to know anything about this group except the names of some of the members and what they did. Jack's flipping out trying to get something. And here you sit calmly telling me . . . "

She shook her head. "Don't get the idea that I know every little detail about them. What I heard was only what everybody else heard."

I ate a slice of tomato drenched in vinaigrette. "What was that?"

"Oh, just that there was this new urban guerrilla group that was really committed to revolutionary violence." She finished her chili and pushed the bowl away.

"When did you first hear about them?"

She thought for a moment. "I'm not really sure. Sometime around the beginning of my junior year, which would have been 1969, I guess."

"Were they affiliated with any of the other radical organizations?"

"Not that I heard. I think they formed more or less on their own. They borrowed a lot of Weatherman rhetoric, but other than that there was no connection I know of."

"What kind of support did they have?"

"Not a hell of a lot in SDS, as I recall. The official line was that the PRC were adventurist."

"Adventurist?"

"Yeah. That was the word PL and SDS used for the Weathermen and all the other terrorist groups. The feeling was that the guerrillas were just a bunch of lunatics out to sabotage the whole antiwar movement."

"So there wasn't a lot of widespread sympathy for the PRC, then."

"No. And they never bothered to solicit any support. Anybody who wasn't one of them was one of the pigs, you know? God, they were really paranoid."

"So where did they go when they went underground?"

"Oh, hell, who knows? Maybe to the Weatherpeople. The only people who *do* know anything about the underground are the ones already in it. Everybody else is by definition the enemy." She shook her head. "Bunch of summertime soldiers."

"What?"

"Summertime soldiers. That was what the Black Panthers called all the white student revolutionary groups. You know, rich honkies playing urban guerrilla when the weather got warm."

I finished my salad. "So why do you think the PRC resurfaced now?"

"I have no idea. Didn't they say something in that first letter about taking up the struggle against the forces of reaction?"

"Mmm-hmm. Support antimilitarism—kill a defense worker."

"Tell me about it. I work for American Aerodynamics."

I peered at her. "Yes, I've been thinking about that. Makes you a potential target, doesn't it? Are you worried?"

She grinned. "I'm not going into hiding."

"I didn't think you would." I reached over and switched off the tape recorder. "Listen, I really appreciate you telling me all this."

"Oh, that's okay. I kind of enjoyed it." She paused for a moment, her face thoughtful. "Makes me feel sort of nostalgic."

"I know." I put the tape recorder in my bag. "It was a bad time in a lot of ways, but . . . I don't know. It was more alive. Real? Something like that, I guess." I sighed. "Or is it just that we were younger? Anyway, I kind of miss it. I'm glad I was there. To see it, even if not to be part of it."

Abby looked up at me. She was smiling, but her large blue eyes were steady and serious. "Aren't we all?"

June 15

Abby may not have been concerned about her own welfare, but a lot of other people with her kind of job were running very scared in the wake of Morgan and Burmester's deaths. In the greater Boston area alone, there were about a zillion industries and think tanks and university-affiliated research labs that did one form or another of defense work. On top of that, the term "defense work" itself was one that, by all indicators, the PRC seemed inclined to interpret loosely. Which suggested that even a part-time secretary to an electronics engineer who'd fourteen years ago participated in developing a transistor for a satellite communications system was a potential target.

There was no way the cops could bodyguard everyone who might be in danger. And so, the bigger companies, like Honeywell and General Dynamics and Avco and Wang, made private arrangements for the protection of their executives and senior research personnel. The need for some kind of action was underlined when the director of Lincoln Labs received a misspelled but undeniably menacing death threat in his morning mail. The letter didn't appear to have been sent by the PRC, but that hardly mattered. Massachusetts was host to as many weirded-out political fringe groups as it was to defense contractors, and half of them probably wanted in on the revolutionary action.

A local newspaper columnist known in the past for his opposition to police surveillance of suspected political extremists now took the cops to task for not keeping closer tabs on suspected political extremists. The strongest reaction his article elicited around the Cambridge P.D. was a few sour smiles. They'd been through all this before.

The governor's office was in a real swivet, it was hard to tell whether out of genuine concern for the welfare of the citizens of the commonwealth or terror that all those heavy tax-paying defense contractors might pack up and move to New Hampshire. In any event, the state police lieutenant that the governor had appointed head of the antiterrorist task force promised a swift crackdown on the PRC and all groups like it.

Jack, being Jack, didn't.

He and I were having an afterwork drink at Ryles in Inman Square. It was the first time I'd seen him in a week, although we'd spoken on the phone a number of times. He was working sixteen-hour days now and, I guessed, catching sleep and meals when he could. It was showing in his face, although he looked as good to me as he always did. I thought there was a little more gray in his hair than there had been three weeks ago. Maybe that was my imagination.

"Why are they all that much harder to catch than other criminals?" I asked.

"Well, they're not *like* other criminals," Jack said. He reached into his jacket pocket and took out a package of cigarettes. He shook one from the pack and lit it with a match from a book that said "The Channel Two Auction—May 29—June 6." That he'd started smoking again was a sure sign that things weren't copacetic. As far as I knew, he hadn't smoked since a year after Diana's death. At least the cigarettes were low-tar.

I picked up my vodka martini and sipped. Ryles served mixed drinks in brandy balloons the size of buckets. It made me feel relaxed even to look at one. "Okay. In what ways different?"

"Lots," Jack replied. "Look, most criminal behavior is predictable. It falls into patterns. Like a guy robs a liquor store, and, afterward he tells somebody about it. He *has* to. It's like he's got this compulsion to blab."

I smiled at the word.

"All right," Jack continued. "So the guy talks. And then he gets picked up, because sooner or later somebody he tells about it tell us about it. That's what happened with Charles Mitchell."

"Oh-ho," I said. "Now that's interesting. I've been wondering how his arrest came about."

"Yeah. Well, the night after that Somerville bank robbery, he split from the rest of the group and went to a bar in Revere. He got loaded and gave everybody an earful about this big heist he masterminded." Jack paused and shook his head slightly, in a kind of reminiscent disgust.

"So?"

Jack drank some of his bourbon. "Well, it just happened that one of the stiffs in the bar who overheard all this crap was some small-time hood with a drug charge pending against him. So he went and made a phone call to this Revere narcotics cop—"

I laughed and clapped my hands together. "Of course. Figuring that if *he* gave the cops Mitchell, the cops would drop the drug charges against *him*. Good trade."

Jack nodded. "Yeah. That's the way it went." He grimaced. "You have no idea what an incredible crew of morons most criminals are."

"Mmmmm," I said. "But it's more than just stupidity, isn't it? There must be a kind of . . . " I stopped speaking, searching for the proper word. "Is it ego? No. Narcissism, maybe, that's involved? The feeling on the part of a criminal that whatever I do is right? Or that no matter what I do, I won't get caught?"

"That's it," Jack said. "A big part of it, anyway." He smiled at me. "You have a real cop's mind. Why don't you take the civil service exam for the next recruit class?"

That remark was an institutional joke between us, but I felt absurdly flattered by it, the way I always did when he complimented me on my skills of observation or reasoning. Probably because I knew that cops, whatever else they might or might not put up with, suffered fools a hell of lot less gladly than almost anyone else I could think of. Certainly much less than academicians or business folk.

"You know I'm too old for that," I said, giving my standard response to the question. "But—getting back to the original subject. Granted Mitchell may have been the classic criminal jerk, but the rest of the PRC wasn't, was it?"

"No." Jack lit another cigarette. "No. They were never dumb the way he was. If they talked at all about the bank robbery and the bombings and the other stuff, they sure as hell didn't do it in bars with total strangers. And anybody they told in the underground wasn't going to inform on them." He looked at the cigarette in his hand, made a face, and mashed it out half-smoked in the ashtray.

"They're very loyal to each other, aren't they?" I said.

"Oh, Christ, yes. Fanatically. It's part of their code."

"The old Nathan Hale routine," I said. "To die without speaking."

"Yeah. You can't trick them into talking, you can't pressure them into talking, and you can't bribe them into talking. So what's left? The usual rules don't apply."

"Rules?"

"Well, they're not written down anywhere." He smiled and picked up his glass. "You know that most of the cases that get solved get solved because of information that somebody bought or traded. But nothing like that is happening here, or going to happen as far as I can tell. Maybe I'm wrong. I hope so. But I really can't see anyone who knows anything about Morgan and Burmester coming forward at this point. They aren't the kind that would." He set his glass down on the round table top and began turning it, idly. "We've asked around on the street. Nobody knows anything."

"Maybe somebody does," I suggested. "And they're just too scared to talk."

He sucked in his upper lip, thoughtfully. "Possible," he said. "But I doubt it."

I finished my drink. "Couldn't the original PRC have been infiltrated?"

He gave me a strange look. "How are you supposed to infiltrate a group if you don't know who's in it or where to find it? The PRC isn't the Ku Klux Klan. They don't dress up in funny clothes and hold regular public meetings. No terrorist group does. They blend in. They have to if they want to survive."

I nodded. "You know, that state police lieutenant the governor put in charge of the antiterrorist unit seems to think he's gonna clean all this up right quick."

"Sure he does," Jack said. "He's a horse's ass." He finished his drink and reached across the table and pinged my empty glass with his index finger. "You want another?"

I shook my head. "No thanks."

"Okay." He put some money on the table for the tip. "Let's go, then."

When we were outside, he said, "You mind walking over to that drugstore?" He pointed across Hampshire Street. "I gotta get a prescription filled."

"Sure," I said. I glanced up at him curiously. "Prescription? You not feeling well?"

"I'm fine," he said. "It's nothing."

We waited for a break in the traffic, which was always horrendous in Inman Square at commuter time, and then hurried across Hampshire Street.

The drugstore had recently been remodeled and had huge plate glass windows. I stood by one and gazed out at Cambridge Street while Jack went to the prescription counter.

Cambridge Street at this end was a heavily Portuguese neighborhood, and while it didn't exactly have the flavor of Lisbon, you wouldn't mistake it for Harvard Square or the Brattle ward. The shops had names like Nobrega or Muralo or Ribiero. Outside the sporting club, a group of dark-haired men in undershirts lounged against the parked cars, drinking beer and chaffing each other in a language that I wouldn't have understood had I been able to overhear it.

Jack joined me at the window. "What you looking at?"

"Nothing," I said. "The passing scene."

On the curb by the bus stop huddled an elderly drunk, head pressed against his knees, swaying back and forth as if in time to some interior melody. Songs unheard are sweeter far. A pair of heavily made-up junior-high-age girls giggled past him, wobbling a little on far too spiked heels. They were wearing miniskirts of some shiny fabric and looked like apprentice hookers. A short, heavy woman in black babushka, black dress, black stockings, and black shoes plodded across the street, dragging a wire-wheeled shopping cart behind her. Two birds of paradise and a crow.

"Nice contrast," I said. "The jailbait and the—"

"*Holy Jesus,*" Jack exhaled, softly but with a great deal of emphasis.

Startled, I glanced up at him. He was standing rigid, staring out across Cambridge Street at the hardware store next to the sporting club. I looked over that way myself. A medium-sized man with curly dark hair and a mustache and full bushy beard had come out of the hardware store carrying a bulging paper bag. He paused for a moment on the sidewalk, hefting the bag into a more comfortable carrying position. Then he set off down Cambridge Street, in the direction of Lechmere.

"What—" I began.

"Stay here," Jack said, and was out of the drugstore and walking down Cambridge Street, on the opposite side of the street from the dark-haired man and just slightly behind him.

"Hey," the pharmacist said in aggrieved tones. I turned to him. He was holding up a brown plastic pill bottle.

"Don't worry, my friend'll be back," I said. "He's a cop." Then I was out the door and trotting down the street, half a block behind Jack. I really obey orders to the letter.

That we were following the curly-haired man seemed obvious. Why was a little less so. Jack didn't look like he was following anyone. He looked like somebody strolling down to the corner package store to pick up a six-pack of Bud. The fine art of nonchalance.

The curly-haired man went into a greengrocer's a block up from the hardware store. Jack stopped outside a bakery, took his little radio from his jacket pocket, said something into it, and slipped the radio back into the pocket. The whole action was performed so fluidly and so unobtrusively that I doubt if anyone noticed it but me. Jack resumed sauntering up the street. Or at least pretending to. Damned if I knew how he did it, but he was able to give the impression of forward movement without actually going anywhere. I had to loiter in front of a sub shop so as not to catch up with him.

About two minutes later, the curly-haired man came out of the greengrocer. He was carrying a second, somewhat smaller bag with a bunch of celery protruding from the top. Then he continued on down Cambridge Street. Jack ambled along after him, hands in his jacket pockets.

The two of us trailed after Curly-Top another four or so blocks, until he decided to cross the street. Jack had reached the corner of Cardinal Medeiros Avenue, in front of an ultra-modernistic church that looked like a cross between Three Mile Island and a sewage disposal plant. Around the perimeter of the church lawn there ran a low stone fence. In a recessed section of it on the Cambridge Street side were benches, now occupied by a group of elderly men.

The curly-haired man was standing on the dividing line in the middle of the street, waiting for a break in the traffic to complete his crossing. Jack looked at his watch like a guy who was going to be late for a date. The curly-haired man finished crossing the street and passed about ten feet in front of Jack. The man stopped, set his hardware store bag on the sidewalk, and reached into the other bag as if rearranging its contents. Out of the corner of my eye, I saw a police cruiser glide into a parking space about two blocks down Cambridge Street.

And then the shit hit the fan.

7

One of the codgers on the bench got up and hobbled toward Jack, creased face breaking into a happy grin. "Hey," he said. "Hey, Lieutenant, I ain't seen youse around for a while. Whatcha been doin witcha self?"

The curly-haired guy's head jerked up and he stared at Jack. Jack stared back at him, and for the briefest of moments the two of them were locked into a kind of tableau of mutual recognition. Jack was the first to break it.

He didn't move quite fast enough, though. The older man stepped in front of the curly-haired guy. Curly dropped his sack of groceries, lunged forward, and rammed into the old guy with his left shoulder. The force of the blow lifted the old man from the sidewalk and sent him lurching and flying into Jack. Jack staggered slightly, grabbed the man, and then eased him gently down onto the sidewalk. The curly-haired guy ran diagonally across Cambridge Street, back in the direction of Inman Square. Jack was after him in a millisecond, dodging cars. The two cops who had emerged from the cruiser down the street were running now, too.

The old man was sprawled on the sidewalk, moaning. Two of his friends were hunkered down beside him. One was patting his hand. The other had removed his cardigan and wadded it up and placed it under the man's head. The rest were milling around and yammering

43

at each other in what sounded like a minimum of three languages.

I ran over to the old man and knelt down beside him. His eyes were closed, and the moan had become a whimper. His color looked okay, though, and when I put my ear to his chest I could hear a regular if rapid heartbeat. Gently, I pushed up his eyelids with my thumbs. The pupils were the same size. Probably he'd just had the wind knocked out of him. Not that that was a trifling matter for a guy of his years.

I could have stayed with him, I suppose, until help arrived, but I had other priorities. I stood up and said to the crowd at large, "I don't think he's badly hurt. But somebody call 911 and get an ambulance right away." Then I started running back up Cambridge Street after Jack.

Jack was gaining on the curly-haired guy, but the curly-haired guy was really moving, slamming into the people in his way and spinning them aside. It was like watching chickens on a country road scatter before a speeding pickup truck.

They were in front of Roosevelt Towers now. Roosevelt Towers is an enormous sprawling red-brick housing project built after World War II for returning vets and their families. Now it's occupied by anyone in the low-income or no-income bracket. A number of Cambridge cops had grown up there. So had a number of Cambridge bad guys. Maybe Curly was one of the latter.

The curly-haired guy swerved sharply, vaulted over a waist-high iron railing, and was off across the Towers courtyard. On an early summer evening it was mobbed with kids on bicycles and kids with stickballs and bats and kids with ghettoblasters, plus a scattering of grownups relaxing on lawn chairs and drinking beer and overseeing the fun.

The curly-haired man stopped in the center of the courtyard, spun around, and reached under his shirt. Jack was about thirty feet away from him. The man pulled a gun from his shirt and pointed it at Jack. In one long motion Jack bent down and threw out his arms, scooping up the two kids nearest him and throwing them and himself to the ground. The curly-haired man fired, and a window in an Oldsmobile parked on the opposite side of Cambridge Street shattered. The two uniformed cops hove into view, guns drawn. They were yelling at everybody to get down and get away.

It was pure screaming chaos, then. A thin woman in jogging shorts and T-shirt and headset of pink plastic rollers flew by me, dragging two small children by the hand. The younger of the two she was literally dragging; his little legs bumped and scraped horribly along the sidewalk. A black man built like a sumo wrestler had grabbed three children at random and was squashing them beneath his bulk as he huddled beside the iron railing. The kids were shrieking and trying fruitlessly to wriggle out from the encirclement of his massive arms.

Jack shoved the two children he'd scooped up into a doorway, put his hands on their heads, and pressed them down into a crouch. Then he turned and yanked his gun out from under his coat. He raised it at the same moment a young dark-haired woman ran screaming in front of him. With his free arm he swept her aside as if she were a cobweb. The curly-haired man dodged behind an elm tree and fired a shot at one of the uniformed cops. It hit an elderly woman standing catatonic with terror beside the lawn chair she'd risen from when the shooting had started. The woman stayed motionless for just a second longer and then sort of melted to the pavement. The uniformed cop fired a return shot and it smacked into the tree, spraying bark. The second cop raced over to the old woman and dropped to his knees beside her. He put his hand on her neck and then knelt down and began giving her mouth-to-mouth.

The curly-haired guy ran toward a group of teenagers, grabbed one of them by the arm, and yanked her around in front of him like a shield. The girl's legs sagged and he had to haul her upright, holding her to his chest. He shoved his gun up against her head. The screaming and yelling in the courtyard died suddenly. The curly-haired man began to move backward, slowly, dragging the girl with him, edging in the direction of one of the apartment buildings.

"All right," he yelled. "Don't any motherfucker move or I blow her head off."

I looked back at where Jack had been poised, gun drawn. He wasn't there.

The curly-haired man and the girl reached the back of the apartment building and vanished. Somebody in the crowd let out a kind of keening wail, and that broke the spell. Two more carloads of uniformed cops arrived and they fanned out, moving to encircle the housing complex. I could hear sirens approaching. I came out from where I'd thrown myself between two parked cars and discovered that I was trembling violently. And crying.

I heard a shot, and then another, and another after that, and cringed as if I myself had been hit by the bullets. The old woman who *had* been shot was being bundled into an ambulance. The attendants slammed the doors shut and raced around to the front of the ambulance. It took off down Cambridge Street, siren whooping and lights flashing. That meant the poor old lady was still alive.

I leaned against one of the cars and wiped the wetness from my face. It was sweat as well as tears. I rubbed my hands down the front of my skirt to dry them. My pantyhose were ripped to hell and gone and my left elbow and right knee were scraped raw and dripping blood. The knee throbbed. Big deal. I pulled out my shirt tail and wiped my elbow with it.

Most of the people who'd been in the project courtyard five minutes ago had disappeared. A blue racing bicycle, its front wheel still spinning, lay discarded on the pavement. Somebody's forgotten radio was blaring Madonna. A brown and white dog of indeterminate breed emerged from one of the doorways and wandered across the lawn, stopping every few feet to sniff the grass. I couldn't spot any cops.

Behind Roosevelt Towers was the Somerville line, and a large vacant lot overgrown with head-high weeds you'd need a machete to cut through. Over to the west, between Windsor Street and Columbia and Webster Streets, sprawled a kind of down-at-the-heels industrial park featuring a colony of auto parts places, a sneaker factory, and a cemetery monument outlet. A good place to lose yourself. Curly-Top and the girl had been heading that way.

The best way for *me* to head would have been home. No doubt about it. I should have gone home, or anyway over to the police station, and waited for Jack to get in touch. I could have even gone back to the drugstore in Inman Square and picked up his prescription. Any one of those things would have been the wise, the practical thing to do.

At the moment, practicality wasn't dictating my actions. I wanted to find Jack; it was that simple. Not for protection—protection from what? And while it was true that I was scared, I was scared for him far more than for myself. I could not just go away and wait for God only knew how long to find out if anything bad had happened to him.

If I kept alert, and jumped into the nearest doorway and scrunched down if I heard or saw anything even remotely threatening, I'd probably be fine. That poor old lady who'd gotten shot had, after all, been right in Curly-Top's line of fire.

I gave another swipe to my elbow and started down Cambridge Street toward the industrial park. It occurred to me after a moment that I'd have had to go pretty much in that direction even if I were about to scuttle on home or over to the police station. One of life's little ironies.

On the corner of Windsor and Cambridge was an Arco station. There was a car pulled up to one of the pumps, but nobody was in it, and none of the attendants were in sight. No other pedestrians, either. Just me, and out somewhere behind the buildings to my right Jack, a gunman, and a teenaged girl.

I walked another block down Cambridge, my stomach heaving with apprehension. Half of me wanted to turn and run the other way. I passed a woman standing in the doorway of a locksmith's shop. Her eyes widened when she saw the blood on my shirtfront and on my leg and she said something that I didn't catch. I shook my head at her.

At the corner of Cambridge and Columbia I paused for a moment, peering down Columbia Street. It, too, was deserted. Of course, the sneaker factory would be closed for the evening, as would the body shops and the monument dealership. The workers would have long since gone home.

Still, where were all the cops I'd seen moving this way?

Where was Jack?

The building to my right was an antique shop, also shut for the night. A little farther up on Cambridge, on the corner, was a triangular patch of grass and juniper bushes, like a miniature park. The bushes would be handy for diving into and dodging flying bullets.

I had limped about ten very cautious feet down Columbia Street, keeping close to the side of the antique store building, when I heard another gunshot. Just the one. I shrank down against the brick wall, barely breathing. A few seconds later, the curly-haired man—alone—emerged from the parking lot in front of one of the auto parts shops. His entire left pants leg was soaked with blood. He stopped and bent down, clutching at it. Then he straightened up and tried another step forward. He stumbled and slumped against the hulk of a rusted-out

Chevy. He was barely seventy-five feet away from me, and I was positive that if he glanced over my way he'd see me. Jesus God. I scrunched down further, as if trying to make myself invisible. He'd be bound to spot me if I made a dash for the juniper bushes.

Out of the corner of my eye, I caught a flash of movement further down Columbia. A uniformed cop sidled out from around the far side of the sneaker factory, gun drawn and raised. Jack appeared from the lot alongside one of the body shops across the street from the sneaker place. The curly-haired guy sagged lower against the fender of the Chevy, his back to Jack and the uniformed cop. I pressed myself still closer to the building wall. Curly-Top raised his head and threw out his left arm, seemingly bracing himself against the side of the car. His mouth opened as if he were about to scream. Jack and the uniformed cop moved toward him, swiftly and silently and with infinite caution.

Everything probably would have ended quietly a moment later if a truck passing through the intersection of Cambridge and Columbia hadn't backfired. I jumped and nearly screamed at the explosion. Curly-Top must have thought one of the cops was shooting at him. Whatever, he threw himself sideways to the ground and rolled over onto his stomach, both legs beneath the front end of the Chevy. He propped himself up on his elbows, facing down Columbia toward Jack and the uniformed cop. He steadied himself, raised his gun, and pointed it at Jack.

Jack made a Baryshnikov leap to his right. He, Curly-Top, and the uniformed officer fired simultaneously. Curly-Top's body jerked and reared up slightly. The gun flew out of his hand and skittered across the sidewalk into the gutter. Curly-Top fell over onto his back and made a flopping motion like a fish out of water. There was a bright and spreading red stain on his shirt front. His injured leg twitched just once. Then he lay still.

I let out a long, shuddering breath and closed my eyes. Then I turned so that my back was resting against the side of the building and, slowly, stretched out my legs. They felt limp and boneless, like the rest of me. My stomach was heaving, and I swallowed as hard as I could to keep down the nausea.

I heard running footsteps and looked up, blinking. Jack was bounding toward me, face dead white and eyes wide with shock.

"Holy Jesus Christ," he said, and dropped down beside me. He yanked at the front of my blouse and the buttons popped open, exposing my stomach and chest.

I shook my head and pushed his hand away. "I'm all right," I said. "I cut my elbow and wiped it on my shirt, that's all. There aren't any bullet holes in my gut."

"Jesus," he repeated. He let his hand drop, and then leaned back and rested his forearms on his knees. His face was streaked with sweat and he was trembling slightly.

"Are *you* okay?" I asked, rebuttoning my blouse.

He nodded.

I looked over to where the curly-haired man lay. He was surrounded by uniformed cops. One of them had retrieved the gun from the gutter and slipped it into a plastic bag. Another two crouched on either side of the body and appeared to be checking it for signs of life. Still another cop stood a little off to the side, talking animatedly into his radio.

An ambulance screeched around the corner and pulled up alongside the group, cutting off my view. I looked back at Jack. He was still staring at me. Some color had washed back into his face, and most of the shock out of it. There was the beginning of anger, too. I could tell by the tightening of the skin around his eyes.

I knew exactly who he was angry at, and why.

"Is he still alive?" I asked hurriedly. "That guy?"

Automatically, Jack glanced over his shoulder. The EMTs were sliding a stretcher with the curly-haired guy strapped to it into the back of the ambulance.

"Yeah," Jack said. "Just barely." He turned back to me. "Listen—"

I held up my hand to silence him. "Don't yell at me, huh?" I said. "Look, I *know* I should have stayed in the damn drugstore. Or at least out of the way. But I didn't. I'm sorry. Okay?" I looked at him with as much intensity as I could muster. "I was worried about you."

He made a disgusted face.

"If you really want to scream at me," I added. "Do it later. I'm too numb to absorb anything now."

He gazed at me a moment longer and then shook his head a little. "Come on," he said. "I'll take you back to the station with me and get you cleaned up." He inspected my shredded kneecap. "That doesn't look all that swell."

"Only hurts when I laugh," I said.

The expression on his face was very sour. He put his hand on my undamaged elbow and helped me to my feet. We started walking toward one of the five police cruisers that had appeared, as far as I could tell, from nowhere.

A crowd of the curious had assembled on the corner of Columbia and Cambridge and were gawking at the proceedings and chattering excitedly among themselves, mostly in Portuguese. A couple of the onlookers were adolescent girls. As I passed them I remembered something important.

"Jack?"

"Yes?"

"The girl that guy dragged off with him," I said. "Is she—is she all right?"

Jack exhaled. "Yeah," he said. "She's okay. She's hysterical, but otherwise all right. They'll take her to the hospital to double-check, but as far as I can tell she's in pretty good shape physically."

"Oh, that's good," I said. "I'm glad. I was really worried that he might have . . . what *did* he do with her, anyway?"

"Dumped her when they got behind the sneaker factory. She was just an encumbrance to him at that point."

"Oh, because I heard some shots. I was afraid . . . "

Jack gave a kind of sardonic snort. "Well, he wasn't interested in killing kids. Just cops."

I nodded. "The soul of discrimination. Lousy shot, though. I hope that poor old lady makes it."

"Yes," Jack said. "So do I."

We got to the cruiser and Jack opened the rear door for me. My elbow and knee had started to bleed again, and it was with some awkwardness that I climbed into the back seat of the car. Jack shut the door behind me and went over to the group of uniformed officers. Their number had increased in the past few minutes. I recognized the captain in charge of night operations. There were also some Somerville cops; the border between the two cities ran right near here, and some of the action must have spilled over onto their turf.

The Channel Five news van came around the corner of Cambridge and Columbia and rolled to a stop in the space just below where my cruiser was parked. A slim young black woman in a well-tailored beige linen suit hopped out of the passenger seat. I recognized her as one of the reporters on the evening news. She strode toward the throng of cops.

Jack broke away from the group and walked back toward me. He got into the front seat of the cruiser and turned to look at me, resting his arm along the top of the seat. "How you doing?"

"Okay," I said. "Fine. 'Cept I'm dripping gore all over the upholstery back here."

"You ain't the first," Jack replied.

"No," I said. "I imagine not."

The Channel Five cameraman was shooting some footage of the section of pavement in the junk car lot where the curly-haired man's body had lain.

"Jack?"

"What?"

"Who was that shithead, anyway? You knew him, didn't you?"

Jack raised his eyebrows. "More or less. I recognized him, sort of."

"Well? Who is he?"

Jack smiled in a way that had no pleasure in it. "If he's who I think he is, sometimes he goes by the name Raoul."

8

(June 15–16)

"He recognized you, too," I said. "The moment he saw you."

Jack shrugged. "He didn't *recognize* me. He made me as a cop. That was enough."

It was well after midnight, and we were sitting in his office at the police station. The past five hours had gone by in a blur for me. I'd spent most of that time hanging around waiting for Jack to get through the massive ritual paperwork and red tape that accompanied any police shooting, justified or not. He'd had to give up his gun for a mandatory ballistics test. He'd also had to speak at length to the captain of detectives and to the chief, the first of whom had been summoned from a backyard barbecue and the second from a dinner party at the mayor's house.

The reporters from the TV and the papers had come and gone.

As for me, a woman officer in the juvenile division had given me some Band-aids and antiseptic, and I'd patched up my knee and elbow in the ladies' room down the hall from the C.I.D. The remnants of my pantyhose I'd discarded. There wasn't much I could do about the blood on my blouse.

Enervated as I was, I was in far better shape than Raoul, a.k.a. Jeffrey Alan Goldman, late of the Peoples Revolutionary Cadre, who as far as I knew was at this moment still undergoing emergency thoracic surgery at Cambridge Hospital.

52

"What beats the hell out of me," I said, "is how *you* recognized *him*. You never saw him in person before tonight, did you?"

"Nope."

"Then how . . . ?"

Jack smiled. "Let me show you something." He opened the top drawer of his desk, took out a manila folder, and handed it across the desk to me. "Here, take a look at what's in there."

I hitched forward my chair and spread open the folder on the top of his desk. The first item in it was a grainy but clear eight-by-ten blow-up of the photograph of Jeffrey Goldman that had appeared in the papers the day after the PRC had robbed the Somerville bank in 1970. The following item was a sketch of the same face, only with somewhat less hair and somewhat more flesh. The sketch after that was of a bearded and bald Goldman. Then there was one of him with glasses and no beard. Another seemed to be the artist's conception of what Goldman might look like after discreet plastic surgery on his eyes, nose, mouth, and chin. Some of the drawings showed him with the big dark mole on his chin, others without it.

All together, there were about thirty sketches of Goldman permutations.

When I came to the last one, my eyes widened with astonishment. The man in this drawing *was* the man I'd last seen lying bleeding from the leg and chest on Columbia Street. It was all there—the abundant curly dark hair tinged just slightly with gray, the bushy beard, the features slightly fuller than those of the kid in the 1970 photograph.

I closed the folder and handed it back to Jack. "Amazing," I said. "Unbelievable, even. Who did them?"

"The sketches? Tommy di Francesco."

Tommy di Francesco was a cop assigned to the Identification Bureau. He was also an artist who'd had a couple of shows around Cambridge in the past few years. I'd have bought one of his still lifes, but I couldn't afford it.

"Incredible," I said. I gestured at the folder. "Do you have the same thing for everyone in the PRC?"

"Just for Sarah Olmsbacher and Prescott Forbes." Jack leaned back in his chair and linked his hands behind his head. "Didn't see much point to having them made up for Linda Spahn and Charles Mitchell."

"No," I agreed. "They being dead and all." I picked up the folder and looked again at the final sketch of Goldman, marveling at its accuracy. "How did Tommy get all the facial detail so *right?* Is he psychic?"

"He's good," Jack replied promptly. "We just went through every possible way we could think of that Goldman might change his appearance. And then Tommy drew him to look fifteen years older in each case."

I slapped the folder shut and dropped it back on the desk. "And then *you* just sat down and stared at every single drawing till you had them all engraved on your mind," I said. "Of course you did the same for the sketches of Olmsbacher and Forbes, too."

He raised his left shoulder in a dismissive half-shrug.

"And then you just happened to recognize Goldman through a drugstore window when he wandered out of a hardware store on the other side of the street. About a hundred feet away from you. At dusk."

"Mmmm."

"You're amazing, too," I said.

"Just routine police work, cookie."

"Uh-huh," I said. "Well, somebody better tell the rest of the PRC that they can run but they can't hide."

He laughed, and then said, "You know, it's possible that the guy in the hospital isn't Goldman."

I blinked. "Huh?"

"There's no positive identification of him. Sure, he looks right, and on the basis of the way he acted at Roosevelt Towers he obviously isn't Joe Average Innocent Citizen, but what does that prove one way or the other?"

I made a face. "Oh, Jack. *Really.* Who else could he be other than Goldman?"

Jack pushed his chair back and put his feet on the desk. "Well, he had a Mass. driver's license and a social security card in his pocket that said he was somebody named Charles Randell from Tewksbury."

"Oh, big deal," I said. "In this state it's about as hard to get phony ID as it is to buy a newspaper."

"True." He smiled at me somewhat wearily. "Let's see what the fingerprints say."

"Oh." That hadn't occurred to me. "Goldman's are on file?"

"Well, not with us. The FBI has them. He was arrested once in New York in 1968."

"Let me guess," I said. "At an antiwar demonstration outside the army induction center on Whitehall Street that got out of hand."

"Christ," Jack said. "You really are a child of the sixties, aren't you? Yes. That's exactly right."

"So how long before you find out if there's a match between Goldman and the guy in the hospital?"

"Tomorrow, I hope." He glanced at his watch. "Today, I mean."

I frowned in surprise. "So soon? I thought it took at least a week to get that kind of information back from Washington."

He shook his head slightly. "Don't have to send to Washington, thank God. The Boston field office has a copy of Goldman's prints."

"Well, that's a help."

"Uh-huh."

"That son of a bitch in the hospital is Goldman," I said. "You know it and I know it."

He nodded, his eyes closed.

"Would you like some coffee?"

He didn't answer me. I looked at him for a moment and then got up and went into the outer office to the coffee machine that was kept going twenty-four hours a day.

A young and brand-new detective named Dennis Riordan was seated at one of the library carrel-like desks, scribbling away at a yellow lined pad. He looked up and smiled briefly as I passed him. He was the sole occupant of the long, narrow room.

Television cop shows, no matter how realistic they purport to be, always and inevitably get one major thing wrong—the atmosphere of a station house or precinct. The single most striking feature of a real police station is its almost monastic silence and order. And emptiness. There are actually very few cops present in the house at any given time. Except for the administrators, everybody's out on the street. And even most of the administrators would prefer to be out riding around rather than reading reports or arranging vacation schedules or negotiating with the patrol officers' union, which is what they spend most of their time doing.

There's another big difference, too. On TV the robbers and the muggers and the rapists and the murderers get dragged in the main entrance of the station, past the front desk, kicking and screaming and yelling obscenities at everybody in sight. In the real world, or at least in Cambridge (the two probably aren't quite the same thing), the bad guy gets trucked in very quietly and discreetly through an underground passage, then escorted to a booking desk well out of the public view. He, she, or it gets processed in the presence of nobody but maybe six or seven cops. The whole mechanical procedure is videotaped from beginning to end to insure that no miscreant suffers any ill-treatment at the hands of one of the officers. The videotapes get picked up at set hours by a security company and are dispatched, under guard, for developing and printing.

The system isn't the meat of high drama, but it usually works.

I asked Riordan if he wanted any coffee. He shook his head and gestured at a thermos on his desk. I fixed two cups and took them back to Jack's office.

He was completely out of it, slumped in the chair, his head resting on his left shoulder. In sleep, his face looked far less lined and complex than it did awake, much the way it must have when he was twenty and had nothing more troubling on his mind than the next keg party and whatever girl.

I tiptoed into the office and set his cup down in the center of the desk blotter. He raised his head and shook it once, vigorously, like someone shooing away a mosquito.

I sipped my coffee. "What do you say we go home?"

He stared at me blankly for a moment, as if I were a stranger just popped in off the street. Then he blinked and said, "What a good idea."

"I'm full of them," I said. "Is there anything special that's keeping you here?" I looked at my watch. "It's getting on for two in the morning."

"Gawd," Jack said. He leaned forward and put his elbows on the desk and rubbed his face. He looked up at me and added, somewhat unnecessarily, "I'm wiped out."

"I never would have guessed it," I said, smiling. "After a leisurely evening like the one we just spent I should think you'd be ready to boogie till dawn."

"You wanna dance," Jack said. "You better go downstairs to the muster room and pick up one of the young studs on the patrol force."

"I would," I said. "If I weren't sexually obsessed with a broken-down middle-aged detective."

"Like who?" he said.

I laughed and finished my coffee. "Come on. Let's go."

As we left the office, I took his arm. We walked down the two flights of stairs, leaning against each other like a pair of drunks. The captain in charge of night operations passed us on the first-floor landing and winked and made a mock military salute.

We took the rear exit out onto Green Street. There was a police parking lot directly across the way, right next to the Division of Employment Security. Somebody had retrieved Jack's car from Inman Square and left it there for him.

As we were crossing Green Street, I said, "We forgot to pick up your prescription."

"It'll wait," he said, yawning. "Right now I just want to get the hell to bed."

"To sleep," I said. "Perchance to dream."

"Yeah," Jack said. "I think I'll skip the dream part."

9

My phone rang at 6 A.M. The sound became part of the end of my dream, and I don't know how long it took me to swim upward out of oblivion and answer the thing. Jack was a long, motionless lump stretched out beside me, and Lucy was sacked out under the bed snoring.

I reached out from beneath the bedclothes to the nighttable, fumbled the receiver from the phone cradle, and brought it up somewhere in the general vicinity of my ear. I said, "Hunnh?"

"Sorry about waking you," a familiar-sounding man's voice said. "Jack there?"

It was Flaherty, the red-headed detective-sergeant. "Oh," I mumbled. "Hi, Sam. Yeah. Just a second." I rolled over and gave Jack a poke in the ribs. He said, "Uh," and twitched a shoulder at me.

I set the receiver on the nighttable and pushed myself into a sitting position. "Jack," I said, more loudly. "Telephone."

No response. I leaned over, grabbed his upper arm, and shook him.

He sat bolt upright and said, "What?"

"Telephone," I repeated. I handed him the receiver and slid back down beneath the covers. My eyelids felt as if they were lined with lead. A few hours' sleep always left me rockier than no sleep at all.

"Yeah, hello," Jack said groggily. He ran a hand back through his hair and gave a jaw-cracking yawn. He listened to Flaherty for perhaps thirty seconds and then said, "When did that happen?"

I reached over and trailed my fingers down the inside of his thigh. He brushed my hand away. All business, even when only half-awake. Whatever Flaherty was saying had his full attention.

"Okay," Jack said. "Okay." His voice grew clearer and firmer with each word. "I'll meet you there in twenty minutes. Okay. See you." He reached across me and hung up the phone. He sat quietly on the edge of the bed for a few moments. Then he said, "Shee-it," and got up and went into the bathroom. A second later I heard the shower start.

I was about three-quarters conscious now, and curious. When he returned from the bathroom, I said, "Something?"

He pulled open my top dresser drawer, where he kept some underwear and socks. "There was a fire in a house on Third Street a few hours ago."

"That's nice," I said, yawning. "What do they want you to do, bring the marshmallows and wienies?"

He went to the closet and got out a pair of jeans and a plaid cotton shirt. "It wasn't much of a blaze. Fire department put it out pretty quickly. Nobody got hurt. There wasn't anyone in the house, apparently."

"So?"

"So when they were poking around afterward, they found some stuff they thought might interest us."

I was fully awake now, sitting up and watching him move around my room. "Like what *kind* of stuff?"

He turned to face me as he buttoned his shirt and tucked the tails into the top of his jeans. "Guns, for one thing," he said. He took his wallet from the dresser and slid it into his pocket. "A whole lot of guns."

I widened my eyes, but said nothing.

"And some—uh, literature," he continued. "A stack of leaflets, anyway. Some kind of mimeographed crap."

"Oh? What about?"

"Well Sam only told me the title of one of them."

I rolled over on my right side and propped myself up on my elbow. "What was that?"

He smiled in that sort of lupine way he sometimes did. "It was something about a declaration of war against the fascist states of America."

59

I stared at him for a moment. Then I said, "*Jesus,*" with considerable feeling, and let myself fall back on the pillow. Jack peered at his reflection in my dresser mirror and ran an exploratory hand over his beard stubble.

"A declaration of war?" I repeated. "Against the fascist states of America?"

"Uh-huh," Jack said. He sat down beside me on the bed and opened the nighttable drawer.

I lay silent for a moment, trying to absorb all this, and what it suggested. My mind never functioned well early in the morning. Jack got his gun from the nighttable and slipped it into the holster that clipped onto his belt.

"Can I make you some coffee?" I asked.

He took his jacket from the back of a chair and shrugged into it. "No. I'll get some on the way."

I nodded. "See you tonight?"

"Hope so." He leaned over and gave me a kiss. "Be good."

"No way, baby."

He smiled at that and left.

I pulled the bedcovers up to my chin and stared at the ceiling, feeling a little stunned.

I spent the rest of the day trying with little success to concentrate on organizing the notes for my article. Jack didn't call, but then, I hadn't expected he would. Both Boston papers had gone to bed before the story about the Third Street fire had broken. When it came time for the six o'clock news, I practically broke my leg getting to the television set.

The news, at least, didn't disappoint. "Good evening," said the female half of the husband-and-wife team who anchored that particular broadcast. "A man wounded in a shoot-out with police in Cambridge yesterday evening has been positively identified as Jeffrey Alan Goldman, an alleged member of the so-called Peoples Revolutionary Cadre, the terrorist group that has claimed responsibility for the recent murders of two area residents."

"And in a related story," the anchorman continued, "a spokesperson for the Cambridge police department told reporters this afternoon that investigators attempting to determine the cause of an early morning fire in a house on Third Street in Cambridge have uncovered evidence suggesting that the occupants of that house may have had close ties with the members of the PRC."

Surprise, surprise.

The doorbell rang at midnight. It was Jack. He looked profoundly weary, but also keyed up, humming with a barely contained interior energy. He had a present for me. My very own copy of the Declaration of War of the Peoples Revolutionary Cadre.

I checked it over while Jack stretched out on the sofa with a bottle of beer and a tuna sandwich.

The Declaration sure made for some fascinating reading. Not *good* reading. The prose style of the document couldn't be described as anything but turgid—a bombastic mixture of Marxist rhetoric and urban American street argot, circa 1968. The content was something else.

The Declaration began with a greeting to "all oppressed peoples" and a description of the PRC as a "federation of men and women joined together to overcome the ruling class of the Fascist States of Amerika and its agents of genocide and exploitation." It went on to affirm the unity of the PRC with the people of the Third World, and to pledge its support to all revolutionary groups elsewhere.

Thereafter came an outline of the goals of the PRC. Chief among these goals, of course, was the destruction of the "U.S. imperialist war machine," which I took to mean the defense industry. This was to be accomplished by the "systematic execution of various representatives of the death merchants." (Andrew Morgan? Stephen Burmester?) Such executions, "performed apparently at random, and with the element of surprise," would result in the "steady demoralization and ultimate collapse" of U.S. military institutions. Once this goal had been achieved, the dawn of an era of true peace and self-determination would be made possible.

This was followed by some paranoid references to attempts by the "jiveass pig media" to characterize the Peoples Revolutionary Cadre as the "last warped holdover of the sixties, a suicidal band of neurotics bent on self-immolation, suffering from the delusion that any kind of widespread public sympathy might be generated by their ludicrously unrealistic aims and barbaric acts." (I thought I recognized the quote as one lifted from a more heated editorial in the *Globe*.) The author of the declaration denounced this as "pathetic bullshit, typical of the lies disseminated by the ruling class to alienate the people from the cause of revolution."

The damned thing was almost too weird to be believed. Yet there it was, right in front of me, in somewhat blurry black and white. I wondered if the PRC had planned to distribute copies on street corners.

When I'd finished reading the Declaration for the second time, I set it carefully on the coffee table, next to my folder of notes for the article on student activism.

"Molto bizarro," I said to Jack.

"To say the least," he replied.

"And there was no one in the house when the fire was reported?"

"Not so far as I know."

"So who called the fire department?"

"A neighbor."

I nodded. "What do you think happened?"

He finished his beer and set the bottle on the coffee table. "Well, the fire started in the kitchen. It was set."

I raised my eyebrows. "Oh? Now that's interesting. I wonder why?"

He held out his hands, palms up. "Why it was set? Don't know for sure. Maybe the folks who were living there were thinking that a fire might cover their tracks."

I thought that over for a moment. "Well, that makes sense, sort of," I said finally. "Burning a house down would certainly be an efficient way of destroying all the evidence in it of your occupancy, no?"

"If it worked," Jack said. "As I say, the fire didn't make much headway."

"When did the neighbor notice it and call it in?"

"A little after midnight."

I nodded again. "So what do you suppose the sequence of events was? Assuming that the place on Third Street actually was the PRC safe house? Which I'm sure it was."

Jack sat up slowly and carefully, like someone whose back is bothering him. "Well," he said. "What I would guess is that when Goldman didn't check in the other night, they must have started getting a little antsy. And Third Street isn't so far from Roosevelt Towers that they couldn't have heard through the neighborhood grapevine that something very heavy had gone down there earlier in the evening. Put that together with Goldman not turning up, and . . . "

"Go on."

He put his feet up on the coffee table, crossing them at the ankles. "Okay. Well, they were probably ready to run at that point. But I would guess they hung around long enough to watch the eleven o'clock news and get confirmation. They *did* have a TV."

"But," I objected. "The news people didn't know that Goldman was Goldman last night. So what kind of confirmation would that be?"

"Sure," Jack said. "But remember that the news *did* say that an unidentified man suspected of having ties with a terrorist organization had been shot and wounded earlier in the evening. If you were as paranoid as they are, wouldn't that give you some reason for concern?" He quirked his mouth in a slight smile. "And, despite the fact that all these urban guerrilla types are supposed to observe a code of silence, I would imagine they figured that Goldman lying in a hospital bed somewhere junked to the eyeballs on sedatives and painkillers couldn't be trusted not to start babbling the secrets of the PRC, including maybe the location of their safe house."

"Has he regained consciousness yet?"

Jack shook his head.

"Well, when he does, you'll have lots of interesting questions to ask him, won't you?"

"Mm-hmm."

"This could be the big break."

"Mm-hmm."

I got up to go to the kitchen and get myself a glass of iced tea. "Would you like another beer? Or anything?"

"No, thanks."

When I came back to the living room, I said, "So where do you think Goldman's fellow—uh, soldiers have gone?"

"I have no idea."

"Anything in the house to suggest it?"

"Not that I could find." Jack shrugged. "But there's a lot of crap to be sifted through and inventoried. Maybe something will turn up. I kind of doubt it, though. These are very goddamned careful people, even if they are loonie."

"Aren't they just," I said. "A fine madness."

10 —

June 17

Jack was right. Despite what must have been their panicked rush, it developed that the PRC had been extremely careful to clear the safe house of anything that might even remotely suggest the identity of its inhabitants. Or where they might be heading.

No personal mail, Jack said. No bills. No magazines with subscription stickers. No diaries, no checkbooks, no address books. No canceled checks. No bank statements. No charge card receipts. Sure as hell, no Christmas card list.

What the PRC *did* leave behind them was interesting, even if it didn't provide any leads as to their whereabouts. The bathroom of the Third Street house was set up like the emergency ward of a small suburban hospital. The chest above the sink held eight rolls of bandages, gauze pads, disinfectants, four rolls of adhesive tape, surgical scissors, tourniquets, a bottle of Percodan, two syringes, even a small probelike instrument. On the toilet tank were a bottle of codeine pills and a box containing an inflatable splint. The inhabitants of the house were evidently prepared to treat their own battlefield casualties.

And inflict some. In a locked hall closet was stored what appeared to be the National Armory of Lichtenstein. An Armalite 180 rifle, a Colt AR-15, a Leader T2 assault rifle, two Browning 9mm. pistols, a Colt .357 revolver, and thirty-two boxes of assorted ammunition. Plus some blasting caps and explosive detonators.

It must have bugged them, having to leave that carefully assembled collection of armaments behind. But they probably hadn't wanted to risk being spotted trying to smuggle all the stuff out of the house at once.

The members of the PRC apparently read a great deal, but, judging from the collection of books in the living room, their tastes in literature were confined to one specific area. Included in the library were a copy of Carlos Marighella's *Mini-manual of the Urban Guerrilla,* something called *How to Fight a Revolution,* an army first aid manual, the Weather Underground's *Prairie Fire,* Mao's red book, and a volume on police procedure. There was a handbook on the assembling of explosive devices.

What clothing was to be found was an interesting mixture of street wear and battle dress. On the floor of the bedroom closet, between a pair of Herman survivors and a pair of Frye boots, was a pair of women's sandals with stacked heels. Hanging next to the jeans and work shirts and fatigue jackets were cotton skirts and blouses. A man's three-piece beige linen suit. On the top shelf of the closet were a straw summer purse, empty, and a blow dryer. Next to that was a jumble of men's and women's underwear. The women's underwear was expensive. All the clothing in the closet was in fact of very high quality.

The day after the fire, I went over to the house on Third Street. The premises were being guarded by a patrolman whom I knew by sight. He nodded at me and I waved back at him.

East Cambridge was in the throes of being what the realtors called gentrified, but the yuppie invasion hadn't yet reached Third Street. Not this part of Third Street, anyway. It was strictly shabby frame three-deckers, auto body shops, doughnut emporia, and asphalt-shingled row houses. The latter would either get leveled by urban renewal or get gentrified by the yups into townhouses.

The PRC safe house was one of the more down-at-the-heels rowhouses, a skinny two-story thing attractively done in chipped and discoloring pale green asbestos and concrete siding. A shutter on one of the first floor windows hung askew. There were no curtains at the windows, only dark shades pulled down to the sill. Except for the boarded-up front door, there was no external trace of the previous evening's mini-holocaust.

The street itself was relatively quiet. An occasional car or truck buzzed by off the McGrath-O'Brien Highway. A dark-eyed kid on a tricycle pedaled industriously past me, chanting something softly to himself in what I took to be Portuguese. An elderly beagle bitch with hugely swollen dugs was sniffing around the base of a dented metal trash can. A seventyish, sunhatted woman puttered around in the minuscule garden of a three-decker a few houses down from the PRC fortress. Her house was one of the few on that section of the street that looked well maintained.

I went up to the patrolman guarding the rowhouse. He was standing in classic cop pose, arms folded and feet slightly apart. His gun belt looked as if it pinched.

"Hello," I said. "Any chance I might be able to go inside and poke around?"

He just looked at me.

"That's what I thought you'd say," I said. "Is it all right if I look in the windows?"

"No."

"Bummer," I said.

He laughed and I moved away.

The elderly woman was on her knees weeding around the flagstone path that led up to her front door. "Excuse me," I said.

She looked up, shading her eyes from the sun.

"There was a fire in that house up the street last night, wasn't there?"

The woman hoisted herself upright, brushing bits of grass and dirt from her knees. "Yes. Did you see it?"

"No. But I heard about it from a—from a friend."

The woman shook her head. "Awful," she said. "Just awful." She sighed heavily.

Awful? I looked at the woman with considerable interest. *Awful* was a very strong word to use in reference to a little nothing fire like the one the other night.

"What do you mean?" I asked, putting on my best ingenuous but puzzled look.

"Oh, not the fire," the woman said quickly.

"Oh?"

She glanced around as if her juniper bushes might be bugged by the

FBI and said, in hushed tones, "Well, you know—the people who were living there."

"What about them?" I said, lowering my voice to the same conspiratorial pitch.

"*Well,*" she said. "What I heard was that they were like some kind of gang." She paused, and then added, "Like *hippies.*" There was genuine horror in her voice.

I bit the inside of my lower lip to keep from laughing.

"And they seemed like such *nice* young people," the woman continued. "A girl and some boys."

To this woman girls and boys were probably anybody under forty-five.

"Did you know them?" I asked.

The woman removed her sunhat and brushed back a stray wisp of hair. "Not exactly. Just to say hello to. They kept to themselves, mostly. I talked to the girl a few times, but . . . " Her voice trailed off and she made a vague little gesture with her hand.

"My name is Liz Connors," I said. "I'm a writer for *Cambridge Monthly*. I don't want to take up your time if you're busy, but I'd like to talk to you more about this."

"Oh, no, that's fine," the woman said. "I'll be happy to. Why don't we sit on the porch, though? It's more comfortable."

"Thank you," I said. She nodded and led the way up the flagstone path. When we got to the front steps, she turned and said, "I'm Louise Costello." We shook hands. She had a nice, perky, vigorous manner about her.

We got settled on the porch, she in a webbed aluminum folding chair and I on a wooden bench. Mrs. Costello leaned back with a little grunt of contentment and said, "You're a real writer?"

"A real writer," I affirmed. "I guess."

She looked at me with something like awe. "I've never met one. A real writer."

I wondered how many fake ones she knew. In Cambridge the possibilities were nearly limitless. It was time to change the subject before the conversation got embarrassing. "You said you spoke to the woman a few times. What did you talk about?"

Mrs. Costello shrugged. "Nothing, really. The weather. I remember once, just after they moved in, she asked me where I did my grocery shopping. I told her the Star Market over in the Twin Cities Plaza. It's the closest. Not the cheapest, though. The Demoulas in Union Square in Somerville . . . "

"When *did* they move in?" I asked.

Mrs. Costello thought for a moment before answering. "Sometime around the middle of March, I guess it was. Yes. Yes, that's when it was. I remember because it snowed that day."

"What did the woman look like?" I asked.

"Oh, she was a pretty little thing." Mrs. Costello looked at me narrowly. "Maybe around your age. Not as tall as you. Maybe about five six or seven. She had dark-brown hair, very short, in little curls. I don't know what color eyes."

I opened my handbag and took out the Bachrach portrait of Sarah Clarke Olmsbacher. I offered it to Mrs. Costello. "Put a short brown wig on that woman and make her ten or fifteen years older," I said.

Mrs. Costello laughed and took the clipping. "You're the second person that's asked me to do that."

I smiled. "Who was the first?"

"Oh, some policeman. Lieutenant something. A German name, I think. He was very nice. My daughter thought he was cute."

"I know him," I said. Cute? Jack? Yowza.

Mrs. Costello looked at the picture in her hand. "Well, I told him I thought it could be the same girl, but I couldn't be absolutely positively sure. She's changed a bit if she is. Although she would, being older, wouldn't she?" Mrs. Costello handed me the picture. "What I can't understand is why anyone would cut off all that lovely blond hair and dye it." She glanced at me. "You have beautiful hair, dear. My mother's hair was that strawberry color, too. Her maiden name was Halloran."

I returned the clipping to my purse. "Did this girl"—I was conscious of using Mrs. Costello's locution—"ever tell you her name? Or what she did?"

"Oh, yes. She told me her name was Kathleen. Kathleen Morris." Mrs. Costello glanced at me again. "Although I guess it really wasn't, was it?"

"Apparently not," I said. "Did she ever mention if she worked anywhere?"

"Oh, yes. She said she was a teacher's aide at a day-care center."

A teacher's aide. Nice, reassuring touch. "What about the people who lived with her?"

"Well, I never really met them. I'm not sure how many there were. There were three or four young men, I know that much. I didn't know their names. One of them was the one who the police shot in that terrible thing at the Towers the other night. It said on the news." Mrs. Costello shivered, I suppose reminiscently.

"Do you recall what they looked like?" I asked.

"Well, as I say, I never saw them up close or very often. One had dark hair and a beard, I think, I guess he was the one the police shot, and there were a couple others."

"And you have no idea what they did."

She shook her head. "No. We never spoke, and Kathleen never said. I guess I thought they were students or something." She flicked a stray blade of grass from her sleeve.

"Who did they rent the house from?" I asked.

"The landlady is Maria Ribiero," Mrs. Costello replied.

I nodded. "Do you know where I can get in touch with her?"

"Oh, Maria's been away for the past week. Her oldest girl had a baby. It's Maria's first grandchild. A little boy. They named him Jason."

Shit, I thought.

"Why?" Mrs. Costello asked, fanning herself languidly with her sunhat.

"I was wondering how they paid the rent," I said. "The police didn't find any canceled checks or receipts in the house, which seemed kind of funny."

Mrs. Costello nodded agreement. "They wouldn't. Maria told me that Kathleen always paid in cash on the first of each month."

I was silent for a moment, digesting this bit of intelligence. "I wonder how they paid for their utilities," I said finally. "It seems kind of awkward to send the gas company a roll of bills and change."

"Oh, the utilities were included in the rent."

"What about the phone?"

"Maria said they didn't have one."

"Didn't that strike her as odd?"

Mrs. Costello laughed and shrugged. "Maria always said she didn't care what her tenants did as long as they were quiet and clean about it and paid the rent on time."

Apparently Mrs. Ribiero hadn't cared if her tenants manufactured bombs and plotted assassinations in her house, either. Well, they *had* been quiet about it. And relatively clean, apparently.

I rose and held out my hand. Mrs. Costello took it and we shook. "Thank you so much," I said. "You've been extremely helpful."

"Oh, I enjoyed talking to you, dear." She smiled. "Bye-bye."

"Good-bye. It was nice to meet you." I started down the steps and onto the flagstone path. When I'd reached the sidewalk, I heard her call to me. I turned.

She was leaning against the porch railing and grinning at me archly. "If you see that nice policeman again, tell him I said not to be a stranger, hear?"

"I certainly will," I promised.

I went from Third Street to the police station. I wanted to compare notes with Jack. It was a sure bet he'd gotten more out of Louise Costello than had I. He knew the right questions to ask.

The cop house was as calm and as orderly as ever, at least on the surface. Up on the fourth floor, in the gym, the recruit class would be learning self-defense from the lieutenant in charge of the Special Weapons and Tactical Squad. Ronnie Mulryne, the instructor, was a guy in his early fifties, about my height, with a hard, wiry build. He'd been a high-school teacher for a few years before becoming a cop. His manner was diffident, almost self-effacing. Not that of somebody who knew fifty-seven varieties of high-tech killing. He was big on vegetable gardening. He and I had once had a chat about how difficult it was to grow cantaloupes in New England. Afterward, I'd asked Jack about him.

"Ronnie?" Jack had said, smiling. "That guy is ten years older and five inches shorter than I am. And he could mop up the floor with me."

"No shit?" I'd replied. "Well, I'll be careful to stay on his good side."

I went up the two flights of stairs to the C.I.D. Midway I bumped into yet another lieutenant (the place was lousy with them), this the one in charge of the police academy. He told me that there had been a schedule change and that my next writing class would be held in the afternoon rather than in the morning. I thanked him for the notice and he apologized for any inconvenience the change might cause me. They were never that polite at any of the colleges I'd taught at.

The outer office of the C.I.D. was vacant, as it usually was at midday. Jack's office door was open. He was seated behind his desk, writing on a white lined pad. I tapped on the doorjamb and he looked up from his work.

"Well, hello," he said. "This is a pleasant surprise."

"It's nice that you think so," I said.

He smiled, and I smiled back at him. Inwardly, I was somewhat startled and more than a little concerned. He didn't look good. Actually, he looked like somebody coming down off a five-day drunk, his face gray and the whites of his eyes red.

"So come in," he said. "Don't just stand there posing in the doorway."

I sat down in the chair across from the desk. "How's every little thing?"

He shrugged. "Same old shit. What about you?"

"I just got back from a trip to Third Street."

"No fooling," he said, leaning back in his chair. "Now whatever on earth would you have been doing down there?"

"Background," I said. "Background for my article."

"Get any?"

"Some. That's what I wanted to talk to you about." I set my handbag and manila folder on the floor beside my chair. "First, though, I think I could use some coffee. Care for a cup?"

"Nope. Just had one." He straightened up in his chair and glanced out at the main office. "I think I took the last of our pot, though. You'll probably have to go down to the muster room. Although the stuff in the machine there tastes like lighter fluid."

"I know," I said. "I've drunk it before." I got up. "Sure you don't want anything?"

"No. But thanks."

I tramped downstairs to the muster room on the first floor. I was careful to knock on the swinging door before I entered. I'd once burst in there to get a diet Schweppes from the soft drink machine and had slapped straight into a patrolman with his uniform pants at half-mast. Since then I'd been careful to announce myself.

The coffee came from one of those vendomatics that purported also to dispense chicken soup, hot chocolate, and tea. The coffee was a sort of beigey gray, with an apparent oil slick atop it. On the sole occasion I'd sampled the chicken soup, it had looked much the same.

The difference in taste hadn't been noteworthy, either. An army of Jewish mothers would have gone on strike.

Cup in hand, I trudged back upstairs to Jack's office. He was leaning back in his chair, hands clasped behind his head, gazing at the ceiling. He really didn't look at all well. I reminded myself that few people would after participating in a shoot-out and going two-and-a-half weeks with virtually no sleep. Still, it wouldn't hurt to ask . . .

I settled down in the visitor's chair and took a sip of coffee. The pride of Juan Valdez. I put the coffee on the top shelf of the bookcase in the corner.

"You're wrong," I said. "It tastes worse than lighter fluid."

Jack smiled a little, in an abstracted way.

"So," I said, keeping my tone carefully casual. "How are you?"

"Okay," he said. "I'm okay."

"You look a little worn."

He shrugged.

"Anything new?" I persisted.

He didn't reply for a moment. A phone on one of the desks in the outer office began shrilling. A fire engine went racketing down Western Avenue. Somebody picked up the phone on its sixth ring. I heard, faintly, the sound of laughter from the corridor. There was a rhythmic thumping from above. The recruits going through their paces.

"Goldman died," Jack said. "About an hour ago."

11

June 22

I spent the following weekend at Jack's place. He spent most of that time in bed. I browsed through a copy of the *Mini-manual of the Urban Guerrilla* and a few other how-to books on terrorism. Lucy settled down in the hallway to work on a new beef neck bone. In our separate ways, the three of us enjoyed ourselves. Sort of.

I was in the living room, reading, Sunday evening when Rip Van Lingemann finally regained full consciousness. He came out of the bedroom yawning and pulling a Celtics T-shirt over his head.

"Role reversal," I said, putting aside Carlos Marighella and taking off my glasses.

"Huh?" He sat down on the couch next to me.

"Role reversal," I repeated. "*I'm* supposed to be the Sleeping Beauty. *You're* supposed to be Prince Charming and wake me with a kiss. Or whatever."

"Whatever." He rubbed his head. "Sorry. I'm a little slow tonight."

"You're entitled," I said, "After the past three weeks. Want some coffee or a drink?"

"Oh, coffee would be good."

I got up. "I'll make it." I'd also put some food together; as far as I knew, Jack hadn't eaten anything since yesterday afternoon.

I went into the kitchen and ran some water in the kettle and put it on the stove. Then I opened the refrigerator to see what might be

73

available in the way of quickie eats. The simplest things appeared to be ham and cheese. Then I rooted around in the cupboard until I found a loaf of rye bread and an unopened jar of mustard. *Voila.* Instant dinner.

I brought everything into the living room on a tray and set it on the coffee table. Jack looked at the plate of sandwiches with something like a slow-dawning wonder. "Jesus, I'm hungry," he remarked.

"I'm not surprised." I sat down on the couch and put cream in the coffee. I handed a cup to Jack.

"Thank you," he said. He picked up one of the sandwiches and bit into it. I put a paper napkin in Carlos Marighella to mark the place where I stopped reading and set the book down on the arm of the couch.

"You're really getting into this stuff, aren't you?" Jack said.

I assumed he was referring to the *Mini-manual* in particular and to terrorism in general.

"Yeah," I said. "It really is sort of a compelling subject."

"Oh, that it is," he said. "That it is."

We munched our way through the plate of sandwiches with little more conversation but with a great deal of appetite. Lucy wandered in from the hallway and lay down before the coffee table and watched us very closely as we ate. Jack tossed her the last bit of crust from his sandwich and she snapped at it like a trout at a fly.

I gestured at the empty plate. "Shall I make some more?"

Jack shook his head. "Not for me, thanks. That was fine." He wiped his hands with a paper napkin, crumpled it, and dropped it back onto the tray. Then he leaned back against the couch cushions and hooked his left arm around my shoulders. I glanced at him quickly, appraisingly, out of the corner of my eyes. He still looked tired, but a lot less harried and tense than he had at midweek. There was definitely more gray in his hair, though. That much I hadn't imagined.

"How are you feeling now?" I asked.

"Oh, better," he replied. "Fine." He took his arm from my shoulders and stretched. "Maybe I'll go back to bed for a while, though." He looked at me. "Care to join me?"

"Well, I don't know," I said. "Maybe if you promise not to fall asleep on top of me like you did last night."

He winced. "Jesus. Did I do that?"

"You don't remember?"

He shook his head.

I laughed. "Boy, you were really out of it. Gonzo."

"Jesus," he repeated, still shaking his head.

"However," I continued. "I'm probably not going to get a better offer this evening. What the hell. Let's go."

He held out his hand and I took it and stood up.

Lucy chose that moment to begin capering around in a highly suggestive manner and to cast urgent looks in the direction of the front door.

"Oh, Lord," I said. "I think Fats here wants to go out for a stroll."

"Swell," Jack said. "Good timing, Luce."

She grinned at him and thrashed her tail back and forth, as if she were being commended for having done something extraordinarily clever.

I got the leash from the hall and clipped it to the metal ring on Lucy's collar. She bounded toward the front door, dragging me behind her. Jack trailed along, rather glumly, I thought.

"Hey, hey, simmer down," I said to the dog. She paused, but gave me an impatient look. Jack slid the bolt on the front door and opened it. I put my free arm through his and we went out onto the porch.

It was a perfect June evening, quite warm and still. In Cambridge you couldn't see the stars, of course, but on a night like this, you had a sense that they were up there somewhere. The exhaust fumes from the street hadn't quite overpowered the scent from the trees and grass. I closed my eyes and took a deep breath.

"Nice night," Jack commented. He put his free hand on my forearm and rested it there. Lucy yanked at the leash and I lurched forward.

"Dog needs to be obedience trained," Jack said, sounding disapproving. "She's got you programmed to do whatever she wants. Why don't you take her to one of those classes at the Center for Adult Ed?"

"When I get up the ambition," I said. "Lucy, will you cut the crap, please?" She was really hauling on the leash now, straining to get at the jungle of rhododendron in front of the house.

"This is stupid," Jack said.

"Yeah," I muttered. "Lucy, dammit, knock it off." In reply, she gave an almighty tug and the leather handle of the leash snapped in my hand. Thus freed, she dashed into the rhododendron bank. There was a violent thrashing in the bushes.

"Oh, for God's sake," I said, and took a step forward.

At that moment, the dog gave a low growl that terminated in a peculiar sort of whine. She backed out of the bushes and stood rigid for a few seconds, staring at something only she could see. Then she turned and hustled past us, her head lowered and her ears crossed behind her skull. As she flew by, I caught a glimpse of her eyes. They had the glazed, staring look of fear they get when she hears a loud, scary noise like thunder or backfire.

Lucy halted before the entrance to the house, alternately panting and whining. Then she began scratching furiously at the front door, evidently on the supposition that she could thereby claw her way to safety. Jack and I stared at each other, mystified.

"What's going on?" he said.

"I don't know," I replied. "I've never seen her act quite this funny." I peered at the bank of rhododendrons. "Maybe there's a dead squirrel in the bushes. Although that wouldn't frighten her, would it?"

"She's your dog," Jack said. "You ought to know. Anyway, she's a hunting breed, isn't she?"

"Allegedly," I said. I looked back at the bushes. "Weird."

"Maybe I should check it out," Jack said.

"Wouldn't do any harm," I replied.

He walked over to the rhododendrons and pushed aside some of the branches. He bent down and peered around the base of the shrubs. Then he said, "Oh, *Christ.*" He straightened up and repeated, "Christ. Jesus Christ."

I felt a little thrill of alarm. "What is it?"

He didn't turn around, but remained frozen in place, staring at the rhododendrons. "There's something dead in there, all right."

"Well, what is it?" I took a step forward.

"Don't come any closer," he said sharply.

"What *is* it?"

He looked over his shoulder at me. Even in the dim light I could see the pallor of his face. "It's some guy."

I put my hand over my mouth and stared at him.

He walked back to me and put his hand on my shoulder. "You really don't want to see what he looks like. Why don't you go inside and call Sam, okay?" He squeezed my shoulder.

I nodded and went into the house. As I opened the front door, Lucy shot past me and made a beeline for the living room. I watched her wriggle under the couch, as good a place as any to hide. I wished I could do the same, but instead, I went to the phone and called the police.

It didn't take them long to respond. An army of them showed up— in addition to Sam Flaherty, there was a fellow with a doctor's bag, a medical examiner I assumed, seven other cops, some technicians, and a photographer who pranced around recording the scene for posterity. I sat on the front steps and watched the show, along with the usual throng of ghouls who'd materialized from nowhere and hung around on the sidewalk gaping at the Police in Action. I wondered if eventually somebody with a pushcart might show up and start hawking hot dogs and ice cream bars.

When they dragged the body out of the bushes, I averted my eyes. The spectators loved it. "Somebody tell those assholes to take a hike," I heard Flaherty say. One of the cops detached himself from the group around the rhododendron and strolled over to the cluster of onlookers. "Okay, folks, let's move along, all right?" he said, pleasantly enough. "Show's over. There's nothing else to see." Most of them moved off, but with considerable reluctance.

Flaherty came over to me and said, "You okay, doll?" His basset hound face looked even sadder tonight.

"I think so," I said. "Thank you."

He nodded and rejoined the others. The medical examiner had closed his bag and was getting to his feet. He was talking to Jack, although I couldn't hear any of the exchange. Flaherty had squatted down beside the body and was rummaging through its clothing. With a pair of tweezers, he removed something from the shirt pocket—it looked like a piece of paper—and squinted at it. After a moment, he said, "Holy shit." He stood up and showed whatever it was to Jack. Jack glanced down at it briefly and then back up at Flaherty. They stared at each other for a few seconds. Flaherty shook his head and handed Jack the tweezers and paper. One of the other cops peered over Jack's shoulder at it, recoiled, and said, "Jesus H. *Christ.*"

The Greek chorus was getting on my nerves. "Jack," I said.

He glanced up at the sound of my voice, said something softly to Flaherty, and walked over to where I was sitting. He dropped down on the steps beside me.

"What is it?" I said.

Jack held the paper before me, about six inches away from my nose. I blinked.

"Read it," he said.

I did. It was a note written in a graceful, almost Italianate hand, and it went:

Lingemann:
    This little piggie makes three.
    And you're next, motherfucker.

                                              Alexa

12

The little piggie's name was Harvey Whitcomb, he was thirty-seven years old, and in life he'd been an engineer at Roper Labs, involved in missile guidance system design. He'd been shot twice in the back of the head, just as Morgan and Burmester had. Then he'd been carted from wherever it was he'd been killed and dumped in Jack's landlord's rhododendrons. He hadn't been dead all that long when Lucy found him.

We didn't get much sleep that night. The medical examiner, the photographer, and three of the cops and the technicians left with Whitcomb's body around midnight. There were yet more cops still out canvassing the neighborhood, trying to turn up someone who'd heard or seen *something* funny going on around Jack's place earlier in the evening. It would seem incredible that what must have been a minimum of two or three people, even operating under the cover of darkness, could remove a body from a car or van or truck, carry it across a front lawn, and drop it in some shrubbery without being spotted by at least one of the neighbors.

And yet the whole grisly business had been carried out virtually under my nose, and I'd been oblivious to it. Even Lucy, whose intruder alert system didn't let much slip by it, hadn't noticed anything until she'd actually gotten outside.

I went into the kitchen. Jack and Flaherty were sitting at the table, talking. Flaherty had a lined pad in front of him and was making notes on it. He'd interviewed me earlier. It made me feel bad, and a little stupid, that I had nothing useful to tell him.

I opened the cabinet over the refrigerator, rummaged in it, and found a bottle of bourbon.

"You two are drinking a lot of coffee," I said. "Maybe you should have something to neutralize it." I held up the bottle. Jack and Flaherty shook their heads.

"Well, I'm going to," I said. "If nobody has any objection." I didn't wait for an answer, but put some ice in a glass and added some bourbon and a little water. I leaned against the counter and sipped my booze and watched Jack. He was lighting yet another cigarette. If this didn't end soon, he'd be up to three packs a day.

Flaherty left about 2 A.M. I walked with him to the door. He tugged a lock of my hair and told me to be good. I told him I couldn't make rash promises.

I locked and bolted the door behind him, and then went into the darkened living room. I parted the curtains across the front window just a fraction and peered out at the street. Now that most of the police vehicles had cleared out, it looked just as any residential neighborhood would at that hour—lifeless. But it wasn't, quite. Although I couldn't see them, there were cops staked out around the house. It was a freaky feeling, being under armed and invisible guard, but no more grotesque than anything else that had happened this evening.

I let the curtains fall into place and wandered back to the kitchen. Jack was still at the table, smoking. He looked up when I came into the room and smiled with some effort and considerable weariness. "You ought to go to bed," he said. "You must be exhausted."

"Me?" I said. "You must be kidding." I flopped down in the chair Flaherty had vacated. "What about you?"

"Never felt better in my life," he said.

We both laughed, then, but in a kind of forced and constricted way.

"You want something to drink now?" I asked.

He looked as if he were going to refuse, then changed his mind. "Oh, okay. Thank you."

The nearest thing to hand was the bourbon, on the counter where I'd left it. I poured some into a glass with ice and brought it to the table and set it down in front of him. He picked it up and took a swallow.

"What are you going to do?" I said.

"Finish this," he replied, rattling the ice in his glass. "Maybe have another. Then hit the sack."

I looked at him for a few seconds, sucking on my upper lip. "You really are something," I said. "You know that? Mr. Cool strikes again."

He smiled a little. "Well, it's not as if this were the first time somebody threatened to kill me."

"I'm aware of that," I said drily. "But I somehow think that sweet Alexa and her cohorts might be better at carrying out threats than the average dirtball is."

"Oh, so do I," he replied. "I do indeed."

I got up and went to the counter and made myself a second drink, a weak one. I brought the bourbon bottle back to the table with me.

"Why does it have to be you?" I said.

He looked mildly surprised. "What do you mean, why does it have to be me?"

I made a gesture with my right hand as if I were trying to slice the kitchen air lengthwise. "Why are *you* suddenly the target for all this shit?"

He finished his drink. "Isn't it obvious?"

"Not particularly," I said. "You're not a defense worker."

"No," he agreed. "But I *am* a cop."

"One of many," I said. "If the PRC's going to get into assassinating cops again, why not start at the top? Go for the gold. The Big Pig. The chief, say. They seem to like flamboyant symbolic gestures like that."

Jack made himself another drink. "Well, the chief didn't kill one of them, did he?"

I was silent for a moment, watching him. Then I said, "You really didn't have a choice about that."

He gave me another slight smile. "I sure didn't think so at the time. But"—he shrugged—"the PRC wouldn't see it that way."

Of course they wouldn't. Nor would they care how many cops had been involved in the shoot-out at Roosevelt Towers, nor would they care that the bullets that had hit Goldman had come from three different guns. They wouldn't know, nor would it matter to them if they did, that the shot that had killed their comrade had actually been fired by one of the patrolmen. The bullet from Jack's gun had hit Goldman in the shoulder, causing a serious wound, but not a fatal one.

But all that was immaterial. Jack was the one heading the investigation. Jack was the one who'd been interviewed by the papers. Jack was the one whose face had been on the TV news four times in the past two weeks.

Ergo, that made Jack the obvious target. Vengeance is mine, saith Alexa.

I finished my drink and glanced at the bourbon bottle. There was about an inch left in it. Might as well split it with Jack. I did so.

"How do you suppose they found out where you live?" I said presently. "The papers didn't say. And you're not listed in the phone book."

"No," Jack agreed. "But my address is in a file at city hall. One of them could have bought a look at it, I suppose."

"Very possible," I said. "Our public servants being the incorruptible lot that they are."

"Or," Jack continued. "They could have been watching me."

I stared at him, horrified. "And one of them followed you home one night?"

"Sure. Why not?"

"But ... " I scratched my head. "That would have been an awful chance for them to take. Suppose you spotted the person following you?"

"If you use more than one person to tail somebody," Jack said, almost didactically. "It can be hard to spot. And they know about clever stuff like that."

"But you'd recognize Sarah Olmsbacher," I said. "Or that other one, that Prescott Forbes character."

"Of course," Jack said. "And I'm sure they know that. Or they do now, anyway."

"So?"

"So I don't know what the others in the group look like. I don't even know how many of them there are. Sure, I got some half-assed descriptions of them from some of the other people on Third Street. But it's the usual contradictory crap. Practically useless for identification purposes."

I nodded. "So Alexa sent one of her new recruits to spy on you. Knowing that you'd have no way of recognizing whoever it was."

"Well, that's one possibility." He yawned hugely, and pushed away his glass. "Come on. What do you say we try to get some token sleep?" He looked at the kitchen clock. "Jesus, four A.M."

I got up and put the glasses in the sink and tossed the empty bourbon bottle into the trash. Then I went over to him and gave him a hug. He put his arm around me and we leaned against each other for a few seconds. All of a sudden, I was exhausted.

As we were walking down the hall to the bedroom, I said, "Well, there's one good thing come out of all this mess."

"What's that?" Jack asked.

"Maybe we can go somewhere for a few days and relax," I said. "A week, even. To Maine. Maine's really nice this time of year and—" I broke off in midsentence. Jack was staring at me in astonishment.

"What's the matter?" I said.

"I can't go anywhere now," he said.

It was my turn to look surprised. "You can't?" I said. "Why not? Some very bad people have just threatened to kill you. Surely the captain's going to take you off the investigation. He's not going to deliberately endanger your life."

Jack stared at me a moment longer, a look of utter disbelief on his face. Then he sat down on the bed and started to laugh. "Honey," he said, shaking his head. "If a police officer got taken off duty every time somebody threatened him, there'd be about twelve out of three hundred people working in the department at any one time."

"What?" I exploded. "You mean you—"

"Ssshh," he said, putting his index finger to his lips. "You'll wake the poor folks upstairs."

"Fuck the poor folks upstairs," I yelled. "What about you?"

He got up from the bed and came over to me and covered my mouth with his hand. "Relax," he said. "I'm fine. I *will* be fine. Nothing bad will happen. I just have to be a little more careful, that's all."

I jerked my head back, out of his grasp. His hand didn't drop, but hovered about six inches away from my mouth, ready to clap over it if I started yammering again. I took a deep breath to compose myself.

"Come on," he said. "Let's get to bed."

I eyed him for a moment. He was smiling a little. I opened my mouth and then shut it. I knew from past experience that there was absolutely nothing more to be said.

We undressed, in silence, and got into bed. Jack slid his arm around me and I edged closer to him. "That's nice," he said. His voice sounded only half-conscious.

Five minutes later he was sound asleep. It took me a lot longer.

13

The following morning, one of Jack's bodyguards drove Lucy and me home. It was the dog's first ride in a police cruiser, and she loved every minute of it. I kind of got a kick out of it, too. Or I would have if I hadn't been so tired and so worried about Jack.

It occurred to me, when I got back to my apartment, that I might have some reason to be concerned about my own safety as well as his. The PRC could well have seen me with him, or watched me go in and out of his house. In their eyes, a pig's woman probably occupied the slot just above slugs and just below cockroaches in the hierarchy of being. And since they seemed to view their role as that of exterminator . . .

The hell with it. If Jack wasn't going to be intimidated by Alexa and company, than neither was I. Besides, I realized with a certain degree of fatalism, there wasn't much I could do to protect myself. So I'd keep on teaching my academy class and researching my article and trying to find out more about this entity that called itself the Peoples Revolutionary Cadre.

With that in mind, I made a date to have lunch Wednesday with a friend of Jack's and mine, a psychiatrist named David Epstein. It would be interesting to get his perspective on the phenomenon of terrorism.

We met at a Mexican restaurant in Harvard Square. Epstein had gotten there earlier than I, and had grabbed a table for two by the window. He was drinking a bottle of Carta Blanca when I arrived. He hopped up from the table and gave me a kiss on the cheek and a big hug.

"Who do you think you are?" I said. "Leo Buscaglia?"

He laughed.

Epstein isn't unique among shrinks in that he's not only physically attractive, but full of exuberance and humor. I had met another therapist, once, who'd had similar qualities. He'd turned out to be a homicidal rapist. I don't know what that said about the breed in general. Epstein himself had once told me that an abnormally high number of cuckoos went into the so-called mental health professions. Probably trying to figure out what made themselves tick. Anyway, I was reasonably sure that Epstein was normal.

Over his beer and my glass of red wine, I described to him the research I was doing for the article I was writing. He'd read in the papers and heard on the news about what had happened at Jack's place Sunday night. He'd probably have a question or two for me about that at some point. He was Jack's friend, but he was also, among other things, a consultant to the police department on stress. He'd counseled a lot of cops who were under pressure. Finding a corpse stuffed into your rhododendrons with a threatening letter in its shirt pocket probably ranked high in the order of stress situations.

The waitress brought Epstein his black bean soup and me my tacos. I know it's un-chic to order tacos in a Mexican restaurant, but I can't help myself. They're the only kind of Mexican food I really like.

"David," I said. "What do you know about terrorists? From a psychiatric standpoint, I mean?"

He was busy with his soup. "Not a hell of a lot, I'm afraid."

"No?"

He put down his spoon. "Well, there have been a lot of studies done. And some tentative profiles set up. But we don't know what makes people into terrorists. Or whether their behavior is psychotic in origin."

"David, shooting up defense workers and dumping their carcasses on cops' front lawns is not the action of a healthy, stable person."

"Of course it isn't, chickie," he agreed. "But we don't know what the motivation behind the action is."

"Sure we do. The PRC wants to bring military spending to a halt and get the U.S. out of the Middle East and Central America. They're going to grease one defense worker for every million dollars spent on weapons and missiles and aircraft and such. That's a big job considering what the defense budget is now. Why don't they just blow up the Pentagon? Their expectations aren't exactly realistic. Doesn't that say something about their mentality?"

"Sure it does, but the point I'm trying to make is that you can't generalize about the impulses that create a terrorist. What may be valid in one case won't be in another. We know what *kind* of people become terrorists, but we don't know why they do."

"Okay. What kind of person becomes a terrorist?"

He finished his soup. "Oh, generally a young one. Early to middle twenties. From a well-to-do or at least a comfortable background. Well educated, usually, either in the liberal arts or some profession like law or journalism. They tend to get politicized in school. Rather rapidly, I might add."

So far what Epstein was saying sounded like a capsule biography of Sarah Olmsbacher. "Can you generalize about any quirks they might have?"

"Well, they all seem to suffer from some degree of paranoia. They have a strong sense of mission and strong feelings of persecution."

"I'll say." I thought for a moment. "But, David, even though what they do seems irrational, they do it in a very rational way, if you follow me. *What* they do is nuts, but *how* they do it doesn't seem to be. And they don't appear to be wild-eyed crazies to the people who meet them and who don't know what they are." I recalled Mrs. Costello's description of "Kathleen Morris," teacher's aide.

"No, because paranoia doesn't cause the kind of personality disintegration that's associated with other forms of mental illness."

The waitress brought Epstein a plate of enchiladas and another bottle of Carta Blanca. She looked at my empty wine glass and I shook my head. I'd been drinking a bit more than I usually did, lately, and I was determined to cut back. Damned if I'd let the Peoples Revolutionary Cadre make a lush out of me.

I put the taco down on the plate and wiped my hands on a napkin. "Tell me something, David."

Through a mouthful of enchilada, he said, "If I can."

"Why is it always rich kids? Or at least, mostly rich kids?"

He sipped some beer. "Who knows? There are lots of theories to explain that. The most popular one is guilt. The kids who become guerrillas are brought up with everything handed to them on a silver platter. But ghetto babies starve. They feel the contrast. I can give you some readings on this, if you want."

I nodded and finished my taco. The waitress brought us some coffee.

"Terrorists tend to be absolutists," Epstein continued. "They need to be attached to a movement or to a cause, and when they are, their dedication to it becomes total. It's a kind of fulfillment for them. Almost a religious experience. The sense of belonging may fill some kind of void."

I smiled. "You know, everything you've told me so far fits perfectly with what I've found out about the people in the PRC. Sarah Olmsbacher, particularly, fascinates me. I'd like to find out more about her. About the others, too, and I wouldn't mind knowing who the hell Leilah is or was. Neither would the cops, for that matter. But Olmsbacher . . . Jesus, she must be a real screwball."

Epstein gave me a curious look. "Why her more than the others?"

"Oh, I don't know. I just have this funny feeling that this whole thing, killing defense workers in the name of anti-imperialism and anti-fascism, is some kind of bizarre game for her. You didn't read the note that was stuffed into Harvey Whitcomb's shirt pocket. It hasn't been released to the press. Not only was the thing addressed to Jack, but instead of all the usual crappy revolutionary rhetoric, it was half a nursery rhyme. Something about poor Whitcomb being the little piggie that made three. Olmsbacher even signed it with her code name."

Epstein scooped up the last of his enchiladas. "Like a personal vendetta."

"Exactly," I said. "That's just what it is."

"It's almost as if she's daring Jack to catch her and telling him that he can't," Epstein said. "Catch me if you can." He sipped his coffee.

"David," I said. "*I* was a kid in college in the late sixties. *I* was a liberal arts major. *I* saw what was going on in the world. *I* don't care much for war or racism or militarism or sexism. My parents aren't poor. So why didn't *I* become a terrorist?"

He shook his head. "If I could tell you that, I could tell you anything."

"No easy answers," I said.

"There never are," he said. "You want dessert?"

"No, thank you."

"Well, I do." He signaled the waitress. Then he turned back to me. "You sure about dessert? They have a great chocolate thing here."

I shook my head, smiling.

"How's Jack?" Epstein said abruptly.

"Fine," I said.

"Fine," Epstein repeated, nodding. "He just had a corpse hand-delivered to his front door with a gift card enclosed, but he's fine. And somebody threatened to kill him. He's still fine. Good show."

I laughed, unwillingly.

"So what's the deal?" Epstein said. He put his chin in his hand and gazed at me. His dark eyes were very bright and probing, like miniature lasers.

"I am a little worried," I said.

"No shit. I would be, too. What's going on?"

I hesitated a moment. Then I said, "Nothing I can put my finger on."

"So try."

I made a little helpless gesture with my right hand. "I don't know. He says he's okay. But he's tired all the time. He looks lousy, you know, all sort of gray in the face."

Epstein nodded. "Has he been drinking more than he usually does?"

"A little. But we both have."

"Sleeping a lot?"

"Gawd, no. Well, over the weekend he did, but he was making up for what he's lost."

"Having trouble getting to sleep or staying asleep?"

"Not that I've noticed. But his schedule's been insane. Some days I think he works sixteen hours."

"Okay. Any sexual dysfunction?"

I choked on my coffee. "I beg your pardon?"

"How's your sex life?"

"Oh. Oh, fine. When we get the chance to have one."

Epstein leaned back in his chair. "Well, that doesn't sound too bad, so far."

"Maybe," I said. "I don't know. He's taking some kind of pill. I don't know what, or what for."

Epstein shrugged. "Could be just a mild tranquilizer. Did you ask?"

I nodded. "He wouldn't say."

"Typical," Epstein replied. He tugged at his short dark beard. "When are you going to see him again?"

"I don't know."

"Oh?"

"I didn't mean it that way," I replied hastily. "He may not come home from work till one o'clock tomorrow morning. Then he'll maybe sleep for five hours and go back again. That's another thing bothering me. He's not a teenager, you know. I don't know how long he can keep going like that." I finished my coffee.

"How are you?" Epstein said.

"Huh?" I was startled.

"How are you coping with all this?"

I shrugged. "It's not me who has to cope. Nobody's threatened to kill *me*."

"That's true," Epstein replied. "But there are worse things. Believe it or not." He dug into his dessert. "God, this is incredible. Whoo-wee. You *sure* you don't want some?" He held out a spoonful of chocolate glop for me. "Here, try it," he urged. I waved away the spoon.

"How does it sound to you?" I asked. I was looking for a reassurance that nobody, even Epstein, could give me. "Jack's condition?"

"Not serious," Epstein said. "According to what you say. But, I don't know. I'd like to talk to him myself. I don't make long-range diagnoses."

"I know."

The waitress brought us more coffee. Epstein asked her for the check.

"Do me a favor," he said.

I widened my eyes. "Sure. What?"

He put cream in his coffee. "Let me know if anything happens. With Jack, I mean."

I frowned. "Like what?"

"Oh, anything." Epstein picked up his coffee cup. "Let me know how he's doing."

I gave Epstein a hard look. "I'm not going to report on him."

"I didn't ask you to. I just want to know if—well, just tell me if anything at all funny or unusual happens with him, okay? For your sake as well as his."

The waitress brought the check. I reached for my handbag. Epstein said, "My treat."

"But I asked *you* to lunch."

"Sure you did," Epstein said genially. "But I make a lot more money than you do."

I gaped at him for a moment, and then started to laugh incredulously. I opened my bag and got out my wallet.

"My treat," he repeated. He put some money on top of the check.

I sat there, holding my wallet and feeling like a dummy. "Well, thank you," I said, finally. "That's very nice of you."

"Well, I'm a very nice person. And you're a very cheap date. Let's go, huh? I got a pack of the walking wounded waiting for me back at the office."

I dropped my wallet back into my bag and we got up and left the restaurant.

When we were out on the street Epstein turned to me and poked me in the collar bone with his index finger. "You," he said.

"What?"

"Remember what I said about Jack." He cocked his head and gave me another of those bright, probing looks. "I mean that."

I smiled. "Sure."

14 —

(June 25)

After I left Epstein, I did some grocery shopping and then went back to my place. No armed insurgents were lying in wait for me. As I was unlocking the front door, the phone began ringing. Naturally, the key stuck, and it wasn't until the sixth ring that I was able to get inside and dash across the living room and grab the receiver. The caller was Abby Henderson.

"Are you okay?" she demanded, without preamble.

I dropped the bag of groceries on the sofa and it fell over on its side, spilling half its contents. "I'm fine," I said. "How are you?" A grapefruit fell off the sofa and rolled across the rug.

"I was away over the weekend," she said. "I just heard about what happened Sunday night."

"Oh, yeah," I said. "*That.*"

"So tell me about it."

I did.

"Unbelievable," was her comment when I'd finished. "How's Jack?"

I gave a mental sigh. Abby meant well, and if I were her, I'd be asking the same question. Still, I'd just gone over the whole thing with Epstein. Once was enough for one day.

"He's fine," I said. "They've got a guard around his house now. So I guess he's pretty safe." I changed the subject. "So where'd you go over the weekend?"

"The Cape."

"How was it?"

"Great. Listen. I have some information for you, for your article. Well, I don't have it, exactly, but I know where you can get it."

"Oh?"

"Uh-huh. Last Thursday night Cal and I were at a party at some friends of Cal. We met some guy, I forget his name, from the Boston bureau of *Newsweek,* and got into a real long conversation with him. Anyway, the subject of the PRC came up, and he happened to mention that he knew a woman who was real tight with Sarah Olmsbacher when they were at Vassar."

"No kidding." I was already reaching for a pen and paper. "He didn't give her name, did he?"

"Well, of course he did. I asked him for it. You don't think I'd bother with this kind of build-up if I hadn't, do you?"

"No," I admitted. "Okay. Go on."

"It's a woman named Shana MacCormack."

"How can I get ahold of her?"

"You know that feminist bookshop on Bow Street? The Winds of Change?"

"Sure."

"Well, MacCormack runs it."

"Son of a gun," I said. "That ought to make it easy to track her down. Abby, thank you. I really appreciate this."

"Not at all," she said. "Glad to help."

"I hope Shana MacCormack feels the same way."

"Tell her you'll give her shop a plug in the article," Abby suggested. "She'll talk your ear off."

"Thanks for the tip."

"You're welcome. Want to have lunch again some time soon?"

"Sure. Maybe some day next week, okay?"

She agreed, and we said good-bye and hung up. I looked at my watch. It was exactly three. More than enough time for me to trot down to Harvard Square and the Winds of Change bookstore and introduce myself to Shana MacCormack as a member of the capitalist press. Too bad I couldn't say I was from *Ms* magazine. Oh, well.

I stashed my groceries and gave Lucy some water and a dog cookie. Then I walked down to Mass. Avenue to catch a bus. A 73 came along after about five minutes and I boarded it. It was jammed with pre-adolescent girls in lightweight blue blazers and plaid skirts. Parochial school uniforms. The decibel level of the shrieking and giggling would have drowned a chorus of jackhammers. I took a seat near the front so as not to get hit by a flying rosary.

The bus let me off at the Cambridge Common, near the tree under which General Washington is supposed to have taken command of the Continental Army in 1775. I had my doubts. The tree didn't look more than seventy-five years old. Perhaps it was a descendent of the original.

I trekked across Harvard Square, playing the customary game of human dodgems with the traffic, and turned down Bow Street. The Winds of Change Bookshop and Coffeehouse was sandwiched between a T-shirt emporium and a place that sold used stereo equipment. I paused outside and looked in the display window. The prominent item was an arrangement of Virginia Woolf's diaries. Next to that were some copies of Marge Piercy's latest novel, and towering over *that* an easel on which rested a poster advertising a poetry reading by Denise Levertov for the benefit of the Clamshell Alliance. Heavy.

As I pushed the door open, a bell above me tinkled. I looked around, feeling my pupils dilate in the dim light. The shop couldn't have been more than fifteen feet long by ten feet wide. Three and a half of the walls were shelved from floor to ceiling. Against the empty half of the rear wall was set a high, wide bench on which a coffee urn and a cash register rested. Beneath the bench was a miniscule refrigerator. The floor space was taken up by four small tables around which were grouped bridge chairs. It was as hot as hell in there.

"May I help you?" a voice above me said.

I looked up. Standing on a step ladder, rearranging the books on a high shelf, was a tall, almost anorexically thin woman. She was wearing a blue, short-sleeved, scoop-necked cotton top, a shin-length Indian print wraparound skirt, and flat leather sandals with a loop to accommodate the big toe. Her skin was pale and her hair light brown, drawn back into a loose knot. Some strands had come loose and partially hid the gold hoops in her ears.

"I'm looking for Shana MacCormack," I said.

"I'm Shana MacCormack," she replied, climbing down from the step ladder. "What can I do for you?" No smile. No expression of any kind.

I told her. She listened to me carefully. As I spoke, I kept my eyes on her face, alert for any trace of hostility, curiosity, or even interest. There was none. She said nothing. Her impassivity was disconcerting. Could anybody be *quite* that blank naturally, or did you have to work at it?

When I'd finished my recital, Shana MacCormack gestured at one of the small round tables and said, "Why don't we sit down?"

"Can I buy you a coffee?" I asked.

"You can buy me an ice tea," she replied.

"Sounds good," I said. "I'll have one, too." I was straining for joviality. The woman made me edgy.

She went to the refrigerator, bent down, opened it, and took out a half-gallon plastic pitcher. From it she poured iced tea into two tall pebbled glasses. She brought them back to the table and sat down. A good sign. If you can get someone to drink with you, you can usually get them to talk with you.

Shana MacCormack sipped at her tea. "Where did you get my name?"

"From a woman I know who met someone who knows you," I explained.

She nodded. I had the feeling she didn't much care.

"Anyway," I continued. "I *am* writing this article, and I *would* like to know something about what Sarah was like before she became an activist." Activist wasn't quite the right word, but what was? Terrorist? Urban guerrilla? Revolutionary? Psychotic killer?

"You were close to her, weren't you?"

MacCormack shrugged slightly. "We roomed together freshman and sophomore years."

"Then you must have gotten to know her fairly well," I encouraged.

"As well as anyone else ever did, I suppose."

I put my chin in my hand. "Meaning what?"

For the first time, MacCormack's face showed the faintest trace of human animation. A corner of her mouth quirked. It wasn't a smile. "Sarah wasn't someone you got to know that intimately. At least, no one at school did that I know of."

"Oh?"

MacCormack shook her head. "She actually didn't care that much for other women."

"No?" I thought back to all those PRC communiques with the references to the smashing of sexism. Sisterhood is powerful. "That's surprising."

"Is it?"

The question threw me a little off balance. "I find it so," I said. "From what I can tell from her, uh, writings, her sentiments seem to be radical feminist."

MacCormack ignored the comment. "If she had a close friend at school, I was it. But I think that was proximity more than anything else. We really didn't have a great deal in common. No one did, with her."

"Uh-huh," I said. "I take it Sarah never got elected Miss Congeniality or whatever."

"Hardly. But she did have a tremendous amount of influence over other people. She was very good at getting what she wanted."

Somehow that particular revelation didn't surprise me. "How did she go about doing that?"

MacCormack shook her head again. "Force of personality. She wasn't precisely aggressive, but . . . I don't know, it was a sort of manner she had. She *expected* people to do things for her and to give her what she wanted, so they did. Arrogance. Is that what you'd call it?"

"Probably as good a word as any," I said. "Okay. You say she wasn't fond of other women. How did she behave with men?"

MacCormack laughed drily. "That was different."

"I suspected it might be," I said. "Go on."

MacCormack had another sip of iced tea. "She had anyone she wanted."

"And I assume that there was more than one or two."

"Oh, yes. She told me once that she'd lost her virginity when she was thirteen. She seduced her piano teacher."

"She started earlier than most of her generation did," I commented. I was only a few years younger than Olmsbacher, but in my high school there'd still been such things as good girls and bad girls. I'd been one of the good ones, but less out of a high moral position than from sheer lack of opportunity to be otherwise. Also, I'd been a romantic and backseat gropings had never appealed.

"Well," MacCormack said. "Sarah was always in the vanguard. Or at the center of things. Whichever would bring her the most attention."

I nodded. I'd met a lot of people like that in my life. The cheerleader or pom-pom girl who'd pupated into a spokesperson for the huddled masses. And when *that* lost its charm, on to something new.

"So what else can you tell me?" I asked.

"What else do you want to know?" MacCormack finished her tea.

"What was she like when she came back from France? Didn't she do her junior year there?"

MacCormack nodded. "Yes. That was when I lost touch with her. She went to France and came back . . . different. Not her personality, but—"

"Her interests?" I suggested.

MacCormack deliberated. "That was it, I suppose," she said finally. "Sarah was in France during the student uprising in Paris. It gave her some sort of new direction, I think. I don't know. That must have been it. I know she was involved with a man who was a leader in the strikes."

"Came back afire with revolutionary zeal, did she?" I asked, smiling.

MacCormack didn't return the smile. "Before that, she'd been apolitical. I don't think she knew that there was a war in Vietnam. No, that's not true. She knew. It just didn't touch her, though. It wasn't anything that was relevant to her life." MacCormack sighed. "I met her just once after she came back from France. She told me she'd learned the meaning of commitment over there. I never saw her after that." MacCormack's voice faded and she gazed out the window at the street.

"I see," I said, after a moment. I knew the rest of the story. Or at least the bones of it. Maybe that was all anyone would ever know.

"Is there anything else?" MacCormack asked. "I really do have to get back to work."

"I know," I said. "And I'm very grateful for the time you've given me."

She didn't say anything.

"Could I ask you just one more question?"

MacCormack nodded.

"Thank you," I said. "It's just this: if you had to describe Sarah in one word, which would you choose as the most appropriate?" Corny, but useful. And revealing.

MacCormack thought for a moment. Then she opened her mouth as if to say something, and paused. I looked at her. Finally she said, "Cold."

"Cold?"

"Yes. Excuse me. I have to finish arranging the stock." She got up and crossed the room to the step ladder and mounted it.

I put three dollars on the table for the tea. My contribution to the feminist cause. MacCormack was busy with the books and didn't notice. I got up and headed for the door. MacCormack didn't say good-bye, nor bid me to have a nice day.

When I got to the door, I halted, my hand on the knob. I turned and looked back at Shana MacCormack. She had a copy of Louise Bogan in her hand. "You know, you were supposed to have been Sarah's friend," I said. "But you don't seem to have liked her very well. Even before she went to France. That kind of confuses me."

"It does?"

"Yes, it does."

MacCormack turned her head and looked at me, without expression, for perhaps ten seconds. Then she turned and slid the Bogan into a space on the shelf in front of her.

"*Did* you like her?" I said, rather more sharply than was probably necessary.

MacCormack smiled. "Actually," she said, in reflective tones, "I hated her."

15 —

(*June 25*)

"I met the spookiest woman this afternoon," I said.

"Oh?" Jack said. "Who was that?"

"A person named Shana MacCormack," I replied. "Abby Henderson got her name for me. She roomed with Sarah Olmsbacher at Vassar."

Jack's eyes widened slightly. "Oh?"

"You haven't run across her yet?"

He shook his head. "Tell me about it."

I described to him my conversation with MacCormack. When I'd finished, he leaned back in his chair and said, "Interesting."

"I thought so, too," I said. "But I don't know how useful anything she told me would be for *your* purposes. According to Shana, she hasn't laid eyes on Olmsbacher for—what? Maybe seventeen or eighteen years."

"So she told you."

I raised my eyebrows. "You think there might be something more there?"

He shrugged. "How would I know?"

I laughed. "I really can't see Shana MacCormack as part of any local terrorist support network that's giving aid and comfort to the PRC. She really seemed to loathe Sarah. I don't think she'd give aid and comfort to Sarah if Sarah collapsed on her doorstep."

"Well," he said. "I'll talk to her anyway."

"Best of luck, cookie." I got up to fetch the wine from the refrigerator. "Old Shana isn't exactly the bubbly, forthcoming type."

"I'll charm her."

"You may find that uphill work." I gestured at his glass with the wine bottle and he nodded. I filled it and he said, "Thank you. Why uphill?"

I resumed my seat and poured myself some more wine. "Shana struck me as somebody pretty much resistant to male blandishment."

"She gay?"

"Well, now, how should *I* know, Jack? She didn't make a pass at me, if that's what you mean."

He laughed and drank some wine. We were in his kitchen, eating the dinner I'd cooked. Outside there were four cops guarding the house. I felt a little guilty about the two of us sitting here eating and drinking while the four of them endured the boredom of an eight-hour stake-out. Maybe later I'd make some coffee and sandwiches for them.

"You know," I said. "I got a bit of background stuff on Sarah today, I think, but I'd like to take it much further. It would be nice to know what she was like as a child."

Jack ate his last bite of steak. "How are you going to find out?"

I frowned. "I'm not sure. I have to figure that out. I'd love to talk to her parents, but I don't know how far I'd get there. Why would they want to talk to someone like me? I wouldn't, if I were them." I sipped my wine. My teetotaling impulse seemed to have died a-borning. "Do *you* know anything about her family? Other than what you've already told me, I mean?"

"Well, the mother's dead."

I put down my glass. "She is? When did that happen?"

"A couple of years ago."

"What was it?"

Jack shook his head. "A combination of things. Mostly booze and pills. She spent the last few years of her life in and out of Silver Hill. Mostly in."

"Silver Hill," I said. "It figures. Isn't that the place in Connecticut where they have one nurse for every half patient? Where the elite go to dry out?"

"Something like that. Anyway, she died. Left all her own money to Sarah."

"What about the father?"

"Olmsbacher? He's still around. Still with Global Airlines. He remarried."

"When?"

Jack gave me a modified version of his wolf smile. "About two months after the first Mrs. Olmsbacher kicked it."

"My, my. Didn't waste any time, did he?"

"Nope."

I sat back and twiddled with the stem of my glass. "So Sarah is heiress to a considerable pile, isn't she?"

"Yup."

"But she can't get at it."

"Uh-uh."

I poured myself a little more wine. "So how the hell has she been financing herself all these years? That Somerville bank robbery money couldn't have lasted this long, especially if she split it with five other people."

"She could have worked."

"Doing what? Knocking over liquor stores?"

"No. But with a phony birth certificate and social security number she could have gotten a job somewhere. It's not hard. In fact, it's very easy to do something like that."

"I know, I know," I said. "I read all the mysteries. You get a birth certificate for someone who was born around the same time as you, but who died in infancy, and you just pass yourself off as that person. Simple."

"Well, it works. What can I say?"

I stood up. "I think the coffee's ready. Want to have it in the other room?

"Sure." He rose, leaned over, and gave me a kiss on the cheek. "Very nice dinner."

"I know," I said. He laughed and left the kitchen. I heard the springs in the couch creak. I hoped he wouldn't lie down and fall asleep before I could join him.

He didn't. "Coffee's still dripping," I announced. "Want to listen to some records?"

"All right."

"Anything special?"

"You pick."

I went to his stack of records and flipped through it. The collection was large and eclectic, heavy on jazz. No New Wave. No disco. No crap. I selected a record I'd given him, something called *Tanzmusik der Praetorius-zeit,* and put it on the turntable, keeping the volume low. If I turned it up, I might be tempted to break into a *branle de Bourgogne.* Sixteenth-century music is as catchy as hell.

I sat down next to Jack on the couch and put my feet up next to his on the coffee table. Despite the fact that it was a warm summer night, we had all the windows closed and all the curtains drawn. We couldn't see out, but no bad people could see in, either.

"You know," I said. "I was kidding around before about Shana MacCormack not being part of any local terrorist support network, but do you think there could actually be such a thing around here?"

"Oh, sure," Jack said. "In fact, it would surprise me if there weren't. That's probably one of the main reasons they resurfaced here." He made a face. "Other than Cambridge being such a hell of a great place to start the revolution, of course. But, yes, they probably *do* have a number of contacts in the area."

"Contacts?"

"Well, sympathizers. People who aren't actively involved, but who might give them money, or food, or find them another safe house. They sure as hell can't go back to that place on Third Street."

"No," I agreed.

"Cambridge is full of ex-militants," Jack continued. "And a lot who maybe aren't so ex. Some of them would be more than happy to lend a hand to the cause."

I looked at him sharply. "You have names?"

He shrugged. "We've been digging back into the files on all that crap that went down here in the late sixties and early seventies. Nothing really has surfaced so far."

He hadn't really answered my question. I wondered if the ambiguity were intentional.

I went to see if the coffee had finished dripping. It had. I prepared two cups and brought them to the living room.

I handed Jack one of the cups and settled back down on the couch, drawing my legs up underneath me. "If the PRC wants to replace all those guns they lost on Third Street, they'll have to do it illegally, won't they?"

He laughed. "Well, they sure as hell can't stroll into Roach's Sporting Goods and buy the place out and put it on their VISA card."

"So won't that work to your advantage? I mean, if there's an illegal gun sale of that magnitude, chances are you'll hear something about it, won't you?"

"It depends on who's doing the selling," he said. "If they go through the usual route, yeah, there's a chance we might hear something. If not . . . " He made a palms-up gesture with his right hand. "They're probably too smart to ask around on the street for a gun dealer, which is the way it usually happens. They didn't survive this long by being stupid or careless about things like that."

"Well," I said, reaching over and patting him on the thigh. "Maybe they'll make a mistake this time."

"Yeah," he said. "Maybe."

Tanzmusik der Praetorius-zeit clicked off on a diminuendo.

"Your turn to pick the record," I said.

"I don't have the ambition," he said.

"Me neither."

"Then the hell with it."

I laughed and rolled my head to the right so that it rested on his shoulder. He finished his coffee and set the cup on the end table.

"Want to hear something ironic?" he said.

"Sure. What's that?"

"Well," he said. "Here you are, running around trying to get the lowdown on Sarah Olmsbacher. And here I am, doing pretty much the same thing in a different way. But, you know, there isn't a shred of evidence that ties Sarah to anything that's been happening around here lately."

I raised my head slightly and stared at him. "Oh, come *on*. Who else could it be other than Sarah? That last letter was signed by Alexa. You yourself told me that was Olmsbacher's code name."

"Sure. But someone else could have adopted it. Olmsbacher could be dead or married and living in Indianapolis with two kids for all I can prove now."

"What about what that woman on Third Street, Louise Costello, told me?" I demanded.

"Louise Costello knew a woman calling herself Kathleen Morris, who may, just may, bear some resemblance to a picture of Sarah Olmsbacher taken—when? Almost twenty years ago? That's no identification."

I put my head back against the couch cushion. "What about Morris's landlady? Couldn't she be more definite?"

"She was even vaguer than Louise Costello was."

I sighed. "But do you, yourself, have any doubt that Kathleen and Sarah and Alexa are all the same person?"

"No. What I'm saying is, at this point, I can't prove it."

I smiled. "You will, Oscar," I said. "You will."

16 —

The following morning, I taught my academy class. That afternoon, I schlepped back to the Tufts library to resume my quest into the background of Sarah Olmsbacher/Kathleen Morris/Alexa. Starting with 1947, the year of her birth, I combed through each volume of the *New York Times Index,* looking for any reference to her or her family, no matter how minuscule. There were quite a few. The Clan Olmsbacher was apparently more prominent than I'd assumed. They weren't Whitneys or Auchinclosses, but they weren't far behind, either.

Most of the family's money and position, I discovered, came from the mother's side, the Clarkes. I traced them back as far as the *Index* mentioned them, which was as far as the *Index* itself went. When I had all the citations I thought I could stand following up at one shot, I went up to the microtext room, commandeered a reader, and settled down to crank my way through twenty-seven reels of filmed newsprint. Clarke Pharmaceuticals had been founded in 1888 by one Elijah Ebenezer Clarke, formerly a major in the Army of the Potomac. Ebenezer had married, in 1870, a hot number named Adelaide Andrews Hoover. Together they produced nine offspring, six of whom survived infancy. One of the six was Sarah's great-grandfather. He married in 1895, and had a son, John, the following year. John married in 1921 and was killed in a riding accident in 1923, although not before he managed to sire Janet Hoover Clarke, who in *her* turn married navy lieutenant (j.g.) James Robert Olmsbacher in a plush but tasteful Episcopalian ceremony in June 1945. Little Sarah Clarke, light of her parents' lives, had been born in Lenox Hill Hospital almost exactly two years later to the day. No siblings.

Sarah's childhood and adolescence, as reported in the press anyway, had been relatively uneventful. She'd copped some ribbons and trophies at various horse shows. There was a photograph from 1965, showing her smiling and holding the bridle of a really gorgeous mare, an Arabian named Fatima. In the same year, she was presented to society at the Junior Assemblies and at a big private party at her parents' place in Tarrytown. The Meyer Davis Orchestra, with Meyer himself conducting, had furnished the entertainment. I imagined that a good time had been had by all. Up until 1965, then, Sarah hadn't done anything to violate the dictum that a lady's name only appears in the papers when she's born, when she marries, and when she dies. Or when she makes her debut or collects a trophy at the hunt club.

One item in the next reel made me sit up and take notice. This was an announcement of the engagement, in November 1966, of Miss Sarah Clarke Olmsbacher, daughter of blah blah blah, to Bradford Dexter Kingsley of Beverley Farms, Mass. The photo of Sarah that accompanied the article was the Bachrach of her in dark sweater and pearls. The next time it had appeared in the paper it had run alongside that of a convicted felon and underneath a headline about armed robbery and murder in Somerville. A far cry from "Miss Olmsbacher to wed Mr. Kingsley" in twelve-point type.

Bradford Dexter Kingsley. From Beverley Farms. Beverley Farms's idea of down and out was anyone who made less than $175,000 a year. I thought for a moment. What very little I knew about the New England rich and prominent suggested to me that they tended not to stray too far from the family fold, even in adulthood. Unless of course they became terrorists. I wondered if B.D. Kingsley was still in the area. Well, there was one way to find out.

I went downstairs to the section of the reference room that kept telephone directories and found one for Beverley Farms. It had a listing for one Chester Wright Kingsley, but none for a Bradford Dexter Kingsley. In itself, the absence meant nothing, but I was operating on the assumption that B.D. was old enough to have his own home and telephone. I checked the Boston book. There was a

B. Dexter Kingsley residing on Chestnut Street. B. Dexter. Zounds, as my father used to say. I copied down the address and phone number.

Okay, what was I going to do with the information now that I had it? Call B.D. and ask him if he were the Bradford Dexter Kingsley once betrothed to Sarah Clarke Olmsbacher? Shit. I'd sleuthed my way right up a dead end street.

Or maybe I hadn't. I got up, put the Boston directory back approximately where I'd found it, and went to the reference desk. The woman behind it told me where to find the public phones. I located one that worked, dropped a dime in it, and called a woman I know who works as a leg person for the *Herald* gossip columnist. It's useful to have heavy contacts in the media. Anyway, she owed me a favor.

It took Sharon five rings to answer.

"Hope I didn't drag you out of the shower," I said.

"No," she replied. "Who's this?"

"Liz."

"Oh, *hi,*" she said, in the italicized breathless rush characteristic of her. "I've been meaning to *call* you. How *are* you?"

"Fine," I said. Her exuberance had the curious effect of reducing me to monosyllables. If I talked to Sharon for any length of time I started sounding like Clint Eastwood.

"How's Jack," she said. "You still seeing him?"

"Yes."

"Oh, *damn.* Let me know if you *stop.* *I* don't mind catching him on the rebound."

"You'll have to get in line," I said. "Sharon, could I ask you a question?"

"Probably. What?"

"I need to know something about a guy called Bradford Dexter Kingsley."

"Cute name," Sharon said. "What'd he do, get cashiered from the Myopia Hunt Club?"

"You tell me."

"Why do you want to know?"

I told her about Kingsley's connection with Sarah Olmsbacher, and my interest in both of them.

"Sure," she said. "I'm familiar with old B.D. Or Dexter, as he's known to his friends and associates. He's forty-one, loaded—"

"I figured he wouldn't be collecting welfare."

"Shut up and let me go on. Okay. He's divorced. No children. Has a *very* nice place on Chestnut Street. Straight, as far as I know. What you might call your basic eligible bachelor type. Doesn't seem to have too much luck with women, though."

"It works both ways," I said. "Maybe the women didn't have too much luck with him. Does he have a job or anything, or does he just clip coupons all day long?"

"You should have checked the college catalogues as well as the phone books. He teaches English at UMass/Boston."

"No kidding," I said. "With a name like that, I'd figured he'd be a stockbroker or an investment banker."

"Well, maybe he's the rebellious type," Sharon replied. "Anyhow, that's the sum total of what I know about him. He's not gossip column material."

"Heaven forfend," I said. "Sharon, thanks a lot. I appreciate the help."

"No trouble."

We said good-bye and hung up.

I now knew how to get hold of Bradford Dexter Kingsley, but had no idea of what to say to him when I did. Am I the only interviewer who's bothered by questions like that? If I were Jack, I'd have an official reason to be tactless and abrupt. But I didn't have the mighty weight of the Cambridge P.D. backing me. I'd felt somewhat the same way going to see Shana MacCormack. Only talking to someone about an ex-college roommate seemed a little less sensitive than talking to someone about an ex-fiancée.

I also wondered why Shana herself hadn't mentioned to me anything about the existence of Sarah's intended. Sarah had become engaged the first semester of her sophomore year at Vassar. Surely she hadn't kept that a secret from her roommate. And surely Kingsley must have visited Sarah at school some weekends. Or she'd have gone to see him.

I went back to the reference room and located a UMass/Boston catalogue. I flipped to the section where the English faculty were listed. Associate professor Bradford Dexter Kingsley fell between full Professor Kenwood and instructor Lamont. In addition to a Yale undergraduate degree, he had collected an M.A. in 1967 and a Ph.D.

in 1969 from Columbia. His specialty was Milton and the seventeenth century. Oh, good. If I spoke to him and we ran out of things to say about Sarah, we could always discuss *Areopagitica*.

I looked in my coin purse and discovered that I had another dime. Interpreting that as a directive from Divine Providence, I went back to the functioning phone and called UMass/Boston. The switchboard operator put me through to Kingsley's office.

Somewhat to my surprise, he was in. Even more to my surprise, his voice and manner remained pleasant after I'd finished telling him who I was and what I wanted. He was quite willing to talk about Sarah, but said he'd rather not do it on the phone or in his office. Could I meet him somewhere? I could. The bar in the Parker House? At 5:30? Fine.

"How will I know you?" he asked.

"You probably won't have any trouble picking me out," I said. "Wherever I go, I'm usually the only five-foot-ten-inch redhead on the premises. But I can wear a tigerlily in my buttonhole, if you like."

"That probably won't be necessary," he said.

As hotel bars go, Parker's isn't half bad. It looks like what you'd imagine a Hollywood set designer's conception of an English gentlemen's club to be. Dim lights, paneling, and lots of overstuffed chairs and sofas grouped around marble cocktail tables. The waitresses wear prim longsleeved blouses and long skirts. It's not the place to go if you're looking to get picked up, which is probably the nicest thing I can say about it.

B.D. Kingsley was waiting for me when I got there at 5:35. I had no problem recognizing him, because he looked exactly like what he was. Tall, slim, fair-haired, and wearing a linen jacket and open-necked light-blue shirt that had probably come from Brooks Brothers seven or eight years ago. The jacket could have used a pressing; despite that, Kingsley made the flashier dressers in the bar look like models for an Anderson-Little catalogue. I went up to him and held out my hand.

"Miss Connors?" he said.

"Mr. Kingsley," I said. I hoped we wouldn't progress to a first name basis. I wasn't too sure I'd be able to address someone as "Dexter," or, God forbid, "Dex," and still keep a straight face.

Kingsley offered me one of the overstuffed chairs and said, "What would you like to drink?"

"Vodka martini," I said. "On the rocks." I could have asked for a club soda with a twist, but it didn't seem like that kind of occasion.

Kingsley gave an order for two vodka martinis to the waitress, a blonde who somewhat resembled Kim Novak in *Moll Flanders*. She put a bowl of dry roasted peanuts on the table and rustled away to the bar.

Kingsley said, "How did you find out about me?" They *always* ask that.

"From the engagement notice in the *Times*," I said.

He nodded.

"Frankly, I'm a little surprised you were willing to see me," I said.

"Why?"

I was a bit taken aback at the abruptness of the question. "I thought the subject might be—uh, uncomfortable. Or disagreeable. Something like that."

He smiled and shook his head slightly. "It was a long time ago."

The waitress appeared with the drinks. Two short-stemmed glasses with olives and ice, and two carafes of martini embedded in stainless steel bowls of crushed ice. The waitress poured the drinks and whisked away. Kingsley and I reached for our glasses simultaneously.

"I feel terribly awkward," I said. "It's hard to know where to begin, with something like this."

He nodded slowly, as if considering some intellectual proposition I'd just brought forth.

"I suppose the logical question to ask you is, how long did you know Sarah before you got engaged?"

Kingsley sipped some more of his drink and crossed his legs. He was so fucking elegant I was beginning to feel like Tugboat Annie. "About a year, I think. A little more, perhaps. When we met she was in her last year at Brearley."

"I see. What was she like at that point?"

Kingsley thought for a moment. "Well, she was very beautiful, but you must know that. Quite intelligent. Fairly independent, considering her age and circumstances. Not especially happy, I should say."

"No? Why not?"

"She had a real dislike for her parents. Particularly for her father."

I smiled. "She and about twenty million other adolescents."

"That's true," Kingsley said. "But Sarah was more intense about it than most." He spoke in a very precise, measured fashion, as if lecturing to a class on the background to *Lycidas.*

I fished the olives from my drink and ate them. "Go on."

Kingsley made a small waving motion with his hand. "She was immature in a number of ways. Easily swayed."

I raised my eyebrows. "That's interesting. Someone else described her to me in a way that suggested she was fairly strong-minded."

"Willful, I think, would be more accurate," Kingsley replied. "There's a difference. Sarah was always insistent on having her way. But her way had a tendency to change rather frequently."

I studied him covertly over the top of my glass. Was this the spite of a disappointed lover, or was Kingsley merely being ruthlessly objective in his appraisal of his former fiancée? His tone was certainly neutral, as was his facial expression. That could be a cover-up, of course. On the other hand, he'd had a long time to get over Sarah.

Some hurts have a tendency to linger on, though.

The more I thought about it, the clearer it became to me that what Kingsley was telling me didn't really contradict what I'd heard from Shana MacCormack. In fact, the one enhanced the other.

The thought of Shana MacCormack brought to mind the question I most and least wanted to ask Kingsley. Perhaps I should just do it and get the whole thing over with. He didn't have to answer if he didn't want to. No one was holding a gun to his head. I took a substantial sip of my drink, set the glass on the table, and leaned forward slightly.

"Mr. Kingsley," I said, "I spoke to Sarah's roommate at Vassar. She told me a lot, but not once did she mention that you and Sarah had been engaged. I find that a bit strange. Do you?"

"Not in the least," Kingsley replied.

I cocked my head, as if I were hard of hearing. "You don't?"

Kingsley smiled a little wryly. "No. Whoever you talked to probably wasn't aware that I was anything else but one of Sarah's visitors, of whom there were many. By the time it came about, I don't think the engagement was one of Sarah's paramount concerns. It wouldn't have occurred to her to mention it to anyone."

I didn't know what to say, so I didn't say anything. I tried to look thoughtful and sympathetic. I hope I succeeded.

"I was serious about it," Kingsley continued. "Sarah wasn't. I had a sense she wasn't, even at the time, but . . . as I say, she was someone whose interests changed rapidly. Well, she was very young."

"So what happened next?" I asked quietly.

"Nothing. We drifted apart. There was very little I could do about it. Sarah was seeing other men."

I nodded. "Did you ever see her again?"

"Oh, occasionally." Kingsley *still* sounded as if he were discussing allegorical imagery in *Paradise Lost.* "She was pleasant, but distant. We didn't have a great deal to say to each other. But I suppose we never really did."

I nodded again. Then I said, "Mr. Kingsley, why are you telling me all this? I appreciate what you're doing, but it can't be easy. Or especially enjoyable."

He smiled in a way that was almost indulgent. "It isn't important. I hadn't thought about Sarah at all until recently."

"Yes," I said. "We've all been given some pretty strong reminders lately. Tell me: what was your reaction when you found out that Sarah had joined a terrorist organization?"

He laughed, but not like he thought anything was funny. "It didn't surprise me. I thought it was an entirely logical step for her to take, given the kind of person she was."

"It shocked a lot of other people, though."

"That's true."

"What about her parents?"

"They were stunned. Terribly grieved. What you would expect. Mr. Olmsbacher made some sort of public plea for Sarah to give herself up."

And a lot of good that had done. "Did you ever have any sense of why Sarah hated her father?"

Kingsley arched an eyebrow. I'd never been able to do that. Probably there was a gene for it. "I think she resented his treatment of her mother. Mrs. Olmsbacher was an alcoholic. Sarah seemed to hold her father responsible for that."

"Was he?"

"I don't think he helped the situation. Sarah was convinced that he'd married her mother for the Clarke money. He apparently didn't do anything to discourage the notion. I don't know. I never knew him very well." Kingsley finished his martini and looked at my glass. "Shall we have another drink?" He didn't wait for my answer, but signaled the waitress and ordered two more. Hurriedly, I ate some peanuts. Maybe they'd soak up the booze.

"Let me backtrack for a moment," I said. "When I asked you what your reaction was when you found out that Sarah had joined the PRC, you told me you thought it was an entirely logical step for her to take. Why? Just to get back at her family?"

"That was certainly part of it," Kingsley said. "But there were other factors involved."

"Such as?" I picked up my new drink.

"It's difficult to be specific at this point," Kingsley said. "But at base I think there was a kind of emptiness in her that responded to the idea of being committed to something that required total allegiance. She'd never had that kind of demand made on her. Also, there was a question, I think, of her finding some kind of identity."

"And it was an outlet, too," I added.

"Oh, yes. Maybe that more than anything else."

We fell silent for a few moments after that, each occupied with our own thoughts. Bits of my conversation with David Epstein were coming back to me. *Terrorists tend to be absolutists. They need to be attached to a movement or cause, and when they are, their dedication to it becomes total. It's a kind of fulfillment for them. Almost a religious experience.*

I glanced over at Kingsley. It was impossible to tell what was going on in his mind. His face was remote, expressionless. Like Shana MacCormack's.

17

Kingsley and I talked for another fifteen minutes, mostly desultory chit-chat about the article I was writing. Kingsley didn't seem to have much else to say about Sarah, and I didn't press him. He'd already told me more than I'd expected to hear. Best to leave it at that.

At 6:30 Kingsley signaled the waitress and called for the check. When it arrived, there was some genteel dispute over who would pick it up. I won. The tab came to well over twenty dollars, excluding tip. Paying it left me with just enough change to buy a subway token back to Cambridge. But I figured the money was well spent.

Outside the Parker House, Kingsley and I shook hands and said good-bye. I thanked him for his time and helpfulness, and he wished me luck with the article. Then I darted for the subway station on Park Street. I was supposed to meet Jack at 7:00, and given the spasmodic way the trains were running, I'd be lucky to be only fifteen minutes late.

During the ride to Cambridge, I thought about Sarah Olmsbacher. What had she been like that last crucial year at B.U., the year the Peoples Revolutionary Cadre had come into being? How had she gone about the business of daily life? Had she spent her days no differently from the ways her contemporaries spent theirs, going to classes, sitting around drinking innumerable cups of coffee with friends, studying in the library, organizing antiwar demonstrations, attending rallies, participating in strikes and moratoria, and then gone back to her Marlborough Street apartment at night to map out revolution? How had the PRC itself been conceived? Had she been the moving spirit? And *how* had she managed to hook up with a sleazebag like Charles Roy Mitchell, much less fall in love with him, as Mitchell had claimed?

Nothing in what I'd gotten from Shana MacCormack or B.D. Kingsley answered any of those questions.

It was five past seven when the subway let me off at Central Square. Central Square is the municipal heart of Cambridge—hence its name, I suppose—and, although it's only a short distance from Harvard Square, it could be in Newark for all the resemblance there is between the two. Harvard Square is Harvard Square. Central is urban America: main post office, commercial high rises, city hall, a lot of banks, the Division of Employment Security, and, of course, police headquarters on Western Avenue and Green Street.

The cop shop has two entrances, the main one on Western Avenue and the rear one on Green Street. If you go in the front door, and the cops at the desk don't recognize you, they'll ask, very politely, if they can help you. It's their nice way of finding out who the hell you are and what you want. The rear door, on the other hand, you can pretty much stroll in and out of unobserved, unless they have a video camera concealed there that I don't know about. The apparent disparity in the security setup had always amused me.

This evening, however, there was a young patrol officer standing outside the Green Street entrance. Maybe he was just hanging out. I kind of doubted it. As I went past him, he said, "Hiya, Liz." I wondered what he would have done if he hadn't recognized me. Asked for my identification? Administered a quick frisk?

As usual, the main office of the C.I.D. looked like the foredeck of the *Marie Celeste*. Jack was in his cubbyhole, leafing through a mountainous stack of reports.

"Lonely at the top, isn't it?" I remarked, lounging in the doorway.

He looked up and smiled. "Busy, too," he replied, pointing at the pile of papers.

"So I see." I pushed myself away from the doorjamb and sauntered into the office. "Not a pretty sight," I said, looking at the reports and shaking my head. "Not *a-tall* a pretty sight."

"Make yourself comfortable," Jack said. He glanced around at the sparse furnishings as if noticing them for the first time. "If that's possible," he added.

I perched on the corner of his desk and grinned at him. "I notice they've tightened up the security arrangements downstairs."

"What?"

"There's a watchdog outside the Green Street entrance."

"Oh," Jack said. "Yeah." He rolled his eyes at the ceiling and made a sour face. "Christ, I feel like I'm being babysat."

"Well, you are, baby."

He snorted and shuffled the papers on his desk.

"So," I said. "What's new in the wide world of law enforcement?"

He leaned back and linked his hands behind his head. "Something good, for a change."

I arched my eyebrows. "Oh?"

"Uh-huh. You know the old lady that Goldman shot?"

"Of course. Jesus, I was there, wasn't I?"

"She's gonna be okay."

I smiled. "That *is* good news. That's great. I'm so glad."

"Yeah, me too."

I slid off the desk and went over to the spare chair.

"What did you do with yourself today?" Jack said.

I settled down in the chair and crossed my legs. My skirt had a slit in it and a great deal of thigh showed in the opening. Jack immediately looked down. I thought it was nice that he still did that, given that he could see all of me minus clothing almost any time he wanted.

"I went drinking with Bradford Dexter Kingsley," I said.

"Oh," Jack said. "Him."

"Yes, him," I said. "Have you and he talked?"

"Well, sure." Jack looked up from his contemplation of my inner thigh. "A couple weeks ago."

I nodded. "I should have known you'd get to him before I would."

"It's my job."

"Uh-huh." I scratched the side of my nose. "Old Dexter claims not to have laid eyes, much less anything else, on Sarah since 1966 or so. I believe him."

"So do I," Jack replied. "What did you think of him?"

"Of Kingsley?" I hesitated a beat, and then shrugged. "I don't know.

An odd, sad guy. He seemed like—"I stopped speaking, searching for a good simile. "Like somebody whose pilot light got blown out a long time ago."

Jack looked at me a moment. "That's a good way of putting it."

"You got the same impression?"

"Uh-huh."

"Maybe that's just his natural manner."

"Possibly."

I could feel my face crinkle into a frown.

"What's on your mind?" Jack said.

I blew out a long breath. "Would it be obnoxiously romantic of me to suggest that maybe Kingsley's the way he is because of Sarah?"

"That's not particularly obnoxious, no," Jack said, smiling.

"I'm serious."

"So am I," Jack said, and sounded it. "Maybe he never got over it. Over her."

"Even after all this time?"

"Even after all this time."

I shook my head slowly. "She must be some kind of woman."

"Oh, yeah," Jack said. "She sure as hell must be."

At that moment, Sam Flaherty walked into the office. He looked at me and said, "I see you around here so much you're like part of the furniture."

I laughed. "Maybe in a way I am."

He sighed. "There's better places to hang out, doll."

"Probably," I said. "But I have low tastes. Besides, it's atmospheric around here."

"Atmospheric," Flaherty said. "I'll have to remember that." He leaned against the open door. "I got some news that will bring a smile to your face," he said to Jack.

"What's that?" Jack took his hands from behind his head and rested them on the arms of his chair.

Flaherty glanced at me and then back at Jack. I said, "Would you two like me to leave so you can discuss whatever it is in private?"

Jack raised his eyebrows questioningly at Flaherty. "Do we want her to leave so we can discuss whatever it is in private?"

"Your office," Flaherty said. "You say."

"She can stick around if she doesn't act up."

I curled my lip at the ceiling. Jack suppressed a smile.

Flaherty reached into his jacket pocket and fished out a package of cigarettes. He shook one out, lit it, and then tossed the pack to Jack. "You know Sonny Manos?"

"Sure," Jack said. "He in trouble again?"

"Yeah."

"What'd he do this time, set fire to his mother?"

"Not that I heard," Flaherty said. "Seems he was picked up a while ago in the company of one Richard Corsell, who happened to have in the trunk of his car a handgun. Unlicensed, of course."

"Of course," Jack said. "That's a parole violation for Sonny."

"Uh-huh," Flaherty agreed. "Anyway, Sonny, being eager to avoid any kind of misunderstanding that might cause him to be put back in the joint, suggested we might be interested in a deal."

"What kind of deal?"

"Well, if we forget about the company he's been keeping, he'll tell us about this big gun sale that's supposed to go down tomorrow night."

"And?"

"Sonny says the buyer's a woman."

I looked up sharply. Flaherty continued placidly smoking his cigarette, his face expressionless.

"Go on," Jack said.

Flaherty shrugged. "That's all I know. You want to talk to him?"

"Yeah, I would."

"Thought so." Flaherty straightened up. "See you." He stubbed out his cigarette in the office ashtray, gave me a wink, and ambled off across the outer office.

"This is my exit cue, isn't it?" I said. "Tell me: didn't you invite me to go out to dinner with you this evening?"

Jack gave me a rueful look. "Sorry about that," he said.

"Well, it isn't as if this is the first time this has happened," I said. "You're just lucky that I'm so goddamned tolerant and understanding."

"I certainly am," he said.

I picked up my handbag and hitched the strap over my shoulder. "Every time Sam comes into this office, I end up losing a meal," I said.

Jack laughed.

"You can come over to my place later," I said. "Provided the watchdogs will let you."

"They better," Jack said.

At the office door, I turned and looked at him. "Jack?"

He was rolling down the sleeves of his shirt and buttoning the cuffs. "Uh-huh?"

"I really hope this—this business about a woman buying guns is what it sounds like."

"So do I," he said. "So do I."

I took the bus back to my place. Lucy was as hysterically glad to see me as ever. To calm her down, I took her for a short walk and fed her. When she was comfortably ensconced on the living room rug with an after-dinner biscuit, I made myself an iced coffee and a plate of fruit and cheese. Then I sat down to make notes on my conversation with Kingsley.

I was rereading the latest newspaper stories on the Peoples Revolutionary Cadre when the doorbell rang. Lucy raised her head and said, "Buf." Startled, I glanced at my watch. It was a little after ten. I went to the living room window and peered down at the front steps. Jack was standing several feet back from the house entrance, grinning up at me. I waved to him and went down to open the front door. Lucy scrambled down the stairs before me, like a good little watchdog. When I let Jack in, she hurled herself at him ecstatically.

"Well?" I said.

"Well, what?" Jack replied. "All *right,* Lucy, simmer down, huh? I'm glad to see you, too."

"You know what," I said. "Did what's his name, that Sonny creature, really know anything about a big gun deal, or did he make it all up?"

"Do you mind waiting until I get inside?" Jack asked, in aggrieved tones. "It's been a long day."

I laughed and said, "Sorry." I leaned forward and gave him a kiss. "Did you get a chance to have any dinner?"

"No."

"Come on," I said. "I'll make you something."

We went upstairs. He headed for the living room sofa and I headed for the kitchen. The cupboard, while not exactly bare, wasn't bursting with goodies. Neither was the refrigerator. Although I *had* made some kind of nice soup the other day that I'd been planning to freeze for a rainy day—quite literally, since we do get the occasional raw, wet day in the summer here in New England.

I dumped the soup into a saucepan and set it on the stove to reheat over a low flame. Then I put some cheese and crackers on a plate and set a place at the table. About five minutes later, Jack wandered into the kitchen.

"Whatever it is you're making," he said. "It smells great."

"Thank you," I said, smiling. "It's an old Scottish recipe. Not exactly a warm weather dish, but what the hell."

He got a beer from the refrigerator. "What's it called?"

"Cock-a-leekie soup."

"Yum," he said, uncapping the beer. "Sounds like a venereal disease."

"Yes," I said. "It's the tartan version of herpes."

"Well," Jack said. "It *does* smell good, anyway." He sat down at his place at the kitchen table. I poured myself a diet 7-Up and joined him.

"So," I said. "Tell me about Sonny."

Jack drank some beer. "Well, he does seem to know something. He's not the world's most reliable witness, and he's got the brains of an artichoke, but he's probably bright enough to know that he's got nothing to gain by bullshitting me in this particular case."

I put my chin in my hands and gazed at him. "What's his story?"

"He said he heard a rumor to the effect that some woman was looking to buy some guns. Heavy-duty stuff, like assault rifles. She asked around, and somebody, Sonny claims not to know who, put her onto Joe Lo Bianco."

"Who's he?"

"Lo Bianco?" Jack took a long swallow of beer. "A dirtball. But somebody who would know how to get his hands on a lot of guns in a hurry. Anyway, Sonny says this deal is all set up for tomorrow night, and that the woman and her people are supposed to meet Lo Bianco's people at midnight."

"Did he say where?"

"Yeah. You know that playing field across from the housing project at the end of Rindge Avenue? There's a bus turnaround there."

I nodded. "Oh, sure. Down near Joyce Chen's."

"That's it."

I raised my eyebrows. "Not bad. That place has to be a desert at night. And those apartments across the street are set so far back from the road that nobody there'd notice anything going on over the way."

"Yeah. It's also very badly lit. Or not lit."

"Perfect," I said. I got up and went to the stove to check on the soup. "So what are you going to do?"

"Be there," Jack said calmly.

For a moment, I wasn't sure that I'd heard him correctly. I stood with my back to him, gazing blankly at the pot of simmering soup. Then I turned and said, very carefully, "I beg your pardon?"

He finished his beer, set the bottle aside, and repeated, "Be there." I stared at him.

"Well, I'm not going by myself, dummy," he added, smiling.

"Jesus H. Christ," I said.

"What's wrong?" he asked, all innocent surprise.

"Are you out of your goddamned mind?" I yelled. I made a fist and banged it against the refrigerator door. "Are you crazy?"

He looked taken aback, and then annoyed. "What the hell's the matter with you?"

"The matter with *me?*" I said. "Nothing's the matter with me. It's you I'm wondering about." I walked over to him and bent down so that my face was about a half a foot from his. "A bunch of people have threatened to kill you. The same bunch of people are very probably going to get their hands on a big pile of very dangerous weapons tomorrow night. And you want to be there when they do it? *Jesus!*"

He looked away from me, shaking his head slightly. I put my hand against the side of his face and pulled it back. "*Listen* to me," I said. "This could be a setup. Some kind of ambush."

"That possibility's crossed my mind," he said drily.

I let my hand drop. "And you're still going to do this?" I said. "The captain's going to let you do this?"

He looked exasperated. "Cut it out, will you? Christ, I shouldn't have said anything at all."

I straightened up and put my hand over my mouth. "I absolutely can't believe it," I said through my fingers.

He shrugged.

"You dumb son of a bitch," I said.

There was a flash of real anger across his face, then. He opened his mouth as if to say something.

"Don't bother," I said. "Whatever it is, I don't want to hear it, okay?"

He stared at me for a moment and then said, "Fine," in a flat voice.

There was a hissing noise behind me and I glanced automatically over my shoulder. The soup had boiled up out of the pot onto the stove.

"Oh, Jesus Christ," I said. I snatched the pot and threw it into the sink and turned off the gas. "Make your own damn dinner," I said. Then I stamped out of the kitchen and into the bedroom, slamming the door behind me.

A few minutes later, I heard him leave.

18

So much anger, and fear, were churning around inside me that I wasn't able to get to sleep until 4:00 A.M. The phone woke me up at 8:00. I picked it up on the third ring. The caller was Brandon Peters, my editor.

"It's the middle of the freaking night," I said thickly, in response to his nauseatingly cheerful greeting.

"Oh, did I wake you?" he asked, in tones of patently insincere apology.

"No," I said. "I just got back from plowing the lower forty. Of course you woke me."

"Gee, I'm sorry," he said, not sounding it. "Want me to call back later?"

"No, no," I replied. "I'm awake now. I think. What is it?"

"How's the article going?"

"You bugger," I said, in disbelief. "You got me up to ask me something you could just as well have asked me four hours from now?"

He laughed. "So how *is* it going?"

"Fine." I was sufficiently irritated to be wide awake now. "I have mountains of material."

"Good, good," Peters said. "Ever hear of a guy called Walter Davison?"

I thought for a moment. The name meant zero to me. "No. Should I have?"

"Probably not. He's an exmember of the Weather Underground. But small-time, you know? He was never one of your celebrity radicals like Abbie Hoffman or Jerry Rubin."

"Jerry and Abbie weren't Weathermen," I explained patiently. "They were Yippies. Youth International Party. Revolution for the hell of it. There's a big difference."

"You know what I mean," Peters said. "Anyway, this Davison character had some kind of federal warrant outstanding against him for mob action at the Chicago convention in '68 and interstate flight to avoid prosecution, plus some other garbage, so he went underground in 1970 and did a fugitive act until 1975. Then the cops picked him up in Philadelphia and he spent about eighteen months in the slam on the old charges."

"Terrific," I said. "Another felon brought to justice. So what?"

"He lives in Cambridge now. He's got a job in the print department at the Harvard Coop."

"That's really wonderful," I said. "I repeat: so what?"

"He knew Sarah Olmsbacher. In Berkeley. In 1973."

"Holy shit," I said. "Oops. 'Scuse me, Brandon. God. How did you find *that* out?"

Peters gave a short laugh. "You won't believe this."

"Try me."

"Okay. Davison's apparently writing, or trying to write, his memoirs. My life in the underground, or some such crap."

"What?"

"I told you you wouldn't believe me."

"Never mind that," I said testily. "It's too early in the morning for games. Davison's writing his memoirs. Okay. I'll accept that. How did you come to find out about it?"

"You know Kenneth Dalton? At the Broughton Press?"

"I don't *know* him. I've heard of him. Why?"

"Okay. Well, what happened was that Davison wrote to Broughton asking them if they'd be interested in seeing what he'd written of his opus. So Ken Dalton wrote back and said, yeah, they'd be happy to take a look at it. Well, Davison sent them the first fifty pages or so and an outline, and the thing just turned out to be total crap. But the point is, I had a drink with Ken yesterday, and he mentioned it to me, and he said there was a section in the manuscript about Davison running into Sarah Olmsbacher in Berkeley in 1973."

"Son of a gun," I said. "Do you suppose Davison would be willing to talk to me?"

"How should I know?" Peters replied. "Ask him and find out."

"I will," I said. "I will. Brandon, I apologize for snapping at you before. You can get me out of bed any time you want."

"The question is," Peters said. "Can I get you into it any time I want?"

"You should be so lucky," I said, and hung up.

I went into the kitchen to make some coffee and think what to do. One obvious thing would be to go down to the Coop and hunt up Walter Davison. If he wasn't working today, maybe I could get his address from the personnel office and catch him at his home. Or at least, call him and set something up for tomorrow or the next day. Or if Davison wouldn't talk, I could get in touch with Kenneth Dalton and ask him if he could remember the gist of what Davison had written about Olmsbacher.

A great way to keep busy and not fret about Jack getting blown away by a pack of terrorists in a vacant lot at midnight tonight.

Jack.

I stood at the sink, one hand on the cold water tap, the other holding the coffee pot. That had been some sweet little altercation he and I had had last night. First fight we'd ever had, in fact. I'd done most of the fighting, though. I probably shouldn't have called him a dumb son of a bitch. Even with all that provocation he'd given me.

I set the coffee pot down on the counter and went back to the bedroom. I looked at the phone for a moment, and then picked it up and sat down on the edge of the bed. I dialed Jack's office number.

He answered on the second ring. "Lieutenant Lingemann."

"Oh," I said, with what I hoped was a good simulation of disappointment. "I thought it was Dial-a-Hunk Phone Phantasies."

"It is," he said promptly. "What's your pleasure?"

"Anything at all," I replied. "Go ahead—make my day."

"Certainly, ma'am. But you'll have to give me your VISA or MasterCard number first."

I lost it then, and started to giggle.

"Hi," Jack said.

"Hi."

"You still mad at me?"

"I was just going to ask you the same question," I said. "I'm sorry I called you a dumb son of a bitch."

"Hey," he said. "I've been called lots worse."

"I know," I said. "Can I come over to your place later? And spend the night?"

"I was just going to ask you if you wanted to do that."

"What time?"

"Six?"

"Okay. See you then." I hesitated a moment, not wanting to ask my next question, but unable not to. "Jack?"

"Yeah?"

"What's happening about tonight?"

I heard him take a deep breath. "Same as I told you before."

"Mmmm," I said. "All right. Talk to you later. Bye." We hung up, both of us rather quickly, neither of us caring to risk our newly reestablished accord.

I went back to the kitchen and resumed making breakfast, trying not to think too deeply about Jack's plans for the evening. He was being awfully casual about this escapade. Too casual. But, statistics were on his side. So was experience. Few cops get killed in the line of duty. Shoot-outs are for television. Most cops never even have occasion to fire their guns off the qualifying range. The ones who *do* get involved in shoot-outs and *do* get killed are usually patrol officers. Not detective lieutenants. And although Cambridge has its share of violent crime, maybe more than its share, it's not Dodge City or the South Bronx. The last time any Cambridge police officer was shot and killed on the job was in 1970.

Sure. By Sarah Olmsbacher, field marshal of the People's Revolutionary Cadre.

And what about that horror show at Roosevelt Towers the week before last? At least one detective lieutenant had been involved in that particular shoot-out.

With these charming thoughts in mind, I finished breakfast and took a shower. Then I dressed in a costume I thought suitable for interviewing a former member of the Weather Underground —

nondesigner jeans and a T-shirt. I didn't have any combat fatigues or work pants.

I occupied myself shuffling through my index cards and pretending I was outlining the article until 11:00. Then I took off for Harvard Square. If Davison were working today, I might be able to persuade him to have lunch with me. My treat.

Every summer day—and night—is carnival time in Harvard Square, and today was no exception. The punk-rockers were out in battalions, looking like trick-or-treaters from another planet. Outside the Unitarian-Universalist Church there was a flea market in progress, and the vendors of home-thrown pottery, junk jewelry, used records, used clothes, used shoes, used books, cotton candy, funny T-shirts, kielbasa on a roll, and God knows what else were doing a land office business. The street musicians were in hot competition not only with the traffic noise, but with each other. A string quartet playing Vivaldi was camped on the sidewalk in front of the Levi's store, trying valiantly to make itself heard over the steel band pounding away in the island in the middle of Brattle Square. A skinny, bearded guy in a loincloth was circling around on a high unicycle, juggling three bowling pins. Some people were dancing. Every third person was eating an ice cream cone from Herrell's or Bailey's or Emack and Bolio's.

I went upstairs to the second floor of the Coop and fought my way through the mob in the record department to the print gallery. That was crowded, too. I edged past a woman contemplating a print of *American Gothic* and peered around the room. Coop personnel wear red name tags that make them easy to identify.

I found Davison rummaging through a bin of Wyeth prints. He was a medium-sized, slim guy, maybe five-nine, with a well-trimmed beard and mustache and not an awful lot of head hair. What remained of it was clipped very short around the ears and neck. He was wearing tinted gold-rimmed glasses, jeans, and a white LaCoste shirt. I went up to him and he stopped what he was doing and gave me an inquiring look.

"Walter Davison?" I said.

"Yes," he replied. "Can I help you?"

"That would be nice," I said, and launched into my introductory spiel. He listened without comment or interruption, just the way Shana MacCormack and B.D. Kingsley had when I'd delivered a similar speech to them. Why did everyone who'd ever been involved on some level with Sarah Olmsbacher turn into a zombie at the mere mention of her name?

When I finished speaking, Davison turned and resumed sorting through the Wyeth prints. I waited. Finally he looked up at me and said, "How do I know you are what you say you are?"

"Do I look like an undercover cop?" I asked, trying to make a joke of it. Apparently my wit was lost on him. I reached into my bag and dug out the press pass Brandon Peters had given me so that I could get into Newbury Street art gallery openings (in the unlikely event I should ever want to go to one) without an invitation. Davison took it and studied it as though it were the Rosetta Stone. Then he handed it back to me with a shrug. I gave him every piece of photographic ID I had, including the faculty IDs I had collected from the various schools I used to teach at. I was on the verge of offering him my library card when he said, "All right. We can talk. But not here."

"Where, then?" I asked.

He glanced at his watch. "My lunch break's in ten minutes. You know the benches by the Gutman Library?"

I nodded.

"I'll meet you there at noon." He turned and walked away without waiting for my response. I stared after him. The Spy Who Came In From the Cold.

I left the print department and threaded my way back through the record section to the escalators. I was careful to look furtive all the way.

19

The Gutman Library is one of the Harvard libraries. It houses the education collection and occupies the block of Brattle Street between Farwell Place and Appian Way. On the Farwell Place corner there's a little grassy nook with flowers and wooden benches, all well concealed behind some evergreens. A great place for a clandestine rendezvous.

I beat Davison to it. I'd been sitting on one of the benches for perhaps ten minutes when he came trudging up Brattle Street, a small brown paper bag in his left hand. His lunch, I supposed.

Davison paused at the corner of Farwell and Brattle and glanced around cautiously. Probably checking to make sure there weren't any Neanderthal fascist undercover operatives of the Cambridge police department lurking behind the spreading yews. Apparently he didn't spot any, for after a moment he crossed the street and headed toward the bench where I was sitting.

As he approached, I smiled at him and said, "Glad you could make it."

He nodded and sat down at the other end of the bench, keeping his distance. I wondered if he suspected I might be wired for sound. Did I look as though I were bugged? And even if I were, what difference would that make to him? He'd done his time. He'd also written about his life in the underground, presumably for all the world to see.

Maybe paranoia becomes a reflexive response. I gave a mental shrug and decided to concentrate on the issue at hand.

"Mr. Davison," I began. "I understand you met Sarah Olmsbacher in Berkeley in 1973. Can you tell me how and where and when?"

"It was in a safe house." Davison opened his brown paper bag.

"I see. Who was running it? The safe house, I mean."

Davison flicked me a brief sideways glance. "I can't tell you that."

"Okay. Tell me this, then: What were the circumstances of Sarah's arrival?"

"What do you mean?"

"For one thing, was she alone?"

Davison shook his head. "No. There was another woman with her. Linda something."

"Linda Spahn?" I suggested.

Davison took a plastic container and a spoon out of the bag. "Spahn," he repeated. "Spahn. I don't know. That could be it. Yeah, I guess so. Linda Spahn." He popped the lid off the plastic container.

"Where had they come from?" I asked. "Linda and Sarah?"

"Some place in the south. Memphis, I think." Davison took a forkful of the contents of the plastic container. It appeared to be several kinds of sprouts and cubed tofu. He didn't offer me a bite. Oh, well—didn't look that appealing, anyway.

I said, "Do you know how long they'd stayed in Memphis?"

"About a year, I think." Davison spoke in a very careful, measured way.

"And before that?"

"New Orleans. That was where they went after they left Boston."

"All five of them?" I asked.

Davison said, "What?"

"There were five of them who got away after they robbed that Somerville bank in 1970," I explained. "Sarah, Linda, two guys named Prescott Forbes and Jeffrey Goldman, and a third woman called Leilah."

Davison's face went from carefully expressionless to completely blank. I couldn't tell if the blankness were real or contrived.

"Here," I said. "Let me show you some pictures. I reached into my bag for the reproductions of the newspaper photos of Goldman and Forbes. I handed them to Davison.

He looked at the picture of Forbes for several seconds. Then he shrugged, delicately.

"You don't recognize him?" I said.

"I know who he is," Davison replied. "I mean, I've seen that picture of him. And I've heard of him. I never met him. He wasn't in Berkeley when I was there."

"Okay," I said. "What about the other guy?"

Davison studied the photo of Goldman. Then he passed it back to me. The blankness on his face had translated into a look of sardonic amusement.

"You recognize *him*, don't you," I said.

"Oh, sure," Davison replied. "He's the one who got wasted by the pigs a couple weeks ago."

I felt a small flare of anger and tried to tamp it down. "Before the cops shot Goldman, Goldman shot a seventy-six-year-old woman," I said, hoping my voice was neutral. "He also almost killed a fourteen-year-old girl."

Davison shrugged again. He looked as if he might be going to say, *Big deal.* Fortunately for him, he didn't, because if he had, I'd have punched him.

Controlling my temper, I said, "Was Goldman ever at Berkeley with Sarah and Linda? Or ever there at any time?"

"No."

"What about the woman called Leilah?" I said. "You ever meet her? Or hear of her?"

"No."

"So she never turned up in Berkeley, either."

"Not while I was there."

Well, that made sense. The five PRCs must have split up right after Charles Mitchell had been captured in Revere, if not right after the bank robbery itself. Of course they would have run in different directions, and stayed well apart in the years after. Until now, of course.

"How long were Sarah and Linda living in Berkeley?"

Davison nibbled a cube of tofu. "About a month. They got there sometime around the end of March, and left sometime around the end of April, the beginning of May."

"Do you have any idea where they went after that?"

"I don't know. I think Sarah might have gone to Florida, maybe."

"Why Florida?"

"She talked a lot about getting to Cuba. Through Florida would be one of the logical ways, wouldn't it?" Davison finished his sprouts and tofu and tossed the empty salad container into a large, heavy, plastic trash barrel a few feet away. Then he reached into the paper bag next to him and withdrew an apple. Organically grown, I was sure. He didn't offer me any of the apple, either.

"What did she say about Cuba?" I asked patiently. Davison made Shana MacCormack look like a positive chatterbox.

He ate about a third of the apple before answering the question. When he finally did speak, it was in the same precise, uninflected tone he'd been using all along. "She wanted to train there, with the army. She thought she could perfect her guerrilla warfare techniques, come back here, and teach others what she learned."

"And maybe get some financial backing," I mused.

Davison gave me another one of those sideways glances. "I wouldn't know."

"A lot of people in the underground went to Cuba or North Vietnam for the same reasons, didn't they?" I persisted.

Davison nodded.

"Did you?"

He shook his head.

"I see," I said. Davison finished his apple and pitched the core at the trash barrel. Should have left it on the ground for a passing squirrel. I had the feeling that now he'd done with his lunch, he might just get up and walk away without saying anything further.

"Tell me about the safe house," I suggested hurriedly. "How many of you were living there?"

"It changed all the time," Davison said. "People came and went. Usually there were about six or seven of us."

"How did you support yourselves?"

Davison shrugged. "Any way we could. One guy sold dope. We worked, sometimes."

"Doing what?"

"Whatever came along. Mostly menial shit. Washing dishes. Street cleaning. That kind of thing." There was an expression of faint distaste on Davison's face at the memory. Workers of the world, throw off your shackles.

"What about Sarah?" I said. "What did she do?"

"She had some money with her."

I nodded. "From the bank robbery, probably."

Davison made a vague gesture with his head, neither confirming nor denying. "I don't know where it came from."

I sighed to myself. Trying to pry information out of this character was like trying to declaw an alley cat.

"When Sarah left Berkeley," I said, "was she alone? With anyone? Did Linda Spahn go with her?"

"Yes."

"Yes what?" This laconic routine was really beginning to get on my nerves.

"Linda was with her." If Davison noted my irritation, he gave no sign of it. "But I don't think they stayed together for very long. I think Linda wanted to go back East."

"She died, you know," I said. "In 1974. She was killed in an automobile accident in New Jersey."

"Oh," Davison said. "I hadn't heard that." He didn't seem affected by the news. I watched him for a moment. Did none of these people, with all their rhetoric about brotherhood and sisterhood and love for humanity, have any feeling for each other? Or was it all expended on the grand design?

I decided to change inquisitorial tacks. "What was your impression of Sarah?" I asked.

Davison gazed at me for a moment before replying. Then he looked away, over at the courtyard in front of the Blacksmith Bakery where some people were sitting under large colored umbrellas eating Viennese pastry and drinking coffee *mit schlag*. "Sarah was committed to the revolution." He sounded as if he were parroting the sentence from his memoirs. He probably was.

"I meant on a personal level," I said. "What was she like? Did she laugh a lot? Cry? Write poetry? Read? Listen to music? Do dope? Do crossword puzzles? Have I hit on anything that rings a bell?"

"She was committed to the revolution," Davison repeated.

I shook my head. "There must have been more to her than that," I said. "Come on. You lived with her for a month. You *must* have some recollections or memories." If Davison repeated one more time that line about Sarah being committed to the revolution,

I'd rip the alligator off his shirt front and stuff it up one of his nostrils.

Again fortunately, I didn't have to get physical. "I've told you everything I know about her," Davison said.

The response was better than I'd expected, but still not satisfactory. I could sense he was holding something back, whether out of discomfort or pain at some memory or simple perverseness I couldn't decide. I figured I'd go for broke. Bluntness would cost me nothing at this point in the conversation.

"Was Sarah sleeping with anyone else at the safe house?" I asked. "I heard she was into heavy-duty sex."

Davison's head snapped around and he stared at me. I stared back. Finally, I'd elicited an emotional response from him. Hostility.

"Was she?" I said.

The left corner of Davison's mouth twitched. "Why don't you go fuck yourself?" he said.

I blinked. Davison got up and walked away. Rapidly. From the rear, his shoulders looked tight and angry.

"You forgot your paper bag," I called after him. He didn't turn around. I sat and watched him cross Farwell Place and slip into the crowd on Brattle Street. After a moment, he was out of my sight.

20

I diddled away the rest of the afternoon in the bookstores and record shops, looking at things I couldn't afford to buy, and went back to my place at 5:00. I tossed some essentials in my overnight pouch, collected the dog, and set off for Jack's. It was about a mile and a half walk—just right for late afternoon or early evening. Sometimes I missed not having a car, but this wasn't one of them.

Whatever cops were lurking in the bushes around Jack's house didn't leap out to challenge me when I arrived there. Probably they had orders to give automatic clearance to all tall redheads accompanied by medium-sized brown dogs. I rang the bell. It was only 5:45, but Jack was home already. He came to the door with a half-finished bottle of Beck's in one hand.

"Well, well," I said. "You look remarkably relaxed for a man who has a midnight date with a pack of terrorists and some Mafia gunrunners."

"That's what us dumb sons of bitches are like," he replied. "Very relaxed. Laid back, even."

I made a face at him. Lucy jumped up and pressed her forepaws against his stomach. He patted her on the head with his free hand. "Come on in," he said. He grimaced. "I'm not supposed to leave the front door open too long, you know."

"With good reason," I replied. I dropped my pouch on the foyer

135

floor, elbowed Lucy aside, and gave him a big hug. "I'm very glad to see you."

"Likewise," he said.

We walked into the living room.

"Want a beer?" Jack asked.

"No. You know I don't like beer."

He shook his head. "That's un-American."

"Okay, so I'm a Communist subversive. Anyway, that's German beer you're drinking. Go make me a vodka and tonic."

He laughed and went off to the kitchen. I sat down on the couch. Lucy, done in by the rigors of our walk, collapsed on the rug. Her idea of a brisk workout was chomping on a beef neck bone.

Jack returned with my drink and a bowl of dry-roasted peanuts. "Thank you," I said. "Aren't you going to have another beer?"

"Nope."

"Oh." I didn't ask why not. Another beer wouldn't make him drunk. Another twelve beers wouldn't—he has an astonishing capacity—but he never, *ever,* drank anything substantial before he had to go on duty. The somewhat increased boozing he and I had been doing recently had taken place strictly after hours.

"When do you have to leave?" I asked.

He looked at his watch. "Forty-five minutes." Lucy rousted herself up and trotted over and looked hopefully at the peanut bowl. "Forget it," Jack said to her.

I sipped my drink. "Is Sonny Manos still sticking to his story?"

"Yeah. He doesn't know a hell of a lot, but he seems pretty insistent about what he does know."

"Where'd he get his information?"

"Around." Jack shrugged. "He says he can't remember where. He might even be telling the truth. Stuff like that *does* get around."

"What's he like?"

"Young Sonny?" Jack smiled. "A little shit-bum. He's on the fringes of things. Nothing big. One of these days he'll annoy somebody heavy and turn up dead somewhere."

I took another hit off my drink. "Funny how this whole thing may turn out to hinge on the word of a little shit-bum."

"That's how it goes." Jack stood up. "I bought some stuff for dinner. Want to go in the kitchen? Or shall I bring it in here?"

"Kitchen," I said, getting to my feet.

I sat at the table while Jack took from the refrigerator some small white boxes that contained either stuff from a delicatessen or goldfish from the Woolworth's in Central Square. In front of me was a brown paper bag. I opened it. Rolls.

Jack tossed a waxpaper wrapped package of what looked like Genoa salami onto the table. "What'd you do with yourself today?"

I picked up my drink. "Interviewed an ex-Weatherman."

"Oh? That must have been interesting."

"It was," I said. "He lived with Sarah Olmsbacher for a month in 1973."

Jack froze in the act of removing some forks from the cutlery drawer and looked at me. I winked back at him.

"Sit down," I said. "And I'll tell you about it."

He did. So did I.

When I'd finished, Jack said, "This guy's name is Davidson?"

I shook my head. "No. *Davison.* D-A-V-I-S-O-N."

He nodded, and unwrapped the package of salami.

"You going to try to talk to him?" I asked.

"Of course."

I raised my eyebrows. "I very much doubt if he has any present connection with Sarah. Or anyone else in the PRC."

Jack shrugged and buttered a roll.

"If he did," I continued. "I'd never have heard about him. If he were still actively involved in the revolutionary movement, he wouldn't be trying to write about it for publication. That's not exactly the best way for someone locked into a terrorist support network to maintain a low profile, now is it?"

"No," Jack agreed.

I put some potato salad on my plate. "So?"

"I'll talk to him anyway." Jack looked up from his plate and gave me that lupine smile. "He might know something he didn't tell you."

"And you think he'll tell *you?*" I scoffed. "A Gestapo pig Nazi torturer like *you?*"

"I haff vays uff making people talk."

I burst out laughing. "That's the worst imitation of a German accent I've ever heard."

"Gee," Jack said. "And here my father's family came from Bremerhaven. I'm hurt."

I reached across the table and patted his head.

"Let's get back to Davison," he suggested.

I made a little sandwich out of a roll and provolone and salami. "I'm sorry you weren't there when I asked him if Sarah had slept with any of the other guys in the safe house. Wow. He really blew up—told me to go fuck myself and then stomped off."

"Why do you think he reacted that way?"

"I'm not sure." I ate some potato salad. "I've been thinking about that all afternoon. I hit *some* sore spot, that's for sure. It occurred to me that Davison might have been in love with Sarah, or at least very attracted to her, and she either wouldn't have anything to do with him, or maybe she went to bed with him a couple of times and then dumped him and took up with someone else. Whatever it was, I don't think it was some kind of ideological or political falling-out he and Sarah had. It had to be something emotional or sexual for him to blow up at me the way he did. That sound like a reasonable supposition?"

"Could be," Jack said. "You think, then, that Davison's still, to coin a phrase, carrying a torch for Sarah?"

"It's possible," I replied. "Whatever happened between them, she sure made one hell of an impression on him." I speared a piece of salami with my fork. "But then, she seems to have done that to everyone she ever knew."

"Yeah," Jack said. "Well, in that case, all the more reason for me to speak to Mr. Davison." He looked at his watch. "Jesus, I should get moving."

I paused in the act of reaching for a dill pickle. "Is it that time already?"

"Almost."

I let my hand fall onto the table top. "Oh, boy."

"What's the matter?"

I looked up at him. "You *know* what the matter is, Jack."

He was silent.

"Tell me," I said, in an artificially light tone. "What are the chances of me seeing you again after tonight? Alive, I mean."

He smiled. "I would say they're pretty good."

"Oh, don't joke about it," I said.

138

"I'm not." He leaned over and grabbed my hand. "Listen to me."

I gritted my teeth. "What?"

"I'd have explained this to you last night," he said. "If you hadn't gotten hysterical and started yelling."

I stared at my plate, chewing on my lower lip.

"That patch of weeds on Rindge Avenue has been under surveillance since last night."

I didn't say anything.

"There's twenty cops involved in this one operation," he continued. "I'm not even one of the important ones."

"You aren't?"

"No," he said. "I'm on the sidelines."

"What are you going to be doing?" I asked suspiciously.

"Watching," he said. "From a very safe distance."

"That's what they all say."

He laughed. "It's true. I have a very secondary role in the whole thing."

Then why do you have to be there at all? I thought.

"I'll be fine," he said, patting my hand.

Humoring me. I closed my eyes and took a deep breath.

"Hey," he said. "Come on. Everything will go like silk. I promise."

Sure you do. I opened my eyes and looked at him. He was smiling at me, comfortingly, reassuringly. Bullshit.

"It'll be fine," he repeated.

"Sure," I said. "Just like silk."

21

"Nothing?"

"Nope. Not a goddamned thing. Six hours we sat in that fucking briar patch and the biggest thing that happened was a fight between two cats. Shit." Jack's face was screwed up with disgust.

It was 4:30 Saturday morning, and the two of us were sitting at the kitchen table, conducting a post-mortem of sorts. Jack had walked in maybe five minutes earlier. I had dozed off on the couch, but the soft thud of the front door had awakened me. I hadn't asked him how things had gone. One look at his face told me everything I needed to know, none of it good. But I wasn't complaining; he was here in front of me in one piece.

I rubbed my eyes. I felt as if I'd run the Boston Marathon in shackles, and somebody'd laced my Gatorade with phenobarbitol. "Did you ask Sonny what happened?"

"Yeah. I asked him for two hours."

"And?"

"He said as far as he knew, everything was all set for midnight. He had no idea why it didn't go down."

"Do you think he was telling the truth?"

"Probably. Why would he set me up? He'd only be screwing himself. He knows that. He's scared shitless."

I sighed. "Maybe Joe Lo Bianco or Sarah got spooked or something and called it off. Or Lo Bianco couldn't come up with the guns, or Sarah couldn't come up with the money, or somebody misconnected somewhere."

"Maybe."

"Or Sonny could have gotten the date or the time or the place messed up."

"Uh-huh."

Another shaft of inspiration pierced the fog in my brain. "What about Lo Bianco himself? Did you talk to him?"

"Somebody's been trailing him around since Thursday evening. That night he went home and stayed put. Yesterday morning, he took his kids to the beach. Friday night, he took his wife to Polcari's for dinner. Got back at nine-thirty and didn't go out again. He's a real family man."

"What does that mean?"

Jack shrugged. "Nothing. Even if the deal had gone through, Lo Bianco wouldn't have shown up for it. He doesn't handle the buying and selling himself. His people do."

"Oh."

"Oh," Jack echoed. He looked ready to fall out of his chair and pass out on the floor. If he did, I'd probably join him. We could sleep until September, and perhaps by then the summertime soldiers would have called it quits, or siezed the Pentagon, or relocated to the Middle East or Central America.

Jack yawned. I gazed at him blearily. The next logical question, of course, was "What are you going to do now?" But I didn't have the heart to ask it. What would have been his answer?

I decided to try for a note of cautious optimism. "If Sarah really wants those guns, she'll try again to get them, won't she?"

"I don't know." Jack seemed just barely energetic enough to move his lips. "Whatever went wrong last night may have scared her off trying to deal with someone like Lo Bianco. She may try something like robbing an armory. It's hard to say." He shook his head. "Christ, I'm tired. I can't think any more. Ask me tomorrow."

"Let's go to bed, then," I suggested. He gave me a funny look and I added, "To sleep. I'm not in any better shape than you are."

He nodded wearily and we got up from the table. I glanced out the kitchen window. The sun was all the way up. Jack or I would have to remember to pull down the shades in the bedroom so the light wouldn't waken us. Although judging from the kind of exhaustion we were feeling, the two of us could have slumbered sweetly through the glare of a thermonuclear explosion.

We were in the bedroom shedding clothing when the phone rang. I yanked my T-shirt over my head and mumbled, "Five will get you ten that's Flaherty."

"No bets," Jack said. He leaned over, still unbuttoning his shirt, and picked up the receiver from the night table extension. "Hello?" I sat down on the opposite side of the bed and kicked off my sandals.

I was in the process of removing my bra when I felt a poke between my shoulder blades. I turned. Jack was half-lying across the bed, the telephone receiver clamped to his ear. With his free hand, he was gesturing at the bedroom door. I scowled at him in confusion. He shook his head furiously and pointed at the door. The light dawned. I sprang off the bed and dashed into the front hallway to the other telephone. I picked up the receiver very quietly and brought it to my ear.

"I told you you'd be hearing from me again, Lieutenant, one way or another," a woman was saying. The voice was young but not girlish, deep, clear, and Manhattan-cultured. There was a tinge of amusement in it. I felt a small lurch somewhere in the region of my diaphragm.

"Hello, Sarah," Jack said. "We missed you tonight. Where were you?"

"Not where you thought I'd be," the woman replied. "I'm disappointed in you, Lieutenant."

"Oh? Why?"

"I thought you'd be too intelligent to fall for an old trick like that."

"An old trick like what?" Jack asked.

"Oh, really. Do you honestly think, Lieutenant, that if I wanted to get some guns, I'd go to someone like Joseph Lo Bianco?"

"It happens."

"Perhaps," the woman said. "But not, however, in this case."

"You set me up," Jack said.

There was a laugh. "That's exactly right, Lieutenant. I set you up. You catch on fast. It makes up for your slowness in other respects."

"Did you have any particular reason?"

"For setting you up?" The woman laughed again. "Of course. I never do anything without a reason."

"Would you like to tell me what it is?"

"I'd be very happy to. It's very simple. I've been feeling sorry for you lately, that's all."

"You have?"

"Oh, yes. You must be feeling sort of helpless in the face of all the action I've been taking. The action that you and your jerk-off pig colleagues haven't been able to do shit about."

"Why don't you get to the point?" Jack said.

"Certainly. It occurred to me that *you* might enjoy taking action, for a change. So I gave you the opportunity."

"That was thoughtful of you," Jack said.

"I know. I'm a thoughtful person. And right now I'm thinking that there's no way you're going to stop me from doing whatever I want whenever I feel like it." She paused for a few seconds. When she spoke again, her voice was sharper, rougher. "I may *still* blow you away, you fucker. Despite that ring of pig bodyguards you're hiding inside now."

Jack didn't say anything.

"Well," the woman continued, her voice once again light and pleasant. "I should let you get some sleep. It's been a long night for you, hasn't it, Lieutenant?"

"Wait a minute," Jack said quickly. "Don't hang up yet."

"Why not?"

"I'd like to talk some more."

"Not now," the woman said. "Some other time. I'll be in touch." She gave her silvery laugh. "Pleasant dreams, Lieutenant." There was a click on the line as the receiver on the other end was replaced.

I hung up and sucked in a huge chestful of air. I hand't drawn a real breath once during the entire conversation, and I felt a little giddy. Shell-shocked, even. But not from oxygen deprivation.

I walked slowly back down the hall to the bedroom, rehooking my bra *en route*. Suddenly it seemed grossly inappropriate to be wandering around the apartment half-dressed. Clothing is a form of armor. It's hard to feel brave and invulnerable when you're naked. It's not all that easy even when you're not.

Jack was sitting on the edge of the bed, his elbows on his knees,

143

staring at the phone. I stood in the doorway and watched him for a moment. He looked worse than tired. He looked old. I had a sudden crawling sensation of apprehension. Not for myself, but for him.

I shifted a little in the doorway and the floorboards creaked slightly. The sound caught Jack's attention and he glanced over at me. "You caught the whole conversation?" he said.

I nodded. "Except for the very first part."

He shrugged. "You didn't miss much."

I crossed the room and sat down next to him. "What did she say?"

"Oh, something along the lines of 'Good morning. Am I disturbing you? I'm sure you know who this is.' " His voice was flat, expressionless, like his face.

I scratched my head. "How the hell do you suppose she got your phone number? It's not listed."

"Same way she got my address. That's no big difficulty." He folded his hands together and rested his chin on his knuckles.

I leaned backward across the bed and picked up my shirt and started to pull it over my head.

Jack looked up in faint surprise. "What are you doing that for?" he asked.

"I'm not sure," I replied. "Back there in the hall I started to get the feeling I was being watched. I wanted to cover up."

"Mmmm," he said, and went back to staring at the phone.

I tugged the shirt down over the waistband of my jeans. Then I looked around for something else to do. It occurred to me to make some coffee or tea. Not much point in getting into bed and just lying there to fidget. I was still exhausted, but the sleepiness was gone, blasted away by the telephone call.

"She's real," I said suddenly. "Sarah. She exists."

"Oh, yes," Jack said. "She exists."

"All this time," I mused. "I've been reading about her, hearing about her, talking about her. I've seen where she lived. I know about her. But . . . " My voice faded.

Jack got up and went into the bathroom, leaving the door open behind him. I heard him open the medicine cabinet and then run the water in the sink. A moment later he came back with a glass in one hand and a little brown plastic pill bottle in the other.

"What's that?" I said.

He sat back down next to me. "Dalmane."

"What are they? Sleeping pills?"

"Yeah."

"Oh," I said. "When did you start on those?"

"A while ago." He held out the bottle. "You want one?"

"No." I shook my head. "Those things never do what they're supposed to for me."

"You sure?"

"Yes."

"Okay." He snapped the lid off the bottle and shook one of the capsules into his hand. I watched him swallow it. He set the water glass and bottle on the night table and then gave me a pat on the thigh. "Scoot over," he said.

I did, and he stretched out on the bed. He closed his eyes. The lines in his face looked as if they'd been scored there by some manic sculptor with a grudge against cops. I reached out and traced a finger gently down his left cheek. The lines didn't go away.

Pleasant dreams, Jack.

---

22 —

June 30

Monday at 5:30 P.M. I was standing outside the Harvard Trust Company on Mass. Avenue in Central Square. I was supposed to meet Abby Henderson here so we could go someplace for a drink and a chat.

Jack had slept nearly all of Saturday, knocked out by the combination of Dalmane and near-total exhaustion. Sunday I persuaded him to spend at home, too. We'd had a late breakfast and lounged around reading the papers and sort of watching a telecast of a Red Sox-Orioles game. Some technicians had come to install a tap on the phone. Better late than never. I broiled some chicken and made a salad for dinner. As if by unspoken agreement, neither of us mentioned Friday evening's fiasco, nor Sarah's call, nor indeed anything to do with the Peoples Revolutionary Cadre. A nice day.

The night had been good, too.

I was peering down Mass. Avenue in the direction of Kendall Square when a voice behind me said, "Sorry I'm late." I jumped a little and turned. It was Abby, looking fresh and fashion-magazzy in a pale-blue silk shirt and natural-colored linen slacks. Her hair and make-up were impeccable. As always when I saw her in her present incarnation, I wondered what went through her mind when she looked at ten-year-old photographs of herself in painter's overalls and denim workshirts.

"Get held up at work?" I asked.

"Yeah, something like that." She rolled her eyes heavenward. "We all had to go to a personal security seminar this afternoon. Director's orders."

"A personal security seminar?" I repeated, puzzled.

She laughed. "What it was, was, we all sat around in a big room and listened to an ex-Pinkerton's guy give us tips on how we can protect ourselves from terrorist attack."

"Ooohhh," I said, nodding. "Learn anything useful?"

"Oh, sure. Like I should lock all my car doors when I'm riding around, and I should also check to see there's nobody hiding in the back seat before I get in."

"Well," I said. "It can't hurt, can it?"

"Guess not. Look, I have to get some money. You mind waiting another minute?"

"Not at all."

The bank had two exterior automatic tellers. I watched idly while Abby inserted her blue and green bank card into one of them and poked the buttons on the console. A moment later she was back, stuffing cash in her wallet. She must have had ten twenties there at the very least. Was all that dough her walking-around and lunch money for the week? Could be—she made an incredible salary.

"Ho-kay," Abby said, dropping the wallet back into her shoulder bag. "Where shall we go?"

I shrugged. "What's close and halfway decent?"

"The Moon and Sixpence?"

"Sure."

The Moon and Sixpence was an aggressively Irish bar a couple blocks down Mass. Avenue in the direction of Harvard Square. The walls were green, and on one of them was a sign proclaiming that no British goods were sold on the premises. Every IRA supporter in Cambridge hung out there. Jack was convinced that it was a front for a gunrunning operation to Northern Ireland.

When Abby and I got there, the place was quiet. Two guys in workmen's clothes were standing at the bar, and another five or six people were at the tables around the room. Abby and I found a comfortable spot in the rear right corner, by the delivery entrance.

She ordered a Harp lager. I was about to order a vodka on the rocks, but changed it to a Bushmill's and water. Might as well go native. Faith and bejesus.

When the drinks came, I said to Abby, "Ever hear of a guy named Walter Davison?"

She frowned at me thoughtfully over the top of her glass. "Davison?" she repeated.

I nodded.

She sipped some lager. "Ex-member of the Weather Underground?"

"Uh-huh."

"Spent some time in jail?"

"That's him."

"Sure I know Walter. Knew him, anyway. He was a heavy in the Harvard SDS just before and after I joined." The left corner of her mouth turned down. "And a *real* asshole."

I snickered.

"Why are you asking about him?" Abby said curiously.

"Met him the other day," I explained. "Interviewed him for my article, in fact."

"Oh. What'd you think of him?"

"A real asshole."

We both laughed, then.

"What's he doing now?" Abby said.

"Working in the print department of the Coop. He's also writing his memoirs of life in the underground."

Abby widened her eyes. "You're kidding."

"Nope."

She shook her head. "That turkey."

"Tell me what you remember about him."

"Not a great deal," she replied. "We weren't bosom pals, as you might guess. He made a lot of enemies in SDS."

I raised my eyebrows. "For ideological reasons?"

"No. Personal ones." Abby spread her hands out in an expansive gesture. "Radicals aren't known for their *joie de vivre,* I admit, but old Walter was really the limit. I mean, the word *killjoy* was invented to describe that guy. He made the people in the Progressive Labor faction—remember those stiffs I told you about? Well, he made *them* look like nightclub comics, for God's sake."

"How so?"

"Oh, he was just an all-around pain in the ass. Prissy, humorless, dogmatic, opinionated—you met him, so you ought to know. Anyhow, he was one of those guys that if you told a joke at a meeting, he'd ream you out for fifteen minutes for wasting good revolutionary time. And he was always accusing people of being closet fascists."

My face must have betrayed some of my confusion, because she broke off her reminiscence and said, "What's wrong?"

"You told me Davison was an SDS heavy."

"He was." Now *she* looked puzzled.

"Well," I said. "If he was such an obnoxious twerp, and he alienated so many people, how'd he manage to become so powerful a figure in the organization?"

"I see what you mean," Abby said. She drummed her fingers on the scarred wooden table top, pensively. "Okay, it was like this. In the first place, Davison was a little older than the rest of us. And he was tight, or claimed to be tight, with the people in the national SDS headquarters. And, you may not believe this, but he was a fantastic orator. A real spellbinder. When he got up to speak in front of a crowd—well, it was really something else. The rest of us were just kids, you know, and we needed a leader, somebody to tell us what to do, and Davison was it. We gave him that power. Actually it was the power that brought out the worst in him. As I recall, he really wasn't such an asshole before he got to be Chairman Walter or whatever."

"Interesting," I said. "Downright fascinating, in fact. I had no idea he had such a glamorous background."

"Yeah," Abby said. "And now he sticks frames around Matisse repros for a living."

"Well, he may yet make a career as a memoirist," I said.

"God help publishing."

We sat quietly for a few moments after that, finishing our drinks. The Irish whiskey went down nicely. Pretty color, too. I held the glass up so that the light from the window filtered through it.

"I think I'll have another beer," Abby said. "What about you?"

"Sure."

She nodded and signaled to the bartender.

When the new drinks came, Abby said, "So what else is new?"

I hesitated, wondering if I should tell her about what had happened, or what had failed to happen, Friday night. No. That was still private police business.

"Nothing much," I said. In a way, that was true.

"How's Jack?"

"Oh, he's okay, I guess," I said. "A little tired and tense. But pretty good, considering."

"He still got a bodyguard around him?"

"Yeah," I said. "His house is staked out, anyway."

"That must be weird. For you, I mean. Having a bunch of cops underfoot all the time."

I laughed. "Well, they manage to stay out of sight. They don't follow us into the bedroom and stand around watching while we do it, if that's what you're getting at."

"Not exactly."

"What about you?" I asked, picking up my drink. "What's new with you?"

She shrugged. "Cal and I are thinking of going away for a while. If he can get some time off."

"Nice," I said. "Where you thinking of going?"

"Oh, I don't know. Vermont? Canada, maybe. Just for a few weeks."

I raised my glass in a small salute. "Have fun."

"Thanks. I'll send you a postcard." She drained her mug and set it down on the table.

"You going to have another?" I asked.

She shook her head. "I'd like to, but I can't. I have to meet Cal in ten minutes. We're supposed to have dinner and then go to the movies." She stood up, brushing some imaginary creases from her slacks.

"Okay," I said, a bit surprised at the abruptness of the departure. "Good to see you."

"Yeah." She smiled. "We'll do it again sometime soon."

"Sure. Well, enjoy the movie."

"For six bucks a ticket, I better. Bye."

Alone, I settled back in my chair to finish my drink. I could take my time about it—I had no particular place to go and no particular thing to do. Funny how sometimes that awareness could be pleasant and at other times profoundly depressing. This evening, it was the former.

No reason I couldn't do a little work, though. The manila folder of material for the article on student activism was in my canvas shoulder bag. I pulled it out, set it on the table in front of me, and flipped it open. The top page contained the notes I'd made after my interview with Walter Davison. I read them over, smiling a little to myself. I wondered if Davison missed his old celebrity. I tried to visualize him on the steps of University Hall, microphone in hand, denouncing U.S. policy in southeast Asia to an army of rapt undergraduates. Or proclaiming to the same group the need for REVOLUTION NOW.

I couldn't. The Davison I'd met, like the Kingsley I'd met, was a man whose pilot light had been extinguished long ago. I closed the folder and pushed it a little to the side.

I sipped my drink and glanced around the bar, checking out the other patrons. None of them looked like obvious IRA supporters, but then, I wasn't sure what an IRA supporter was supposed to look like. Hadn't Mao said something about how all good revolutionaries were able to swim like fish in the sea of humanity? The two guys in workclothes were having a lively discussion with the bartender about the Red Sox pitching staff. A man and a woman at a table a few feet away from me were debating whether to go to a Mexican or Indian restaurant for dinner. By the jukebox (ninety-five percent of the selections were by the Clancy Brothers) stood a young African man in jeans and an MIT T-shirt, diagonal tribal marks scored on his cheeks, sipping a beer. Black Irish, no doubt.

The door opened and a slim, fair-haired man in chinos and a red and white checked shirt and denim jacket entered. He took a seat at the bar, resting his elbows on the countertop. I looked him over casually. Semi-attractive, even if he was a little shorter than I. I looked at him again, more closely, and stopped breathing.

I sat absolutely motionless for perhaps fifteen seconds. Then, very carefully, I reached for the manila folder and opened it. As unobtrusively as possible, I leafed through the pages of notes and newspaper clippings till I got to the very back, where I kept the pictures of the five known PRCs. I slipped one of them out of the folder and onto my lap. I stared at it, inventorying every detail of the face, and then looked back up at the man at the bar. Then I stuffed the photo in my skirt pocket. My hands were shaking.

There was a phone booth in the hall behind me. I fished around in my purse for a dime. I found one, and got up and went to the phone and dialed Jack's office number.

23

Detective Riordan answered.

"Dennis," I said. "This is Liz Connors."

"Oh, hiya, Liz," he replied. "How you doing?"

Jesus, he wanted to socialize. "Fine," I said. "Is Jack there?"

"Yeah. He's in a meeting with the captain."

"Could you get him?"

Riordan didn't answer for a moment. When he did, his voice was hesitant. "Oh, well . . . "

"It's extremely important," I said.

"Well . . . "

"*Please,*" I said. "It's terribly important."

"Hold on," he said. My adjectives must have bowled him over. That or the real urgency in my voice.

There was a wait that seemed equivalent to the Age of Pericles, but was probably only about ninety seconds. When Jack came on the line, he sounded half-irritated, half-concerned. "What's up?"

"Jack," I hissed. "I'm in the Moon and Sixpence."

"Yeah?"

"Forbes is here."

"What?" he said, in a bemused kind of way.

I took a deep breath. "There's a man at the bar. I think it's Prescott Forbes. If it isn't, it's his twin brother."

There was a little silence at the other end of the line. Then Jack said, slowly, "Are you sure? I mean, is the resemblance that close?"

"God. Yes, of course it is. Would I be calling you about it if it weren't?"

"Okay, I believe you. What's he wearing? Describe him."

"Blond hair. About five-eight. Chinos. A red and white checked shirt, and a denim jacket. Jack, he looks just like his picture, only older."

"Okay, fine," Jack said. I had the feeling he was writing down what I said as I spoke.

"So what do I do now?" I almost wailed.

"Nothing," he replied. "I mean, here's what I want you to do. Have you paid for your drink yet?"

"Yes."

"Good. After we hang up, you get your stuff and leave. Don't run out, but don't act like you're trying to be too casual about it, either."

"Right, right," I said excitedly.

"Jesus, calm down," he said. "Don't, whatever you do, look at the guy on the way out."

"Why not?"

"Because you have the kind of face that'll give everything away if you do," he said. "When you get outside, just wait there. A car'll be right along. They'll know who to look for. As soon as you see them, leave. Doesn't matter where you go. Just get the hell out of there as quickly as you can."

"But—"

"Goddammit, do what I say," he snapped. "I swear to Christ, if you pull the same dumb stunt you did that night at Roosevelt Towers, I'll lock *you* up."

"All right, all right."

"What's the guy doing now?" Jack said, in normal tones.

I peered through the phone booth windows at the bar. The bartender was placing another pint of lager on the counter in front of the blond man.

"Just starting on his second beer," I reported.

"Good. Are there many other people in there?"

I did a quick headcount. "About seven or eight. Either in couples or alone. The blond guy's by himself. It's very quiet."

153

"Okay. Liz, I'm going to hang up now. There'll be a car there in under a minute. As soon as we hang up, you go outside." He paused briefly. "Better still, come here. To the station."

"Will you be there?"

"Yeah. I'll meet you in the office."

"Okay."

"Bye."

I replaced the receiver on the hook. The trembling in my hands had spread to my entire body. I took another long, shuddering breath to try to compose myself, and pushed open the phone booth door.

The man at the bar was lighting a cigarette. Feeling as if everyone in the room were staring at me, I went back to my table. I managed to get some change for a tip out of my purse without dropping it all over the floor and put the coins down on the napkin beside my half-finished drink. So far, so inconspicuous. I hoped. I picked up my canvas bag and threaded my way between the maze of tables to the door. On the way out, I passed within two feet of the blond man. He never looked up from his beer.

I couldn't have been out on Mass. Avenue more than ten seconds when a dusty, dark-green 1977 Chevy Malibu rolled to a stop about a half a block up from me. It was one of the police department's unmarked cars. The driver emerged. He was a very tall, thick-chested, bushy-haired guy wearing a revolting hibiscus-patterned sport shirt that hung outside his pants. He looked straight at me and I nodded, just once, and began walking very fast up Mass. Avenue. The other cop got out of the car. He and the gorilla in the flowered shirt walked past me. They didn't look hurried or anxious, but by the same token, they didn't look like two guys out for an early evening constitutional, either.

I, on the other hand, couldn't conceal how pumped up I was. When I got to the end of the block, I started to run. It wasn't that I was scared, it was just that I had to take myself out of the way of the temptation to linger and be a part of the action at the Moon and Sixpence. Or at least a spectator. God, I'd have given up the commission on my next article just to watch. Some people had all the fun.

I raced the rest of the way to the cop shop, ignoring, barely noticing the funny looks I got from passers-by. By the time I got to the Green Street station entrance, I was breathing in great chest-tearing rasps and I had a stitch in my side. Nonetheless, I burst through the entry like an Olympic sprinter breaking the tape and bounded up the two flights of stairs to the C.I.D. two at a time.

I went through the swinging doors to the detective bureau only slightly more sedately and stopped by the secretary's desk to catch my breath. Three cops converged on me from different corners of the room—Sam Flaherty, Riordan, and a guy named George De Feo. I twiddled the fingers of my right hand at them and said, "Hi, fellas." De Feo and Riordan were looking at me as if I'd just dropped down through the ceiling instead of entered the room by the normal route. Flaherty threw his left arm around my shoulders and said, "Good girl."

I laughed weakly and shook my head.

He gave me a hug. Then he scrutinized my face. Over his shoulder, he said, "George, what do we got to drink here?"

"Lemme check," De Feo replied.

"I don't want a drink," I said.

Flaherty raised his right hand in a shushing gesture. "Come on and sit down." He took his arm from around me and led me over to one of the unoccupied library carrels. The sign on the desk said, "Detective-Sergeant Anthony Luccarelli."

I looked across the room at Jack's cubbyhole. The door was open, the office itself dark.

"Where's Jack?" I asked Flaherty.

He gave me a slightly surprised look. "Out."

"Oh?"

"Well, yeah," Flaherty said. "He's down . . . " He jerked his head to the left. Despite the vagueness of the gesture, I understood its significance.

I nodded. "Went off to the big bust, did he?"

"Well, sure. Didn't he tell you he was?"

I made a sour face. "He *told* me he'd meet me right here."

"What's the matter?" Flaherty asked, sounding concerned.

"Nothing," I said. "Nothing."

Cute trick, Jack.

At that juncture, De Feo ambled over to us with a styrofoam cup and a half-full bottle of Jim Beam. He poured a heavy slug into the cup and handed it to me. I smiled my thanks and set the cup on the desk. One hundred proof bourbon straight, at room temperature, isn't my favorite tipple.

"You know, Sam," I said. "If that guy in the bar isn't Forbes, I'm going to feel like a real horse's ass."

"Don't worry about it," he replied.

I rolled my eyes at the ceiling and he laughed. Although Luccarelli's desk had on it a prominently displayed NO SMOKING sign, he took a package of cigarettes from his jacket pocket, shook one out of the pack, and lit it. He blew a cloud of smoke off to the side and said, "Tell me about what happened in the bar."

I gave him a play-by-play of the scene at the Moon and Sixpence. Riordan and De Feo edged a little closer as I spoke, as if not wanting to miss a word. I couldn't quite see why. The story wasn't actually all that exciting in the telling.

At the end, Flaherty said, "You did good."

I shrugged. "Only if that guy does turn out to be Forbes."

"We'll see," he said.

The phone on his desk rang and he went to answer it. De Feo and Riordan hovered, still gazing at me as if I were the Redhead from Another Planet. They were overdoing it a bit, I thought. I hadn't done anything that amazing.

I sipped my drink. It didn't taste any better than I thought it would.

"You want some more?" De Feo asked, holding up the bourbon bottle.

"No, thank you," I said hastily. "This is fine." I looked up at the two of them. "Listen, I'm sure you must have a lot of work to do. You don't have to stay here and keep me company." I gestured at my bag. "I brought my own work with me."

It took a little doing, but I was finally able to convince De Feo and Riordan that I'd be fine left to my own devices. De Feo went back to his carrel and began shuffling through some papers. Riordan drifted over to the computer setup by the entrance to the conference room. He sat down at the terminal and scowled at the blank monitor. After a moment, he poked at the keyboard. The printer beside it hummed into life. Grinding out a breakdown of the latest crime statistics, no doubt.

Despite what I'd said to the two cops, I was far too keyed up to work. In any case, the desk at which I was sitting didn't have an inch of clear space on its surface. Off to one side was a foot-high stack of manila file folders. Opposite that was a pile of yellow sheets—the detectives' copy of the patrol force's crime reports. In the very center of the desk blotter there lay an eight-by-ten glossy of an absolutely gorgeous young brunette woman wearing an extremely low-cut sequined dress. I wondered if she were a suspect. If so, it couldn't be on a concealed weapons charge. All her artillery was in plain view.

I got up, taking my drink with me, and began pacing slowly around the long, narrow, oddly angled room. The right-hand section of the far wall was plastered with wanted posters. I went over to inspect them. It was the usual collection of degenerate morons. Some of the faces looked barely human. Did the criminal element indeed constitute the Missing Link?

A Kelvinator of extreme age stood in the corner. I walked over to it and opened the freezer compartment to get some ice for my drink. There was a nice little kitchen setup in this alcove—a hotplate and coffee maker in addition to the fridge. All they lacked was a sushi bar.

The wall behind the bench on which the coffee maker and hotplate rested was white and blank, except for three wanted posters. Like a shrine. It wasn't the Holy Trinity hanging up there, though. I peered at the posters. One was of Jeffrey Goldman, a reproduction of the 1970 photo. Someone with a bleak sense of humor had drawn a huge black X over the face. Another of the posters featured Prescott Forbes. No doubt it was the same wag who'd drawn dartboard circles over his face, complete with a bull's-eye on the tip of Forbes's nose.

The lovely features of Sarah Olmsbacher were unsullied. I studied them for a moment. The delicate, smiling face stared back at me, almost taunting in its well-bred impassivity.

Lady Madonna. Midwife to the revolution.

There were a couple of copies of the *Journal of Law Enforcement* on the bench beside the coffee maker. I picked them up and went back to Luccarelli's desk. Might as well catch up on my light reading.

Around me, the business of the C.I.D. continued. De Feo and another cop went out on a call. Riordan continued playing with the computer. The phones rang and got answered. Flaherty and another detective interviewed some witnesses to a liquor store holdup. Somebody turned on a radio to a soft-rock station. An elderly custodian came in and emptied the wastebaskets into a black plastic bag. I read.

I had just finished an exciting article on the revolution in fingerprinting techniques when Jack came through the swinging doors. I put down my magazine. Riordan swung around from the computer terminal. Flaherty stopped in the middle of dialing his phone. No one said a word.

Jack leaned against the filing cabinet by the door and looked straight at me for several seconds. Then he raised his right hand and pointed the index finger at me. He brought his thumb down like the hammer of a gun.

He said, "Bingo."

24

"Forbes?" I said, hardly daring to believe it.

Jack nodded.

There was an instant of total silence, and then Riordan let out a sound that was halfway between a yelp and a cheer. I leaped up from my chair and ran across the room and hurled myself at Jack. He grabbed me and, holding each other, we swung around in a half-circle. I barely missed crashing into the file cabinet, but if I had, I probably wouldn't have noticed. Flaherty hopped up from his desk and hurried over to us. I let go of Jack and grabbed Sam's hands and jumped up and down. Flaherty sort of bounced along with me. I was laughing like a crazy woman, but I wasn't making any more noise than anyone else in the room. One of the other detectives was pounding with clenched fist on his desk and chanting, "Son of a bitch, son of a bitch," over and over again. Riordan was still making his strange yelp.

It took us about five minutes to even begin calming down. I still felt like doing high kicks down the stairs and cartwheels across the room, but I had the impulse under somewhat better control. Riordan's yelps subsided. Flaherty got the bourbon bottle and some styrofoam cups. Six of us crowded into Jack's office. Sam poured us each a shot, and very solemnly, we toasted the triumph of justice and brilliant police work. The lukewarm bourbon went down like Château Lafite-Rothschild this time, I noticed.

Then Jack proposed a toast to me, "without whom it would have been impossible." The five men turned toward me and raised their cups. I was sitting in the only spare office chair, and when the others saluted me, I was ready to fall out of it with embarrassment. But I was very, very pleased. Jack gave me a secret smile over the top of his cup. His face was gray with weariness but at the same time vibrant with exhilaration.

"Was there any trouble?" Flaherty said.

Jack smiled very broadly. "Not at all," he said. "It was fucking beautiful."

"Went just like silk, huh?" I piped up innocently.

Jack gave me a quick, sharp look and then started to laugh. He pressed the knuckle of his index finger against his mouth to suppress it.

Flaherty glanced from me to Jack and back again and said, "Did I miss something here?"

"Private joke," I explained, and sipped my Château James Beam.

"Oh," Flaherty said. He looked back at Jack. "Well, how *did* it go, anyway?"

Jack began describing the arrest, and the rest of us listened without any interruption, rapt. From what I could gather, the whole business had, in fact, gone like silk. Jack lapsed into a kind of cop shorthand as he spoke, and I was sure I was missing the finer points of what he was saying. Oh, well—I'd get an English translation from him later. The gorilla cop (his name was actually Joe Mooney) and his sidekick had apparently gone into the Moon and Sixpence and gotten themselves a table and some beers. The blond man was still at the bar, nursing his lager. After a few minutes, Mooney had gotten up and made a phone call. Anyone who overheard him would have thought he was talking to his girlfriend. Some more plainclothes cops moved into the parking lot behind the bar. Another cop took up a post at the corner of Hancock Street and Mass. Avenue. He had a shotgun. There were police cars on Harvard, Centre, and Green Streets. Mooney and friend drank beer and swapped dirty jokes and watched without watching the blond man.

That was the trap. The bait was the cruiser that pulled up in front of the funeral parlor directly across the street from the Moon and Sixpence, in full view of anyone who happened to glance out the front window of the bar. Forbes did. He seemed to stiffen slightly. Then he drank down the remains of his lager, took some money from his pocket, and put it on the counter. He swiveled around on his stool. Before he had one foot on the floor, Mooney and the other cop were all over him. There was no struggle; the two cops had the barrels of their guns shoved up against the blond man's head. He himself was armed, too—he had a .25 automatic in the right pocket of his jacket. That in itself would have been sufficient to get him arrested.

The most fascinating part of the story to me was the fact that Forbes, once taken into custody, had made no attempt to protest his innocence or maintain that he was, say, Joe Blow from Quincy or Malden or Arlington or Dorchester. Not only did he not bother to hide his identity—he proclaimed it to the skies.

"My name is Prescott Forbes. I am a soldier in the Peoples Army." And that was *all* he would say.

The party broke up shortly after Jack finished speaking. He had to get back downstairs, and as for the other cops, crime in Cambridge hadn't suspended itself for the duration. Flaherty offered to get one of the patrol officers to take me home. I told him I'd rather wait for Jack. He told me I might have a very long wait. I said that was okay.

The downstairs was roiling with people from the papers and the television. I had absolutely no desire to join them. I knew that my part in this evening's proceedings would be kept absolutely quiet by Jack and everyone else in the department who knew about it—the best they'd say to the reporters was that an anonymous witness had spotted and identified Forbes and subsequently called the police. Still, I had no desire to risk being set upon by anyone with a microphone or portable tape recorder or steno book in hand.

For obvious reasons, I had to clear out of the C.I.D. well before Forbes was brought up for "interview." Where I would go was a matter of some debate. Flaherty finally resolved the issue by getting a key to the ICAP office on the second floor and installing me there. ICAP did crime analysis and crime prevention. Alone in the big silent room, I inspected a display of locks and deadbolts. I studied some antidrug campaign posters. Then I read every pamphlet in the place on how not to get robbed, mugged, burglarized, or raped. Around midnight, I dozed off behind one of the desks.

Jack shook me awake at 1:00 A.M. I raised my head from my arms and blinked at him. He smiled at me and said, "Quitting time."

I rubbed my eyes and said, "Goody."

He held out his hand and I took it and stood up slowly. I felt as if I creaked when I moved. Sleeping in a swivel chair with an IBM Selectric II for a pillow isn't like reposing on a cloud. In fact, it was only slightly less comfortable than the waterbed I'd once been forced to spend a night in while on a weekend visit to some friends.

"How'd it go?" I asked.

"With Forbes?" Jack shrugged. "Not far. After he stopped giving us his name, rank, and serial number, he said he wouldn't say anything else without a lawyer."

"So?"

"So we got him a lawyer. Hell, what else?"

I nodded. "What lawyer?"

Jack smiled. "Frank Doucette."

"Perfect," I said. Frank Doucette was a public defender and a Marxist. He was also a Quaalude freak. I wondered if he ever argued any of his cases zonked.

"Come on," Jack said. "Let's get out of here."

"Hey, wait a minute," I said. "I just helped to capture a major league criminal. Don't I even get a lousy kiss or something?"

"Something," Jack said. "But not here."

Forbes was arraigned—on charges running the gamut from possession of an unlicensed handgun to first-degree murder—in the courthouse in East Cambridge the following morning. I'd have liked to have gone over there and watched him being brought in, but I didn't need Jack to tell me that to do so would have been less than wise. It was a million-to-one chance that Forbes would spot me and recognize me as someone who'd been in the bar just before his arrest. And if he did, and put two and two together, it was even less likely that he'd be able to effect any kind of retaliation, or get a message through to a person who could. Still . . .

So I settled for watching the proceedings on the noon news. Spectators *did* gather outside the courthouse, but the crowd was small and from what I could see well behaved. In any case, every second person in it was probably a Cambridge SWAT cop, a federal marshal, a state cop, or an FBI agent. The security arrangements seemed to be about twice as heavy as they would have been for a presidential visit. The TV camera caught a shot of a sniper poised on the rooftop of an adjacent building, rifle trained on the crowd. I was sure he wasn't alone. A couple of ambulances stood at the ready. According to the news reporter, the bomb squad was on the alert.

In contrast to all the preparations made and precautions taken for it, the event itself was extremely low-key. Forbes was driven up in a police wagon. As he emerged from the rear of the vehicle, a few people in the crowd cheered. Whether they were for him or against him, I couldn't tell. Forbes himself didn't appear to acknowledge, or even notice, the cheers. Manacled and shackled at the waist as he was, he could hardly have raised the traditional fist, nor even given anyone the finger had he so desired. As soon as he and the escort stepped down from the van, they disappeared inside a ring of cops. If my watch was correct, it took them less than fifteen seconds to hustle Forbes into the courthouse.

I rose from the couch and switched off the TV. Kind of anticlimactic, I thought. Not that I'd been hoping that someone might start hurling Molotov cocktails or incite the spectators to storm the courthouse. But Forbes could have at least yelled "power to the people" or even "off the pigs."

As it turned out, Forbes had chosen to save his histrionics for the courtroom. I heard about them in detail from Jack later that evening. We were sitting in his living room splitting a celebratory bottle of Piper Heidsieck. I hate champagne, even the good kind, but the occasion seemed to demand something other than his usual bourbon or beer and my usual vodka. I'd picked up twenty dollars' worth of caviar at Sage's. That I could gobble up until it started coming out my ears. Come to think of it, vodka probably would have been appropriate.

"So," I said. "Old Forbes put on a good show, did he?"

Jack drank some champagne. "I'm almost sorry you had to miss it."

I raised my eyebrows. "Me, too. What happened?"

"Well," Jack said. "The first thing was that Forbes demanded that the judge handle his case in accordance with dictates of the Geneva Convention. Forbes being a prisoner of war, you understand."

"Who was the judge?"

Jack smiled. "Forrest Furman."

"Oh, God." I started to laugh. Forrest Furman had been on the bench for nearly thirty years. Physically, Furman resembled William Howard Taft. Politically, he made Taft resemble Jane Fonda.

"What else?" I said, wolfing down another helping of caviar.

"Furman denied the request. Said that as far as he knew, there wasn't anything in the Geneva Convention about releasing prisoners on bail."

"So how did Forbes take that?"

"Not too well. He kept interrupting Furman while Furman was trying to read the charges."

"Slick move."

"Yeah," Jack said. "Furman finally threatened to have him gagged if he didn't keep quiet."

"That must have been a blow."

"Well, it didn't stop him from calling Furman a fascist insect and the prosecutor a Nazi pig."

"Wow," I said. "Sounds heavy."

Jack shrugged.

I had barely sipped my champagne. I handed the glass to Jack and said, "Would you like to finish this?"

"Sure."

I got up and went to the kitchen to get myself a vodka on the rocks. When I returned, Jack was lounging back on the sofa, eyes closed, feet on the coffee table. His face was drawn, almost haggard. I felt a small flutter of anxiety in my stomach. He opened his eyes and smiled at me. I smiled back, quickly.

"You seem tired," I said.

"A little," he admitted.

I curled up on the couch next to him and he slid his arm around me. I drank some vodka. Much better. Too bad I'd already eaten all the caviar. I could imagine what somebody like Forbes would have said about my gluttony. For some reason, the thought of his reaction didn't amuse me. I felt, rather, a little sad. And, in some corner of myself, almost ashamed.

It must have showed on my face, because Jack said, "What's wrong?"

I hesitated a moment and then shook my head. "Nothing," I said. "At least, nothing I can really specify."

"Make an effort," Jack suggested, and drank some champagne.

I stirred the vodka and ice with my index finger. "It's Forbes, I guess."

Jack gave me a surprised look. "What about him?"

I sucked in my lower lip and held it between my teeth for a few seconds. "I don't know, exactly. I guess . . . you and I have been sitting here laughing at him, that's all."

"And?"

I shrugged. "Maybe we shouldn't be."

Jack shook his head like someone puzzled. "How's that?"

I let out a long whoosh of breath. "Look," I said. "I know what the guy is. A murderer and a bank robber and a lot of other terrible things. I have no sympathy whatsoever for him that way. I'm glad I helped catch him."

"You ought to be."

I held up my hand. "But."

"But what?"

I turned to look at Jack. "I think he honestly believed in what he was doing."

Jack gave a sardonic snort. "Most murderers and bank robbers do, babe. The ones I've met, anyway."

"That's not what I mean," I said. "I really do think Forbes was convinced he was fighting for the people. Against militarism and racism and all that stuff. For, as corny as it sounds, a better life for everybody."

There was a little pause. Jack took a mouthful of champagne, held it, and then swallowed. "Not everybody," he said. "You think somebody like me fits into his scheme? Or you, even? Who do you think the first ones to get lined up against the wall would be if he had the say?"

I was quiet. I knew what I was thinking, but I couldn't articulate it. Jack was right, of course. Ninety percent of me agreed with him. It was the other ten percent that was the problem. I drank some vodka.

"Look," Jack said. "I don't want a nuclear war. I don't want any kind of war. Who the hell in his right mind does? I'm not all that goddamned crazy about racism and poverty either. So?"

I recalled making much the same comment to David Epstein. But there were things that Jack had the right to say and things that I didn't. He had seen a great deal more of human suffering and its consequences than I ever had, or probably ever would. All cops did.

"I don't know what I'm talking about," I said, finally.

Jack took a deep breath and let it out very slowly. "Who does?" he said. "Who the hell ever does?"

25

Jack polished off most of the champagne, and I had some more vodka, and by the time we got to bed, we were in a far less introspective mood. In fact, we were downright silly. Part of it was liquor, of course, but most of it was letting off steam. We let off even more steam in bed.

I woke up at 7:45 the following morning feeling very good. The other half of the bed was empty, and I could hear sounds of life in the kitchen. Jack would be leaving for work in half an hour. If I got up now, we could have breakfast together. I hopped out of bed and went over to the door and shouted, "Two eggs over easy with rye toast and orange juice in ten minutes, please." Then I took a shower and got dressed.

I bounced into the kitchen just as Jack was setting my plate of food on the table. It was a sort of ritual with us that when I stayed at his place or he stayed at mine, he made breakfast. He had a knack with eggs that I couldn't duplicate, and his coffee was the best I'd ever drunk.

I gave him a kiss before I sat down at my place. He smiled and said, "Morning." He still looked tired, I noticed. Well, we hadn't gotten a full eight hours' sleep the previous night.

Jack poured himself a second cup of coffee and sat down at the table to study the sports section of the *Globe*. I dug into my eggs and toast. I was halfway through them when the phone rang. Jack let the newspaper fall to the table top and pushed back his chair. He got up and left the room. I reached for the marmalade.

I was sipping my coffee when he came back to the kitchen. "Who was that?" I asked idly.

"Sam."

I looked up from my coffee. Jack was standing in the doorway. There was an odd expression on his face.

"What is it?" I said.

He shook his head slightly, as if he were trying to clear it.

"You look funny," I said.

He came into the room and sat down at the table. "Walter Davison is dead."

There was a little silence, in which the tick of the kitchen clock sounded very loud. I set my cup down carefully. Then I said, "What?"

"Davison," Jack said. "The Weatherman. He's dead. Somebody shot him in the back of the head and dumped him in the parking lot behind the Moon and Sixpence."

"Oh, my God," I said.

"There was a note in his shirt pocket," Jack said. "It said that this was what happened to pig informers."

"Oh, God," I repeated. I felt as if my insides were frozen.

"I talked to him Monday afternoon," Jack said. "A couple hours before . . . " He made a vague gesture with his right hand.

I licked my lips. "What did he tell you?"

Jack shook his head.

"He must have known something," I said, half to myself. "Something he didn't mention to you or me."

Jack didn't reply. He picked up his coffee and drank the rest of it. His face was gray and the lines in it seemed to have deepened within the past five minutes.

"I have to go," he said.

I nodded, watching him very closely. He really looked awful. I hesitated a moment and then said, "Jack?"

"Yeah?"

"Are you okay?"

"I'm fine."

"You're sure?" I persisted.

"Yes, yes, for Christ's sake." His voice was ragged with irritation.

I was being warned not to push it any further. "Good," I said, and picked up my coffee cup. My hands were shaking a little.

"See you later," Jack said.

"Right," I said. "Want me to stick around until you get back?"

"No. Don't bother."

That annoyed me, but I kept it hidden. "It's no bother. I don't have to teach today."

"I'm not sure how long I'll be gone. I'll call you when I can."

"Yup. Talk to you later."

"Uh-huh." He left the kitchen. I heard him go down the hall and turn into the bedroom. It was probably my imagination, but his footsteps sounded listless to me. I told myself that I was being paranoid. Looking for trouble. He was tired, that was all. Lucy wandered into the room and over to the table and shoved her muzzle into my lap. I scratched her behind the ears and she swished her tail.

"Have some toast," I said, and gave her what was left on my plate. Then I got up and started clearing the table. The eggs, butter, and milk were on the counter. I put them back in the refrigerator and started washing dishes.

Perhaps five minutes had passed when I realized that I hadn't yet heard the front door open and close. It was a sound I'd been half-consciously listening for. I set the frying pan in the sink and dried my hands on my jeans.

"Jack?" I said.

The apartment was very quiet. I went to the kitchen entrance. "Jack?" I said, more loudly this time. "You still here?"

No answer. I went down the hall to the bedroom. The door was ajar. I hovered on the threshold, feeling alternately silly and apprehensive. A ridiculous coupling of sensations. I opened the door.

He was sitting on the edge of the bed, his arms crossed over his chest and his head bent. He was breathing through his mouth in shallow little gulps. It looked as if it hurt him to take in air. There was greasy drops of sweat on his forehead.

"Godalmighty," I said.

He glanced up at the sound of my voice. His eyes had a glazed and unfocused look, as if he weren't really seeing what was before him. The gray of his face had faded to a kind of oystery whiteness.

I was across the room in two bounds and beside him on the bed. "What's wrong?" I said.

He shook his head.

"Jack, something is." I put my hand up to his face. His skin was cold and damp. I took my hand away and stood up. "I'm going to call an ambulance."

"No," he said. The word was spoken with considerable effort.

"*Yes*," I said. I started to move away and he grabbed my hand. "Jack," I said. "You're sick. I don't know what's wrong, but you have to see a doctor. Now. I'm not kidding."

"I have seen a doctor," he said.

"Good," I said. "You're going to see another one." I pulled free and made for the door. He stood up, one hand still pressed against his chest.

"Lie down, goddamn you," I yelled. Always a calm presence in a crisis.

"I have something to take for it," he said.

"What?" I said. "Take for what? Where is it? Let me get it."

He shook his head again and started across the room. He paused midway, swayed slightly, and took a deep breath. I slumped against the wall, staring at him.

"It's all right," he said. He went into the bathroom and shut the door behind him.

Once I was on a British Airways 747 taking off from Heathrow in London. When we were about two miles up, one of the rear doors flew open and the plane started bouncing up and down like a yo-yo in the hands of God. A stewardess had to hold the door shut until one of the passengers could run forward to the cockpit to get the flight engineer. I thought I was frightened then. It was nothing compared to what I was feeling now.

A minute or so passed. The bathroom door opened and Jack emerged. He'd wiped the sweat from his face and there was slightly more color in it. He gave me a weary little smile.

"Sorry," he said.

"For what?" I said. "For being sick?" I went over and put my arm around him. "Jack, you have to see a doctor. Today. This minute. I'm not kidding."

"I know," he said. "Really, it's okay. This has happened before."

"What's happened before?" I said. "I thought you were having a heart attack. You still may be."

"It's not that."

"So what is it, then?"

He shrugged. "I don't know. A bad case of heartburn, maybe?"

"Oh, Jack. Didn't you ask the doctor?"

He shrugged again.

"Why didn't you tell me?" I asked. "How often does this happen?"

"Not very," he said. I could tell by the expression on his face that he was lying.

"How is it now?" I said.

"Oh, better." I must have looked disbelieving, because he put his arm around my shoulders and gave me a brief squeeze.

"Let's relax for a moment," I suggested. He nodded and we walked over to the bed and sat down. He kept his arm around me and I leaned against him. I had the feeling our positions should be reversed.

We were quiet for several moments, holding each other. Gradually his breathing slowed and deepened and became normal. Trying to be unobtrusive about it, I moved my head so that my right ear was pressed against his chest. His heart seemed to be beating regularly and not too rapidly. But what did I know? He rested his chin against the top of my head.

"That was a scare you gave me," I said presently.

He smiled. "I told you I was sorry, didn't I?"

"That's not the point," I said. "Being scared I can handle." I straightened up and looked him in the eye. "You dying is something else."

He made a face. "I'm not going to die."

"You looked as if you were on the verge of it ten minutes ago."

"You worry too much."

"Maybe so," I conceded. "But you have to admit you gave me good reason."

"You're as bad as your mother," he said, shaking his head. "Worse."

"Well, at least I come by it honestly," I said. "You want to lie down for a bit?"

"No. It's a nice thought, but no."

"Oh, come on," I urged. "Catch up on a little rest. Civilization's not gonna collapse if you take a nap. You have three hundred colleagues to stave off the apocalypse. One or two of them may even be as capable of it as you." I was absolutely determined not to let him stir out of the apartment. Heartburn, my ass. I knew all about the statistics concerning forty-three-year-old men in high-stress jobs and heart attacks.

"Liz," Jack said.

"Hmmm?" I put my face in his shoulder.

"I appreciate what you're doing."

I raised my head and looked at him. "That sounds as if it has a 'but' attached to it."

He smiled. "It does. I have to go."

I closed my eyes. "Jack," I said. "I don't care what you say. You are not well. Don't do this. You're not going to do anyone any good at all if you end up in the coronary care unit of Mount Auburn Hospital."

"That's not going to happen."

"Jesus," I exploded. "A minute ago you couldn't even make it out the bedroom door. You are not in any condition to go chasing terrorists around the greater Boston area."

"I'm not chasing them."

"So what are you doing, then?"

He shook his head. "Liz, please. Try to understand. You know what this job is about."

"Yeah," I said. "I've had several graphic demonstrations of that lately."

He stood up. I stayed where I was, looking at the floor and biting my upper lip.

"I'll call you when I can," he said.

"You do that," I said.

"You're angry," he said.

I looked up at him. "No," I said. "I'm scared to death."

26

He left. I sat on the edge of the unmade bed for another twenty minutes, staring at the wall opposite. My innards were still clenched and frozen. My mind didn't seem to be working properly, either. The thoughts in it were whirling and zipping around like protons and electrons and not really going anywhere but the same circle.

Finally I got up and made the bed. I did it very precisely, as if I were an entrant in a housewivery competition. I finished washing and drying the breakfast dishes and then scrubbed the already immaculate kitchen counter. The rest of the apartment was spotless. Jack had a good cleaning woman.

At 9:45 I called David Epstein. He was with a patient. I left my name and Jack's number with the answering service. Epstein had told me to let him know if anything "funny" happened with Jack. I figured this qualified.

I gathered up the material for my article and sat down at the kitchen table to try and work. I actually wrote a page and a half of introductory material. I read it over and ripped it up and tossed the pieces into the wastebasket. Drivel.

At 11:30 I called Abby and asked her to have lunch with me. She said sure. We agreed to meet in an hour at the Spanish restaurant on Boylston Street in Harvard Square. After we hung up, I took Lucy for a walk. Then I put her back in the apartment with a fresh bowl of water and a biscuit and set off to meet Abby.

When I got to the restaurant she was waiting for me at a table for two on the back patio. She took one look at me and ordered a carafe of wine from the waiter.

"I really don't like to drink in the daytime," I said.

"Neither do I," she replied. "But I can make an exception." She peered at me through brown-tinted sunglasses and said, "What's the matter with you?"

"Oh, God," I said, taking my seat. "Do I look that bad?"

"Like somebody took away your typewriter. What's wrong?"

"It isn't me," I said. "It's Jack."

She frowned in a concerned way. "What is it?"

I took a deep breath. "I don't know," I said. "He's . . . I . . . he's . . . something's wrong with him. He's sick."

The waiter brought the wine and poured us each a glass. He put a basket of bread and a saucer of butter on the table. Abby waited until he'd gone and then said, "Sick? How?"

I told her what had happened that morning.

"That's awful," she said, when I'd finished. "I don't blame you for being scared."

The waiter reappeared with a pad and pencil. Without bothering to look at the menu, Abby ordered gazpacho and a salad. I asked for the same thing, not because I wanted it, but because there wasn't anything else that I did.

"So what should I do?" I said.

Abby was silent for a moment, playing with her fork. "I don't know," she said finally. "I'm trying to think of something, and I can't. It's like you've already done everything that you can." She set down the fork. "He *did* tell you that he'd been to see a doctor."

"Uh-huh."

"So what did the doctor say? About the chest pains or whatever they are."

"Oh, who knows? Jack told me some nonsense about how he just had a bad case of heartburn."

Abby sighed. "Well, that *is* possible. Those attacks can be incredibly painful. And some of the symptoms are a lot like heart attack symptoms."

"Oh, yeah," I said. "I keep forgetting that you once studied to be a doctor."

174

She smiled a little. "I didn't learn about heartburn in a classroom."

At that moment, the waiter brought the food. Despite myself, I had to laugh at his timing.

Abby buttered a chunk of bread. "So what brought all this on?"

"Huh?"

She described a small circle in the air with her bread knife. "I mean, did this attack that Jack had this morning happen out of the blue? Or was there something that might have precipitated it? Other than all the shit that's been going down here the past month or so."

I stared at her for a moment, a little surprised by the question. Then I said, "Of course. You don't know. How would you? Walter Davison's dead. Somebody shot him to death for being a pig informer. Jack got a call about it this morning from one of the other cops."

Abby's eyes widened and her mouth opened slightly. "Jesus Christ," she said softly. She took a big gulp of her wine.

I had a spoonful of gazpacho and a mouthful of salad.

"The PRC?" Abby said.

"Who else?"

She shook her head in a bewildered way. "I don't understand. How. . . ? *Was* Davison an informer?"

I shrugged. "All I know is that Jack talked to him Monday afternoon. I have no idea what, if anything, Davison told him."

Abby ate some soup. Her face had a look of intense concentration, as if she were working out one of her computer problems. She put her spoon in the saucer beneath her bowl. "Wait a minute," she said. "How the hell would the PRC know that Davison talked to the cops? Were they watching him?"

"I guess they must have been," I said. "They probably had—maybe they even still have—Jack under some kind of surveillance. If they could pull off spying on a police lieutenant, then they could swing it with somebody like Davison."

Abby nodded. "And they just *assumed* Davison blabbed to the cops. And so they shot him more or less on suspicion of squealing."

"More or less."

Abby picked up her spoon. "But that implies that Davison knew something to squeal. And he wouldn't know anything to squeal unless he were actually involved with the PRC in some way now, would he?"

"Yeah," I said. I had a sudden thought. "Maybe they figured he had something to do with Forbes being captured. That he set Forbes up so the cops could move in and grab him."

Abby lifted her eyebrows. "Possibly." She drank some more wine. "God, I can't believe that you and I were sitting in that bar just an hour before the whole thing came down there."

I smiled and nodded. Abby didn't know that I'd been the one to turn in Forbes. I'd promised Jack I wouldn't tell anyone. Not that I wanted to proclaim the news to the skies.

"That must have been it," Abby said. She forked up some salad. "Yeah. That *had* to have been it. Olmsbacher or one of the others saw Davison with a cop. Then six hours later, Forbes gets busted. The coincidence must have been too much for them." Abby sighed. "Christ. Poor Walter."

I felt sick. I hoped it didn't show on my face. To cover I drank some wine and force-fed myself some gazpacho. A mistake. I gagged and had to grab for my napkin and press it to my mouth. Abby peered at me in alarm. "You okay?"

I nodded and sipped some water. That seemed to settle things. I let out a long breath and said, "Whew."

Abby finished her soup. I fiddled with my water glass.

"You know," I said presently. "Maybe Davison wasn't really involved with the PRC."

Abby gave me a curious look. "Then why would they have shot him? If he didn't know anything about them, he couldn't say anything to hurt them, no matter who he talked to, or how loudly or often."

I shrugged. "Maybe they found out about the book he was writing."

Abby's face was skeptical. "But you told me there wasn't anything useful in it."

I shook my head. "But the PRC didn't know that."

"But . . . " She waved a hand. "It all goes back to the same thing. If he wasn't involved with them now, then he wouldn't know anything incriminating about them to write about. So what the hell would they care how many books he churned out?"

I took a small, cautious sip of wine. It went down okay. "That's beside the point," I said. "Maybe they killed him to make an example of him. As a warning to others. Maybe they figured that any exrevolutionary who wrote about the underground and talked about it with cops deserved to get blown away on general principle."

"Maybe," Abby said slowly. "Maybe. Jesus. Yeah, I suppose that could be it."

The waiter appeared and asked us if we wanted coffee. We said yes. Abby poured half the remainder of the wine in the carafe into my glass and the other half into hers. I pecked at my salad. I was wondering where Jack was, and what he was doing now. How he was. Half of me was sure I'd get a call from one of the hospitals this afternoon or evening. Or that somebody like Flaherty might show up on the doorstep and tell me . . . He wouldn't have to tell me anything. I'd see it in his face.

The waiter brought the coffee and the check.

Abby said, "What are you doing this afternoon?"

I looked up from my salad and shrugged.

"Why don't you come to my house?"

"Don't you have to get back to work?" I asked in surprise.

She smiled. "I feel a summer cold coming on. I'll call in sick. Come on. You need the company. We'll have a drink and sit around and maybe figure out what to do about Jack."

I nodded. "All right. That sounds good." I smiled at her. "Thanks. You're a good buddy."

We finished our coffee and paid the check and left the restaurant. Abby's red Volvo was parked a block down on Boylston Street across from the JFK school of government. There was a ticket under the windshield wiper on the driver's side.

"Oh, for Christ's sake," Abby said. She ripped the ticket from beneath the wiper and tossed it at me like a Frisbee. "Here, good buddy. Get this fixed for me."

I laughed and picked up the piece of paper. "Jack doesn't do parking violations."

Abby snorted and unlocked the car doors. We took off up Boylston as if we were starting at Le Mans. I put the ticket in the glove compartment.

Abby's place was on a street off Linnaean in North Cambridge. The neighborhood was posh. Her apartment was half the third floor of an enormous frame house that an enterprising podiatrist had bought for next to nothing in the midfifties and converted into six or seven flats.

The place must have been a gold mine. I wondered when it would go condo.

Abby parked in her space at the head of the driveway and we got out of the car and walked to the house. She unlocked the massive oak front door and we went up the two flights to her apartment. The stairs were expensively carpeted and the banister a hunk of hand-carved mahogany.

"Wish my building were as nice as this," I said.

"Get a job in computers," Abby replied. "Then you'll be able to afford all the luxuries." She inserted the key into the lock of her apartment door and started to turn it. She stopped and a puzzled look crossed her face. "That's funny."

"What's the matter?"

She shook her head. "The door's not locked. I could have sworn I locked it when I left. I mean I do that automatically."

"Maybe Cal's home."

"No. He won't be back till six at least."

We stared at each other.

"Burglars?" Abby said softly. "There's been an awful lot of house-breaking around here recently."

"I don't know," I said. I put my ear to the door and listened. "I don't hear anything."

"Oh, the hell with it," Abby said. "Maybe when we go in, they'll go out the French windows. I'm not going to stand around in the hall for the next four hours." She threw open the door and strode into the apartment. I followed her.

"No burglars," she announced. "Come on. Let's go sit in the living room. I'll get—" She stopped dead in the entrance to the living room and I walked right into her.

"Sorry," I said, backing up. She didn't reply.

"Abby?" I said. She was standing motionless in the doorway, still staring into the living room. I moved forward and peered over her shoulder.

A slender, attractive woman with short curly dark-brown hair was seated in a rocking chair by the fireplace, facing us. Her legs were crossed and she was smiling slightly. In her hands was a gun. It was raised and pointed at us, very steadily.

"Jesus Christ," I whispered.

"Come in and sit down," the woman said. I'd heard that voice before. On the telephone at 5:00 A.M. Neither Abby nor I moved.

The woman smiled more broadly. "I didn't expect you back from work so soon. But then, you didn't expect to see me here, did you?"

Abby shook her head woodenly.

The woman gestured with the gun. "So come in and sit down and talk. We haven't had a chance to do much of that lately. I want to hear all about what you've been doing with yourself, Leilah."

27

(July 2)

The walls of the foyer seemed to belly inward and wobble and only after a long time right themselves. I felt a kind of numbness begin in my chest and then spread outward and down my arms and legs. Abby was motionless beside me. I didn't look at her.

"Do as I say," Sarah said. She got up and moved toward us. "Do it or I'll shoot you both right now where you're standing. And you know I can."

Abby and I edged into the room.

"On the couch," Sarah said. "Not too far apart, either."

We sat down next to each other on the couch.

"Fine," Sarah said. "You follow orders better than you used to, Leilah."

"Don't call me that," Abby said.

"I'll call you anything I fucking well want to, you bitch." Sarah stepped back a few paces and leaned against the mantelpiece. Her eyes moved back and forth between our faces. The gun in her hands was still quite steady.

"How'd you get in?" Abby asked. Her voice was mechanical, affectless.

"Your locks are pieces of shit," Sarah said. "It took me about ten seconds to pick them both. You know I'm good at that."

Abby nodded.

"However," Sarah continued. "I didn't come here to discuss the finer points of lock picking." She paused a moment. "You know why I'm here, don't you, Leilah?"

Abby was silent.

"Answer me," Sarah said.

"Yes. I know."

"I thought you would." Sarah pushed away from the mantelpiece and dropped into the rocking chair. The movements of her body were fluid, yet economical. Amazing grace.

"Where were you Monday night?" Sarah asked.

I thought I was beyond shock, but the words hit me like a fist in the stomach. I turned my head just a little and stared at Abby. In profile, her face was white and very still.

"We had a date the other night, Leilah," Sarah said. "You were going to bring me some money, remember?"

Monday evening outside the bank in Central Square. Abby stuffing a wad of bills into her wallet and asking me where I wanted to go for a drink.

"I waited two hours," Sarah continued. "You never showed up. Where were you?"

Abby shook her head slightly.

"You weren't by any chance talking to the pigs, were you?" Sarah asked. "Trying to set something up?"

"No," Abby said faintly.

"I should hope not," Sarah said. "You know what would have happened if you had."

Abby nodded.

"Or if I thought you had anything to do with Pres getting picked up," Sarah added.

"I had nothing to do with that," Abby said.

"Sure." Sarah laughed, a rich, almost good-humored sound. "If you had, you'd have been dead yesterday."

Abby put a hand to her eyes and rubbed them. "If you want money," she said. "Take it." She lowered her hand and gestured at her purse on the coffee table. "There's a couple of hundred there. Just take it."

"Oh, I will," Sarah said. "I will. But before I do, we have some other business to settle, you and I."

I sneezed. I couldn't help myself. I could feel the tickle in the back of my nose and I tried to suppress it, but it came out anyway.

Olmsbacher transferred her gaze from Abby to me. She stared at me for a moment and then frowned slightly, the way you do when you're curious or puzzled. She leaned forward slightly and the frown deepened. Then she rose and walked over to the couch. When she was about three feet away, she bent down and peered very intently at my face. Her eyes were large and green and almond-shaped. "I know you," she said. "You're the girlfriend of that cop, aren't you? I saw you going into his house one night." She straightened up and smiled broadly. A dimple, shocking in its incongruity, appeared in her left cheek. "Well, well," she said. "You two make a good pair. A pig's woman and a traitor. Perfect." She backed away, slowly, and sat down in the rocking chair. I felt as if my throat were lined with glue.

Sarah leaned back in the rocking chair and glanced around the room. "Nice apartment," she said. Idly, she scuffed at the Oriental rug with the toe of her left sneaker. "You live well, Leilah."

Abby didn't say anything.

"You must make a good salary," Sarah continued. "The death merchants pay well, don't they?"

Abby swallowed, loudly enough for me to hear.

"What is it, exactly, you do?" Sarah asked. She sounded genuinely interested. "Work on missile guidance systems? Design bomb parts, maybe? Nerve gas? Something like that?"

Abby shook her head.

"Oh, how good," Sarah replied. "I'm so glad you're not sullying your hands with any of that shit. What is it you *do* do, then?"

"I'm a systems analyst," Abby said, very softly.

"Louder," Sarah said. She cupped her free hand behind her left ear. "Speak up. I didn't hear you the first time."

"I'm a systems analyst," Abby repeated.

"Oh." Sarah nodded. "A systems analyst. That's nice. And what kind of systems is it you analyze?"

Abby was silent.

Sarah arched her eyebrows. "You don't know? Is that it? You don't know?"

Abby hunched her shoulders a little and bent her head so that she was looking at her knees.

"How nice," Sarah said. "You analyze systems, but you don't know what systems. How convenient." She leaned forward slightly. "Is that how you justify it to yourself? Is that what you say to yourself when you pick up that big paycheck? 'I don't know what I'm doing, so it's okay as long as they give me the bread.' Is that it, Leilah?"

Abby scrunched over further. Her face looked as if she were in pain.

"Look at me," Sarah snapped. "Look at me when I talk to you." She jumped out of the rocking chair and came toward us. Abby raised her head. Sarah went down on one knee, the gun in her right hand pointed directly at Abby's face.

"You sold me out," Sarah said. "You sold us out. You sold out the whole movement. If it hadn't been for you, Charlie never would have been arrested after that bank robbery. You were supposed to meet him and me that night, remember? You were going to drive us to New York. You ran off and left us, you bitch. And Charlie got picked up by the cops."

There was a look of infinite weariness on Abby's face. "He would have been picked up anyway," she said. "He was a loser, Sarah. He would have done the same thing in New York he did in that bar in Revere and the New York cops would have grabbed him."

"Shit," Sarah said. "You got him busted and you got him killed."

Abby closed her eyes and shook her head.

"You sold us out," Sarah said. "Why? You were the big revolutionary. The Maoist. You knew what had to be done. Why'd you run off?"

"I couldn't do it," Abby said. "I thought maybe I could. But I couldn't kill people."

"Kill people," Sarah repeated. "Kill pigs, you mean. What the fuck do you think a revolution's about?"

"I couldn't," Abby said softly. "I couldn't kill anyone."

"Yeah, you could," Sarah said. "You killed Charlie. You got him put in a fucking prison and he died."

Abby looked down at her lap. Her hands were folded tightly together. The knuckles were white, like her face.

"It took me a long time to work my way back here," Sarah said. "Fifteen years. Fifteen years I had to run and hide. But I did. And I came back for you."

"Fifteen years," Abby said. "That's a long time to hate."

"Oh, no," Sarah said. "The hate kept me going. It helped a lot when

I was living in some roach hole waiting for the FBI to come through the front door. And now . . . you know what I'm going to do, don't you?"

Abby nodded once.

"I figured you would," Sarah said. "Whatever else you are or aren't, you're not stupid."

She got up and backed over to the rocking chair. As she sat down, she was careful to keep the gun raised and pointed at us. It looked like the kind of gun uniformed cops carried. I wondered how long she'd had it, and how she acquired it. And what she'd done with it.

"Hey," Sarah said. "You."

Abby and I looked at her. She was smiling at me over the barrel of the gun.

"You're a writer, aren't you?" she said.

How the hell did she know that? I hesitated a moment, and then nodded. No point in denying it.

"Worse and worse," Sarah said. "A pig's lady *and* a writer. Don't care much for writers, myself."

"Is that why you killed Walter Davison?" Abby asked abruptly. I jumped, startled less by the question than by the sound of her voice. For the first time, it had some body in it.

Sarah looked nearly as surprised. Then she grinned. "Partly."

I breathed in deeply, and exhaled as softly as I could.

"Wasn't that a little drastic?" Abby said.

Sarah shrugged. "He was supposed to be a fucking revolutionary. Revolutionaries don't write books about other revolutionaries. And they don't talk to the pigs. Not if they want to keep on breathing, they don't."

Abby wet her lips. "How do you know he talked to the pi . . . the police?"

Sarah laughed. "Oh, we were keeping an eye on him. As soon as we found out about the book, we knew we'd have to. Walter always did have a big mouth. Too big." She looked at me. "By the way, did you and he have a nice chat the other day?"

The shock of it must have shown in my face, because she laughed again. "Revolutionaries aren't supposed to talk with writers, either. *Especially* writers who hang out with pigs." She leaned forward and rested her elbows on her knees. The gun was aimed at me now. I pushed myself back against the couch cushions.

"Tell me something," Sarah said.

I kept very still, watching her.

"What's it like?" she said.

Was I supposed to know what she was talking about? I let a moment pass, and then shook my head.

"Fucking a pig," she explained. "I never did that. What's it like?"

I stared at her.

She smiled. "How long have you known him?"

"Two years." The sound of my own voice shocked me. I wouldn't have thought I'd be able to speak.

"Two years," Sarah repeated. She raised her eyebrows. "That's a long time." She rose, abruptly, and went to the French windows and peered out at the street. Abby and I glanced quickly at each other. Abby shrugged minutely, helplessly.

Sarah turned from the windows to face us. For the first time, she wasn't pointing the gun in our direction. The hand holding it dangled loosely at her side.

"You wish you were with him now, don't you?" Sarah said. "Your pig friend. Lingemann."

There seemed nothing but the obvious to reply to that, so I didn't.

Sarah gave me a long, considering look. "Tell you what," she said. "I'll let you talk to him."

I stared at her, feeling my eyes widen. She smiled.

There was a telephone on the end table next to me. Sarah pointed at it with the gun. "Go on," she said. "Call him."

I sat perfectly still.

"Do it," she snapped, and pointed the gun at me.

Robotlike, I twisted around and picked up the receiver. Then I looked back at Sarah, as if awaiting further instruction.

"Go on," she encouraged.

I brought the receiver up to my ear and dialed Jack's office number. He answered on the fourth ring. "Lieutenant Lingemann."

I tried to answer, and realized that my voice didn't seem to be working.

"Who's this?" Jack said.

I swallowed. Then I coughed. "Jack." It came out a creak.

There was a second or so of silence and he said, "Liz?"

"Jack," I repeated.

"Fucking hopeless," Sarah said. She came over and snatched the receiver from me and held it up to her ear. "Hello, Lieutenant," she said. "Guess who this is? I didn't expect to be talking to you again so soon." She fell silent for a moment, listening. Then she laughed. "Now you know I can't do that," she said. "Besides, if I did it would spoil what I have in store for you. I told you we'd be getting together one of these days, didn't I?"

Abby stirred. I glanced at her out of the corners of my eyes. Her face was pinched and drawn, as if the muscles in it had somehow collapsed in on themselves. I looked back at Sarah.

"I'll let *her* tell you that," she was saying.

"God," Abby whispered. "God, God."

Sarah held the receiver out to me. "Here," she said. "Your boyfriend wants a few words with you."

I didn't move.

"Take the fucking thing," Sarah said, irritably. She tossed the receiver at me and I caught it and held it up to my ear. "Hello?"

"Are you all right?" His voice was calm, relaxed.

"Yes."

"Where are you? Your place?"

What would Sarah allow me to reply to that? "I'm with Abby," I answered, carefully.

"You're at Abby's place?"

"Yes."

"She okay?"

"She's fine."

"Okay, that's good. This is what you have to do. Stay away from the windows. Keep down. Don't turn your back on her. If she talks to you or asks you a question, answer her. But, for Christ's sake, don't try to be smart or funny. Don't antagonize her. All right?"

"Uh-huh. Jack, I—"

Sarah grabbed the phone away from me. "That's enough," she said, and slammed the receiver back on the hook. She turned to me. "What'd he tell you?"

I swallowed. "To stay away from the windows."

She laughed. "Good advice. In five minutes there's going to be about fifty trigger-happy assholes out there, and he doesn't want you getting shot by one of them." She backed over to the rocking chair and sat down and grinned at us. "This is going to be fun."

Abby cleared her throat. "Why're you doing this, Sarah?" she asked quietly.

"Hmmmm?" Sarah said. "Doing what?"

"This," Abby said. She raised her right hand and let it fall to her lap. "Why'd you make Liz call the cops? You could have shot the two of us and walked away from it like you did all the others." She paused, and shook her head. "Now . . . they'll get you for sure, Sarah. There's no *way* they won't."

A spot of red appeared on either of Sarah's cheeks. "Shut up," she said. "Just shut the fuck up." There was an edge in her voice that made me feel cold. "I know *exactly* what I'm doing." She sprang up from the rocking chair and went over to the windows and looked out at the street. Then she glanced at the clock over the fireplace. "They ought to be here soon," she said. She looked out the window again, craning her neck so that she could see down the end of the street.

I believed, then, that Sarah did indeed know exactly what she was doing. I knew, also, that the reasons for her being here had nothing to do with Abby or with that long-ago betrayal or even the death of Mitchell. They were merely the excuse.

"Here comes the first one," Sarah said. She looked at the clock and nodded approvingly. "Two minutes' response time. Not bad, not bad." She turned from the window and paced back to the rocking chair. Her stride had an extraordinary quality of loose-limbed grace. Even in the jeans and T-shirt and worn running shoes, and with the dyed hair, she was an elegant-looking woman. Like her picture.

The phone rang. "I'll get that," Sarah said. "It's probably for me, anyway." She went to the phone and lifted the receiver. "Hello?"

I waited, holding my breath.

"I figured it would be you, Lieutenant," Sarah said. "What do you want?"

There was a little pause while she listened to whatever it was that Jack was saying. The apartment was very still.

"What kind of shit is this?" Sarah said. "I have nothing to negotiate. You're not talking to some junkie holding up a liquor store." She fell silent again.

Abby shivered violently and pressed her hands together.

"No," Sarah said. "NO. And listen, Lieutenant, if you call me one more time, I'll throw your girlfriend out the window. But first I'll put a hole in her head. Then I'll do the same with the other one. You understand me? Good." She slammed down the phone and went back to her chair and began rocking, furiously.

"Straight from the police hostage negotiator's manual," she said. She looked at me. "Your friend's really got the technique down pat. Only it doesn't work all the time."

I said nothing. I couldn't think of anything to say.

"You're not much of a talker, are you?" Sarah observed.

"No."

"Neither am I," she said. "I prefer action." She turned her head to look at Abby. "You did, too, once. What happened?"

"I grew up," Abby said. She raised her head and stared back at Sarah. I tensed.

"You grew up," Sarah said quietly. "Was that it?" She shook her head. "I had hopes for you. You could have been great. You and I . . . " Her voice faded.

I shifted position on the couch and the springs creaked. The noise was abnormally loud in the quiet apartment. Or at least it seemed so to me.

"The revolution's over, Sarah," Abby said. "It's dead. It never even was."

"No," Sarah said. "Not true. It was real."

Abby shook her head. "No. The only revolution was the one in your mind. And in mine, for a while. It was nothing else. All those people we knew who were going to change history . . . it didn't work. It never could have. Not the way they wanted it to."

Sarah leaned forward. Her face was pale, the skin drawn tight over the fine bones. "That's bullshit," she said. "We stopped the war in Vietnam, didn't we?"

Abby laughed. "The war would have stopped without us."

"What about Chicago in 1968. Or Columbia? The Days of Rage?"

"What about them?"

Sarah stood up and paced over to us. "They were *real. That* was action. *That* was the beginning of revolution."

"Only to people like us, Sarah."

"You're wrong."

"No," Abby said. "I'm right. You know I'm right, and that's why you're coming apart."

Sarah stared at her. "You never had any commitment at all, did you?"

"Yes. But to different things. Not to killing people."

"Killing is part of revolution," Sarah said. "You can't separate the two."

"I could," Abby said. "You couldn't. You like it. The power of it. You still do. That's all it ever was with you. The power."

Sarah stepped back. "I'm a revolutionary. I kill because I have to, not because I want to."

"That's a crock of shit, Sarah. You kill because you enjoy it. Davison was no threat to you. There wasn't any need to shoot him. You know that. You did it because you liked the idea of showing everybody how easy you could blow someone away. 'Look at me, Sarah, with the power of life and death over all.' And then leaving that poor bastard behind that bar where the cops picked up Pres just so nobody would miss the point." Abby took a deep breath. "Just like those cops you killed, and the girl in the bank. What did any of that accomplish?"

Sarah was silent, staring at her.

"Well?" Abby said. "I'm waiting. You tell me, Sarah. You tell me how killing some kid and some cops helped the poor or stopped the war or prevented—"

"Shut up," Sarah screamed. "You just shut your fucking mouth." She raised the gun and pointed it at Abby. The barrel shook slightly.

Sarah licked her lips. "Okay," she said. "You say I like it. You're right. I do like it. And I'm good at it. You want to see how good?" She looked over at me, and I saw something moving behind her eyes that froze my blood.

"I'm going to blow up that piece of pigshit out there," Sarah continued. She jerked her head in the direction of the French windows. "I've been meaning to do that all along anyway."

I felt as if the air were being squeezed out of me.

It must have shown on my face, for Sarah's eyes widened in mock surprise. "That's your boyfriend I'm talking about, darling," she added in a detestable cooing voice. "Why do you think I let you call him? Why do you think I wanted him here? We have something to settle, he and I."

Her last words I could hear only faintly over the gray buzzing noise in my head.

Sarah smiled, and stepped back a pace. Then she made a sharp half-turn and strode over to the French windows. Her gun hand wasn't trembling any more.

"No," I said, and shoved myself up from the couch cushions.

I was on my feet and ready to lunge across the room after Sarah when Abby said, "Jesus Christ." She hurled herself sideways and snagged me around the waist with both arms. Caught off balance, I staggered, and then tried to wrest free of her hold. She locked her hands together.

"Let *go,*" I said furiously.

She slid off the couch, dragging me with her, and we toppled over in a heap of thrashing arms and legs. Abby's shoulder hit the edge of the coffee table and knocked it crashing over on its side.

Sarah grabbed one of the window handles, pushed it down, and threw open the glass door. She stepped out onto the balcony, the gun upraised in her other hand. She leaned over the short railing and fired a shot into the street. And then another.

Almost simultaneously there was an explosive whining crack from below. Sarah's body jerked and a sort of red mist appeared around her head, like a garnet halo. Something small detached itself from the back of her head and hit the upper part of the closed window. I felt my stomach heave. Sarah swayed and the gun dropped from her hand and skittered across the balcony. Then, in one long liquid motion, she fell forward and went over the balcony railing. A second later there was a violent rustling of leaves and a thud. Then total stillness.

I closed my eyes and took a deep breath. My stomach was still trying to climb into my throat. I felt movement beside me and opened my eyes. Abby rolled over and sat up slowly. Her chest was heaving. She made a sobbing noise and then gagged and put a hand to her mouth.

I pushed myself up on my elbows. "Come on," I said. "Let's get out of here."

She nodded. I stood up shakily and held out a hand to her. She took it and climbed to her feet. My knees gave, then, and I lurched onto the couch. Abby put her free hand under my arm and yanked me upright. Together we made it to the apartment door and out into the corridor. Then we started down the two flights of stairs to the building entrance.

On the first landing, Abby stopped and leaned against the banister. "What's the matter?" I said. I wanted to get outside and find Jack. Quickly.

She looked at me, and what she was going to say was written on her face.

I shook my head. "Don't," I said. "You don't have to tell me anything."

"I do," she said. She put her hand on my arm, then took a long, harsh breath. "I was giving them money."

I nodded.

She looked away from me to the white blankness of the stairwell. Her eyes were wide and unseeing of what was physically before her.

"I heard from her the first time in April," Abby continued. "It was just a little while after she got back here. She said everything would be fine if I gave her four hundred dollars every month." Abby paused and gave a little dry laugh, like an old man's. "If I didn't . . ."

"I can guess," I said.

"No," Abby said. "Let me finish. She didn't say she'd kill *me,* or arrange somehow to have me turned in to the cops." Abby shut her eyes, and her face crumpled as if she were about to cry. I bit my lower lip.

"What it was, she told me she'd kill Cal first," Abby continued. "And after that, she'd go for my family. One, two, three, four. My mother, to begin, and then my father, and then my sister, and then my brother." Abby opened her eyes and looked at me. "And I knew she could do it, too. That she would do it."

I nodded again.

"I couldn't talk to the cops," Abby said. "What could I tell them? That I was one of the ones they'd been looking for for the past fifteen years?"

"I know," I said. "I know."

Abby shook her head. "No," she said. "You don't. There's no way you ever could."

That was true. Abby stood beside me, her head bowed, her hand still on my arm.

"I won't say anything," I said.

She looked up at me.

"I won't," I said. "It's over."

She tried to smile. It was grotesque. "Thank you," she said.

"Makes us even," I said.

She looked at me quizzically.

I pointed upstairs. "You saved my life. Back there when I went bananas and decided to jump Sarah."

Abby made a small dismissive gesture with her right hand.

"Well," I said, "it may be no big deal to you, but it is to me."

We walked the rest of the way down the stairs.

"Ready or not," I said. "Here we go."

Abby smiled slightly.

I opened the door and we stepped out onto the porch. I blinked in the raw daylight and peered around. There had to have been at least fifty cops poised in various groupings in the street and on the adjoining properties. Every single one of them was standing perfectly still and watching us intently. The hush was absolute.

"There's Jack," Abby said.

"Where?"

I looked in the direction she indicated. He was there, motionless like the others, staring at me. I let go of Abby's hand and started walking toward him. When we were about five feet apart, I stopped and held out my hands. He came over and took them and we leaned against each other. He was shaking nearly as badly as I was. Neither of us said anything. What was there to say?

After a minute, he released my hands and put an arm around my shoulders. He led me over to the cruiser and set me down in the passenger side of the front seat. "I'll be right back," he said. Then he walked away to the front of the house. I hunched over, hugging myself and willing the nausea to go away. My head felt weird, as if the very top had been inflated with helium.

I heard footsteps in the gravel and looked up. Ronnie Mulryne, the SWAT cop, was standing over me, his face drawn with concern. "You all right?" he asked.

I forced a smile. "I'm fine."

"That's good. We were worried about you." He put his hand on my hair. "And your friend."

Mulryne gave my head a pat and walked away to talk to one of the other cops. I looked over at Abby. She was sitting on the lawn, Indian fashion, her head bent. A young patrolman was kneeling beside her, patting her on the back the way a mother pats a baby after it's been fed. Perhaps feeling my gaze, she looked up at me. I made an unobtrusive thumbs-up gesture. She caught it and smiled, very faintly.

Mulryne rejoined me. He folded his arms and leaned against the side of the cruiser, watching the mop-up operation.

"And Olmsbacher makes three," he said.

I sighed. "You got them all. The important ones, anyway."

"Forbes is dead," Mulryne said.

I inhaled sharply.

"He hung himself in his cell," Mulryne said. "They found him this afternoon."

I let out my breath. "Where's Jack?" I asked.

Mulryne tilted his head in the direction of Abby's house. I craned my neck. Jack was standing about three feet away from Sarah's body, staring down at it. From where I was, I couldn't see the awful damage to her head. Up close, it must have been devastating. I wondered what was going through Jack's mind. I thought of the piece of skull that had hit the balcony window and swallowed hard.

"Who shot her?" I said.

"Who do you think?" Mulryne said. He looked at Jack.

I nodded slowly. "But she really killed herself, Ronnie. She walked out on that balcony to commit suicide." I closed my eyes and leaned back against the car seat. "It was her last act of revolution."

28

Jack gave the tennis ball an underhand pitch and Lucy went galloping across the lawn after it. The ball hit one of the flagstones on the path that ran down the center of the yard and bounced up in the air once. Lucy caught it on the way down, let it drop, and pounced on it as if it were a squirrel or a bird. Then she lay down in the grass with the ball clutched between her forepaws and began gnawing at it.

"Isn't she supposed to bring it back to me so I can throw it and she can catch it again?" Jack asked.

"Now what fun is that compared to the sheer thrill of shredding it to pieces?" I said.

Lucy ripped a small hunk of chartreuse fuzz off the ball, chewed it, and spat it on the grass.

"You can tell she's German," I said. "She's got a very systematic way of destroying things."

Jack shook his head. "Dumb mutt."

I laughed and drank some iced coffee. I was sitting in a lawn chair in his back yard. He was lounging alongside me, a piece of grass in his mouth.

"How you feeling?" I said.

"Fine," he replied. "Great."

I rattled the ice in my glass. "You sure?"

"Yes," he said. "I'm sure."

It was mid-afternoon. The temperature was about eighty-five degrees and the humidity was low. There were kids playing in the yard next door, and their voices floated over to us through the still air. Jack's landlord was weeding his vegetable garden.

"Do me a favor," I said.

"If I can," Jack said. "What's that?"

"Make an appointment to see a doctor. Tomorrow or the next day."

He started to speak and I reached down and put my hand over his mouth. "Let's not argue about it," I said. "Just do it for me. Please?"

I took my hand away from his mouth and he said, "Oh, Christ, what for? There's nothing wrong with me."

"Yeah, well, you didn't see yourself yesterday morning."

"Look," he said. "I already did go to a doctor. He told me I had a bad case of heartburn caused by nerves. You're making a big deal out of nothing."

"Be that as it may," I said. "It wouldn't hurt to have things checked out again, now would it?"

"Why? You know all anyone's gonna tell me to do is cut out or cut down on the coffee."

"So?"

"So why should I go back to a doctor so he can tell me something I already know?"

"Well . . . "

"There's nothing wrong with my heart, if that's what you're worried about."

"The thought occurred to me," I said drily.

He let out an exasperated breath. "Look, if I had a problem, I'd do something about it. But I don't. Okay?"

I looked at him for a moment, my lips pursed. Then I said, "You really are a stubborn son of a bitch, aren't you?"

"Yup."

I laughed, as much out of resignation as amusement, and put my hand on his head.

Lucy ripped a long green strip off the tennis ball, shook it vigorously, and cast it aside. Then she got up and wandered over to the vegetable garden to see what was doing there. Jack's landlord stopped weeding and scratched her behind the ears. Somebody at the house next door started up a lawn mower. Lucy licked the landlord's chin and went off to investigate some rose bushes. She was still giving the rhododendrons at the front of the house a wide berth. I couldn't say I blamed her.

I got up and moved my chair so that I'd be sitting in the shade of the house. I'm not really a heliotrope. Jack lay back on the grass and crossed his arms behind his head and closed his eyes. Lucy came over and settled down beside him in a sphinx position. She looked at me with her tongue hanging out and thumped her tail on the ground.

"What a difference a day makes," I said.

Jack smiled a little. "Uh-huh."

I finished my iced coffee and set the glass down beside my chair. "Where do you think they've gone?"

Jack opened his eyes and gave me a curious look. "They?"

"The rest of the PRC," I said. "There were more of them than just Sarah and Goldman and Forbes, weren't there? At least there were when they were living on Third Street. Their neighbor said so."

Jack nodded.

"So?" I said. "Leaderless, I can't imagine how effective they'll be, but . . . where do you suppose they've gone?"

"If they have any brains at all, which they do, they'll be halfway to Ohio or Georgia by now."

"What'll happen to them?"

"I don't know." He raised himself up on his elbows and then turned over on his side to face me.

"You think they'll ever be caught?" I said.

"I don't know that, either. Maybe."

I sighed. "You must have been getting close to catching them, the past few days."

He gave me a sharp, curious look. "Why do you say that?"

"Were you?"

He hesitated a moment, and then said, "We had a few leads."

"Like what?"

He shook his head.

"You can't tell me?" I said. "Or you don't want to?"

"Can't," he said. "It's still an open investigation."

"Did Davison tell you anything helpful?"

"No. Not really."

"What about Forbes?"

Jack shook his head again. "I can't answer that question."

I pinched my lower lip between my thumb and forefinger and tugged it, reflectively. "My guess is that he did," I said. "And that's why he killed himself. He broke the code."

Jack didn't say anything.

"Sarah must have realized it was over, then," I continued. "And that's why—or at least part of why—she . . . "

"Did what she did yesterday," Jack finished.

"Yes." I sat silent for a moment, remembering. "She wasn't in control any longer. It was all falling to pieces around her. But all the same, she couldn't just give up or give in."

"No."

"The code again."

I got out of my chair and went to sit beside him. He put his arm around me. Lucy rolled over on her back and waved her paws in the air. Jack's landlord tossed an armful of uprooted crabgrass into his wheelbarrow.

Jack said, in a very matter-of-fact tone, "Abby's Leilah, isn't she?"

I sat very still for several seconds. Then I said, "When did you decide that?"

Jack smiled a little sadly.

"Forbes tell you?"

"No."

I glanced at him. "Then how—"

He looked back at me, the same slight, sad smile on his face. "It wasn't too hard to figure, on the basis of what happened yesterday. How long have you known?"

I thought of the promise I'd made to Abby and turned my head a little, so that Jack couldn't see my face. I said, "Only since yesterday afternoon."

"Uh-huh."

"What are you going to do, now that you know?"

"Nothing."

I jerked around and stared at him. "*Nothing?*"

He shrugged.

"Why not? I mean, I certainly don't want to see Abby get arrested, but why are you just going to let it go?"

"Because there's nothing else I *can* do," he replied. "There's no proof to tie her to the original PRC. Everyone who could identify her as Leilah is dead. Even if she turned herself in, with a good defense attorney ... " His voice trailed off and he made a little gesture of dismissal. "There is no case against her. Not one that would stand up in court. The prosecutor wouldn't touch it."

"Does it bother you that she's going to walk away from it?"

He raised his eyebrows. "She committed a very bad crime."

"That's true," I said. "But you know, Jack, she didn't do anything nearly as terrible as the others. She *did* drive one of the getaway cars after the bank robbery, but she was never in on any of the bombings or assassinations. I mean, I know that technically she's as guilty of that bank robbery and the murder of that teller and the cop as Mitchell and Spahn and Goldman and Forbes and Sarah were, but ... she said it herself. She just couldn't kill people."

He just looked at me.

I let out a long, tremulous sigh. "Tell me," I said. "If you can ever make a case against her, will you?"

"Yes."

I nodded.

"I'm sorry."

I hugged my knees. "Not your fault."

Jack's landlord trundled his wheelbarrow past us. He smiled and said, "Some day, huh?"

"Great," Jack said.

"Enjoy," the landlord said. He shoved the wheelbarrow around the side of the house.

"I could use a beer," Jack said. "Get you anything?"

"What time is it?"

He looked at his watch. "A little after four."

"All right. Vodka and tonic."

He got up, brushing grass from his jeans, and went into the house. I sat with my arms around my legs, huddled like someone cold, trying not to think. I hadn't heard from Abby since last night, since before she'd finished telling Jack and a state police investigator and an FBI agent that the only reason she could think of for Sarah to come after her was that she, like Morgan, Burmester, and Whitcomb, was involved in defense work.

That was the tale that had been in today's papers and on the news, anyway.

Sometime, I'd tell Jack about the blackmail. And about how Abby had refused, finally, to make that last payment.

I wondered what would happen to her. Bad as I felt now, I knew that the memory of what had taken place yesterday would recede, become muted. Even the worst parts. Because in a very real sense, none of it had had anything to do with me. I was just there, watching. And so my life would go on pretty much the same as it had before.

For Abby, no matter what became of her, things would never be right.

I heard the screen door open and then slam shut. Jack appeared with a bottle of beer and a glass. He handed me my drink and dropped down beside me on the grass.

"You okay?" he said.

I smiled. "I'm fine."

"Good."

For a while after that, we were quiet. The game the kids next door were playing got more uproarious, and finally a woman—the mother, I supposed—came out and told them to hold it down. Lucy resumed savaging the tennis ball. Jack's landlord turned on the sprinkler in the vegetable garden. We watched the streams of water arc slowly back and forth over the tomato and pepper plants.

"Jack?"

"Hmmmm?"

"Do you think anything like this will ever happen again?"

"What do you mean?" he said.

I took a swallow of my vodka and tonic. "What happened with the PRC. The killings."

He lay back on the grass before replying, resting the beer bottle on his stomach. "Do you want the answer I gave to the papers, or do you want what I really think?"

"What you really think, please."

"Yes," he said. "It'll happen again. Maybe not right here, right away, but, yes. It'll happen again."

I shook my head. "Nothing ever really gets ended, does it? With all the loose ends tied up nice and tight like a Christmas package?"

"No," Jack said. "Not ever."

EPILOGUE

July 3

SARAH CLARKE OLMSBACHER

by Deborah Abramowitz

Special to the New York Times

Sarah Clarke Olmsbacher, sought for over fifteen years by federal and state law enforcement agencies, died late yesterday afternoon in a shoot-out with police in Cambridge, MA.

Miss Olmsbacher, who is believed to have been the leader of a terrorist group calling itself the Peoples Revolutionary Cadre (PRC), had taken two women hostage in an apartment on Washington Avenue in Cambridge. Neither of the women was injured in the two-hour-long confrontation.

Miss Olmsbacher was born in New York on June 7, 1947. She attended the Brearley School and was graduated with honors from Vassar College in 1969. While a graduate student in political science at Boston University, she helped to organize the PRC, a small group of self-styled urban guerrillas dedicated to the violent overthrow of the U.S. government. Before it went underground in November 1970, the PRC claimed credit for bombings at Logan International Airport in Boston and police headquarters in Cambridge, MA, for the assassination of two Cambridge police officers, and for the robbery of a

Somerville, MA, bank, during which a Somerville police officer and a bank employee were shot to death.

In recent months, the remnants of the PRC, apparently under the leadership of Miss Olmsbacher, resurfaced in Cambridge to initiate a new campaign of violence, this time directed at employees of Boston-area corporations and research facilities holding defense contracts. A mimeographed leaflet found in a Cambridge safe house occupied by the PRC described the group's goal as "the destruction of the U.S. imperialist war machine." In the pursuit of this end, the PRC is believed to have shot and killed three persons employed by Boston-area firms holding defense contracts, and a fourth whom they believed to have been a police informer.

Miss Olmsbacher's movements between her flight underground in November 1970 and her return to Cambridge in March of this year are largely unknown, although she is reported to have lived for brief periods in New Orleans, Memphis, and Berkeley during the early 1970s. Gerald Tomlinson, an agent of the Federal Bureau of Investigation involved in

200

the pursuit of Miss Olmsbacher, has described her as "possibly the most intelligent and dangerous woman criminal in American history." That assessment was echoed by Chief Louis Santoro of the Cambridge, MA, police department, who characterized Miss Olmsbacher as "ruthless and totally amoral."

Miss Olmsbacher leaves her father, James, and stepmother, the former Ann Marie Engstrom. Mr. and Mrs. Olmsbacher are said to be in seclusion at their home in Tarrytown.

A cousin, Sheridan Hoover, told reporters late yesterday of the family's reaction on learning of Miss Olmsbacher's involvement with the PRC. "We were shocked," Mr. Hoover said. "Nothing we knew of Sarah prepared us for what happened to her. None of us ever understood it. She was a lovely, radiant young woman."

Funeral services will be private.

July 4

SEATTLE, WA (UPI)

An explosion caused severe damage to the sixteenth and seventeenth floors of an office building early this morning in downtown Seattle. No injuries were reported.

The blast, which demolished the executive offices of the Northport Corporation, was caused by charges of dynamite placed in the building's ventilation system. The Northport Corporation, headquartered in Seattle, manufactures aircraft and is a major contractor with the Defense Department.

Fifteen minutes after the explosion, Seattle police received a telephone call from an individual claiming that a group known as the Peoples Revolutionary Army was responsible for the bombing. The caller added that the attack on the Northport Corporation offices was performed in the memory "of the late freedom fighter" Sarah Clarke Olmsbacher . . .

If you have enjoyed this book and would like to receive details of other Walker mystery titles, please write to:

Mystery Editor
Walker and Company
720 Fifth Avenue
New York, NY 10019